W9-CZB-936

Hey,
White Girl

Hey, White Girl

JUDITH BICE

atmosphere press

© 2021 Judith Bice

Published by Atmosphere Press

Cover design by Senhor Tocas

No part of this book may be reproduced without permission from the author except in brief quotations and in reviews. This is a work of fiction, and any resemblance to real places, persons, or events is entirely coincidental.

Atmospherepress.com

For my daughters, who get it.

Chapter One

I didn't care much about science or rockets, even if I did like to watch *Lost in Space*. As a girl, I wasn't expected to. But like everyone else in the world, I was captivated as I watched the *Eagle* get closer and closer to the moon and glide onto its dimpled surface. I feared for the fuzzy gray image of Neil Armstrong as he stepped down the ladder of his spaceship to walk on the moon. I thought he might drift away into the immense black; but instead he bounced around with that pack on his back, like a carefree kid.

We didn't keep a TV in our living room; its sleek shininess wouldn't have looked right next to the piano and the wing-back chairs and the cut glass bowls on the narrow end tables. But on that hot night in July of 1969, my father rolled our black and white set from its place in the den to the center of the living room. The casters made parallel trails across the carpet before it stopped in front of the fireplace. The four of us squeezed onto the brocaded mint green sofa, waiting. My mother made us stand so she could put a beach towel across the cushions to protect them from the sweat behind our knees.

It was the last night before my brother Donald left for camp; his departure had been delayed because there were no

TVs there. My mother had bribed him with fried chicken and rice with white gravy to keep him around that night. So we had an entire evening together, watching the men of Houston in their skinny black ties anticipating what had never happened before. Except for the stickiness of the night, the buzz of cicadas on the other side of the screened windows, and the absence of stockings hanging from the mantle, being together felt like Christmas Eve. Even the rule about no dogs in the living room was relaxed to allow Skipper, our sandy-haired mutt, to watch with us.

"I don't understand how we can actually see what is happening that far away," my mother mused without quite asking a question.

"Marjorie, you don't understand how we can see pictures from Washington, either," my father teased.

"I feel sorry for the guy who's circling around, instead of getting to step on the moon. I sure wouldn't want to go that far and not be allowed to even set foot on it!" Donald slid off the crowded couch and onto the floor beside Skipper without taking his eyes off the TV.

"Why can't he go too?" I asked.

"Nell, he's got to keep the spaceship going! Without him, nobody gets home."

My dad, more used to reading his news than seeing it, leaned forward, gripping his knees the whole time we watched, the same way he listened to baseball on the transistor radio—like he was ready to jump in and assist. He loosened his tie, but little rivulets of sweat still trickled down his neck and soaked into his white undershirt.

"Aren't they hot in those spacesuits?" I asked. My dad launched into an explanation of how far the moon was from the sun and how cold it had to be there, and added some scientific concepts that made me wish I hadn't asked the question. I just wondered if the astronauts were hot like we were.

We stayed up past midnight. By the time the sun came up, Donald had left for camp, Skipper had been sent back outside, and my mother had sealed herself into the den, cooled by a window unit, where she continued to redecorate our house curtain by curtain with her sewing machine. Just like life returns to normal the day after Christmas, the magic of the moon landing evaporated into the ordinariness of the morning.

I woke to the roar of lawnmowers and the stickiness of sheets tangled around my feet. One could hardly breathe when humidity made bangs cling to foreheads and iced tea glasses sweat pools onto kitchen tables. The thrill of adventure that had accompanied the first day of summer was now suppressed by the Virginia heat. Most Augusts, our family vacationed at one of the Carolina beaches, and Donald and I rode the waves and built sandcastles without our usual bickering. There were two years between us. The summer he hit the bump of adolescence his moods kept me at a distance. When I joined him as a teenager, he became my friend again, commenting on cute girls as we walked the beach, or giving me tips on how to ride the waves on our floppy raft. I envied the way his skin turned bronze after a day in the sun, while mine freckled and burned. He envied how fast I could read through a stack of paperbacks, while he stuck to his comic books way past the age when he should have given them up. That summer my parents moved up our beach trip to accommodate Donald's camp assignment as a junior counselor, so I was left to figure out how to spend the month of August in a quiet house, and an even quieter neighborhood.

My best friend, Sally, had always lived around the corner. There wasn't much moving in or out of our sleepy neighborhood. The kids that waited at the bus stop with me in first grade were the same ones that got off the bus with me our last day of junior high. We were classmates and expected to graduate from Lee High School together. We were white. I guess we were middle class, though I never considered either one of those circumstances. Our dads went to work and our moms did everything else. My family went to Mass on Sundays, and my mother had bridge club on Thursdays. Sally's family had five children, so I felt a little cheated sometimes having only Donald.

When Sally's family wasn't away camping that August, we rode our bikes. Sometimes to the air-conditioned library to sit in bucket chairs of fake orange leather and pore over teen magazines. Sometimes on zig-zagging routes through side streets to get to the pool, towels draped over our shoulders, searching for sprinklers to catch their spray. When the pool water grew tepid and we tired of the same magazines, the only cool places to go were the cement-floored basements beneath our houses. We plotted for our first year as sophomores at Lee High School in Sally's basement. Her older sister, Nancy, drilled us for the JV cheerleading squad. We jumped and yelled, fixed peanut butter sandwiches for lunch, and earned sore throats by late afternoon. I was more at home at Sally's house than my own. There was always a brother or sister or other friends around and their dog was allowed in every room. Mrs. Carpenter never seemed to leave the kitchen. She did all the cooking and ironing while keeping up with the goings on in *As the World Turns* and *General Hospital*. There was never a shortage of homemade chocolate chip cookies or lemon pound cake. If I was there at dinner time I simply squeezed in on one of the benches they used instead of chairs. My mother had a rule that she needed to know at lunchtime whether one of my friends would be staying for dinner, so she could "prepare appropriately." That rule made me nervous: I didn't want to ask a friend by lunch, in case we would be tired of each other by dinner, and I didn't want to face my mother's temperamental response if I delayed the ask until late afternoon, so I rarely invited anyone to eat with us.

"Nell, what does your father say about all this busing talk?" Mr. Carpenter asked when I stayed for dinner. That summer the papers were full of terms like desegregation and annexation.

"He thinks it could still blow over," I answered.

"Hmmmm. I'd like to think that too, but now I'm not so sure." He nodded to Nancy with his eyes on the bowl of mashed potatoes, and she passed them.

"Of course, if they do decide to bus, nothing will change for Nancy and Donald, since they would be allowed to finish high school at Lee." He sipped his iced tea, put down his glass, and searched my face.

"But you realize you and Sally and the rest of my crew here would be sent to different schools." He spoke gently as if he was preparing me for some great disappointment.

"Oh, I understand," I reassured him, "But if all of our friends are bused too, won't we just be going to a different school, all of us together?" That's how I'd reasoned it. New school, same friends.

"I guess we'll have to wait and see, won't we?" Mr. Carpenter surveyed all the children seated at his table. "Now I hear we have dessert made by our resident chefs, tonight. I think I'm brave enough to try some."

He flashed a smile at Sally and me. We hopped up to serve the brownies we'd made that afternoon, and the heaviness of the busing conversation dissipated into the sultry summer air.

Sally's family left on a camping trip the next weekend. I kept hoping for an invitation to join them, but it never came. There were enough children in that family that they didn't need the entertainment of extra friends. Our family had never gone camping even though Donald and I had begged our parents to take us. My mother didn't understand why anyone would want to sleep outside with the bugs or have to pee in the woods.

I was setting the table when I brought it up again. "We could go to one of those campgrounds with bathrooms."

"Do people park their campers right next to each other? If they do, it's no different than a cheap motel." She lifted the top off the butter beans, tasted them, and added salt.

"They're further apart than that. When I went with Sally's family last summer they set up away from anyone else and you could see the lake at night. You like seeing the ocean from your room at the beach."

"My ocean-view room has a hot shower and ice in the freezer and a TV." She pressed her lips together. "And what do they *do* after they've set up camp? It's not like you can look for shells or walk to a restaurant or get ice cream on the boardwalk."

"They build a fire and cook hotdogs and make s'mores. During the day there are trails to hike, and you can swim in the lake, and Skipper could go with us." I'd always wanted to take our dog on vacation, but he wasn't allowed at the beach house. "And at night Sally's family plays cards and charades."

My mother's lip curled up.

"It's really fun," I added.

She pulled the pot of potatoes off the stove and carried them to the sink to drain.

"I don't think our family is the camping type, Eleanor."

She was probably right. Still, I wished we could have tried it at least once.

"How about I take you shopping this weekend? We can go downtown to Thalhimers and Miller & Rhoads." Her voice turned bright and cheerful. "Get you some new school clothes and have lunch in the Tea Room." She added a chunk of butter to the potatoes and looked at me with a hopeful expression. "Wouldn't that be fun?"

I knew not to dismiss the opportunity of good-mood time with my mother. "Sure."

She untied her apron and her heels clicked in a perky rhythm as she carried the serving bowls of hot food to the table.

I kept planning on Lee, even though the newspapers said I would probably be going to Stonewall High School. It was hard for me to imagine anything different from the neighborhood where I'd grown up. My world was a few blocks of stucco and brick houses with sprawling yards that had enough room between them to keep us from hearing the neighbors settle their differences, but were close enough for the mother next door to keep an eye on us. My father had less than a ten-minute drive to his law office in downtown Richmond on the boulevard lined with statues of Confederate war heroes. The local newspaper was delivered twice a day. Milk carriers came before dawn on Tuesdays. Every family had a cat or a dog, or both. Every kid had a way to be called home that wasn't as uncouth as yelling off the back steps. My mother rang an old cowbell; the Carpenter kids each had a whistle signal, like the Von Trapps in *The Sound of Music*. There was the piano teacher down the block where children suffered through interminable lessons, the wealthy widow who lived on the corner and gave out the best Halloween candy, and Mr. Thornton, who let his grass grow too long in the extra lot he owned and yelled at children if they cut through it to get to the creek behind his house.

But my curated life was about to be challenged. Each night

the local news showed crowds of angry white parents outside the court holding "NO BUSING" signs and yelling *"No, no, we won't go!,"* the sweltering heat antagonizing their swarms, like insects before a storm. One night the judge hearing the case had to call for police protection. Before retiring for the evening he let his dog out, and a bullet killed the poor animal while he relieved himself.

My parents weren't part of the angry mob, but the idea of busing dominated their conversations with each other, with the neighbors, and with our new priest. As the neighborhood families returned from their camping trips and beach vacations, impromptu meetings were held in living rooms and church halls. There was a collective holding of breath; a tension in waiting for the judge to overturn the busing ruling and validate our freedom to choose where we went to school. And then there was planning for what could be done if that freedom was stripped away.

The air of anxiety was mirrored in the brief but violent thunderstorms that threatened each day, when the sharpness of the breeze and the subtle scent of earth replaced the stale hot smell of the afternoon. My mother almost always foretold one of those storms with a migraine headache.

"Eleanor, would you crack me some ice?" she would ask, with a palm pushing on one side of her head.

I would get the aluminum ice tray out of the freezer and jerk the lever back with practiced speed so as not to get my fingers stuck to the frame. I'd wrap ice cubes in a washcloth and tiptoe into her room with the makeshift ice pack. The dull drone of the oscillating fan and the closed curtains made her room a tomb. The more intense her pain, the tighter a circle her body made, stoking an anxiety in me. I felt guilty to be glad to leave her alone with her misery.

My father came home from the office in a downpour on one of those stormy, headachy afternoons. My mother had instructed me on what to pull together for supper: leftover fried chicken, potato salad, sliced tomatoes. She was too sick to eat, so my father and I ate our cold supper to the flashes and claps outside.

"Nell, I'd like for you to go with me to the neighborhood meeting tonight."

"I thought it was just for parents."

"The decisions made will affect your life more than mine, so you're entitled to go if you'd like."

My father had often let me try things when my mother thought I wasn't old enough. She disapproved when he let me taste beer. She cringed when he took me past where the waves broke and the ocean was over my head. She would show her distaste when he bought me a pair of platform shoes before I left for college.

"Okay." I liked being treated like an adult.

The meeting was run by our new priest, who looked much younger in the church hall than he did in the sanctuary. His blonde hair touched his clerical collar and his Keds seemed to propel him around the room, greeting our neighbors as if they were old friends. But his congeniality became suspect for them when they realized that he was not opposed to busing the way they were.

"Folks, you've already taken the harder step and integrated

11

your schools. And your children have been fine, right? What's the worst thing that can happen if the schools are made more equal across the city?" Father Richard asked.

"Sir, our children have been in good, upstanding, rigorous schools. Why should we mess with that? What does it accomplish to bus our kids out of the neighborhood, and bring other kids in? It's a waste of time and resources to make *all* the schools subpar!" Mr. Palmer wasn't Catholic and had no trouble speaking his mind to Father Richard.

"What do you see as your options?" Father Richard asked. Voices called out across the room.

"Keep our kids home."

"Start our own schools."

"Petition City Council. Didn't we elect them to protect our interests?"

"But, what if it's the *right* thing to do for the good of the community? What terrible thing are you afraid of?" Father Richard scanned the faces around the room. Rumbles rolled, their words undistinguishable.

Mr. Palmer stood up again, his face now looking sunburned with its red splotches, his tone not as diplomatic. "Sir, I mean no disrespect, but I don't think you've been here long enough to know what you're talking about. The coloreds in this town are slow, lazy troublemakers. How is forcing our children to be with them *good* for the community?"

Silent tension quieted the room. Father Richard tilted his head and crossed his arms like he was struggling to comprehend this point of view. Dr. Thomas stood.

"As a pediatrician I don't have too many qualms about putting young children of different races together, as long as it's fifty-fifty. But I have concerns about sending our teenaged girls to school with mature colored boys. And we all know why."

I stole a glance at my father, but his face was unreadable.

"Is there scientific evidence for what you're referring to?"

Father Richard asked.

"I'm sure there is somewhere," Dr. Thomas said. "There's plenty of anecdotal evidence." There was universal nodding across the room.

"Will the ratio be fifty-fifty with the proposed plan?" someone asked.

My father stood. "I can speak to that, Howard." He paused. "It's my understanding that if we all consent to staying in the schools the numbers will be close to fifty-fifty. Most schools will be closer to sixty-forty."

"Which way?" someone called out. "More white, or more colored?"

"There are more Negro children than white children within the city limits." More rumblings. "But we don't know how this could turn out unless we try."

"Mr. Randolph, you willing to risk busing that pretty little daughter of yours across town?"

All eyes focused on me and I shifted in my seat.

"I trust that Nell can take care of herself. And I believe that this busing strategy can only work if we all support it."

"Well, I've heard all I need to hear." Mr. Archer turned to leave the room, followed by his wife. Others started moving around, chatting in small groups, the meeting never formally ending.

Mrs. Hazelton walked over to me. I'd played at her house often in elementary school, with her daughter, Debby. "How do you feel about all this, Nell?"

"Well, I'd rather go to Lee, but if all my friends are bused with me, I guess it will be okay."

Her mouth made a flat line and she shook her head up and down as if confirming some truth about me that she had suspected before. My answer had not impressed her.

My father and I were among the last to leave. The rain had stopped, but instead of clearing the air, it had left an oppressive humidity. I rolled down the window as soon as we got in the car.

"Let me show you something," my father said.

He pulled out of the church parking lot and turned the opposite way from our house. As he drove the houses got smaller, the roads narrower. We hadn't gone but a few minutes when he stopped the car at the end of a street and we faced a massive stucco building with red double doors. The words Stonewall High School framed the arch that stood at the top of a broad set of concrete steps. I stared at its three stories of paned windows, some of them taped. or made of cardboard instead of glass. A lone basketball goal on a metal pole stood inside a chain-link fence. There were no trees, no grass, no green except for the random clusters of weeds sprouting up between cracks in the asphalt.

I'd imagined Stonewall as a smaller version of Lee, just in a different place.

"Is this where I have to go?"

"I believe it is," my father answered, regarding the school and not me.

We sat for a few minutes. The car got steamy and my father rolled down his window and loosened his tie. My legs stuck to the seat where my shorts stopped. My ponytail was damp on my neck.

"Who gets to go to Lee?"

"They're taking some kids from this school and sending them to Lee. The plan is to make both schools the same. Both half white, half Negro. Equal."

"Will they fix the school? I can see why people are upset if the schools look this bad."

"Yeah—we have a lot of work ahead of us." He put the car in gear and we drove the short distance back to our own neighborhood, lost in our own thoughts.

Chapter Two

Donald's return from camp meant the end of summer. On Sunday my mother roused us early for Mass. Donald's impassioned pleas for staying home had no effect on her.

"You haven't been to a proper Mass in a month. We're *all* going this morning. Besides, we have a new priest, and you're really going to like him."

Sundays gave my mother the opportunity to showcase her good taste in clothes. Her sleeveless navy knit dress with its dropped waist and white trim defied her role as the mother of teenagers. Her white patent leather pumps click-clacked on the trips between the stove and the kitchen table as she delivered pancakes.

When Donald tried to prod our father, he didn't even glance up from his newspaper. "As your mother said, we're *all* going this morning."

Although my father made the rules of the house and inflicted whatever punishment deemed necessary if they were broken, when it came to church, my mother was the leader and we did not dare to not follow. My father had been raised a relaxed Presbyterian, but had agreed to raise us as Catholics in order to marry my mother. She had attended a Catholic all-

15

girls school, and though we only heard uncomplimentary words about the severe nuns that rendered her an education, she referred to the priests with overly positive superlatives.

My mother was counting on Father Richard's electric voice and youthful good looks to encourage my brother's church attendance. After Mass, she orchestrated our exit so Donald could meet him.

"Mr. and Mrs. Randolph! So glad to see you this morning!"

My mother beamed. She turned back to him with the brilliant smile she reserved for company.

"Father, I'd like for you to meet my son, Donald."

"Donald, so glad to meet you!" He gripped Donald's hand with both of his. Then his twinkly blue eyes peered into mine, instead of scanning my face like most adults did. "And hello, Nell!"

"Father Richard is from the seminary in California. Aren't we so pleased to have him here?" My mother's company voice made Donald look at me sideways.

"You're starting your senior year, aren't you?"

"Yes, Father."

"You and Nell may be interested in a new idea I have for Mass. Mind if I call you sometime?"

"Sure, Father," Donald said and I nodded. My mother pushed back her shoulders and squeezed her gloved hands together with pride.

Donald and I walked to the car while our parents stopped and talked to friends.

"Man, priests sure make her happy," he said, kicking the gravel with his loafers. He leaned against the car but its sizzling surface made him pop up.

"Why would he want to talk to us about Mass?" I asked.

"Beats me, but I'm not going to have time for any extra Masses in my senior year, I can tell you that. I've already done the altar boy thing."

"I wouldn't know what to say if a priest wanted to talk to just me."

"They're just people."

"Yeah, but they're priests. That's different."

"Not that different."

"Better not let Mom hear you say that."

When our parents finally made it to the car my mother was no longer sporting the radiant smile she'd given Father Richard. We took her cue and dropped all conversation. I grabbed the towel we kept in the back and put it under my thighs to protect them from the blistering vinyl. Donald took off his tie and wrapped and unwrapped his hand with it like a bandage. My mother swiveled her head and addressed me.

"Did you know Polly and Lisa are going to St. Mary's for high school?" she asked.

Polly and Lisa were friends from school, but not the spend-the-night kind. We'd eat lunch together sometimes, but only when other girls were with us. I liked them fine, but they were more popular than I was, so I had to wait for them to make the first move. Since they didn't, we had stayed on the "sign your autograph book" level and had never advanced to the "talk on the phone" level. They were not the type of girls who went to St. Mary's.

"Really? Are you sure? I can't see them going there."

"Lisa's mother told me, so I guess they are." She turned to my father. "She said there was no way they were going to let Lisa go to Stonewall; she didn't think it was safe."

My father kept his eyes on the road but granted her a half nod.

"She says policemen will have to be stationed there in case fights break out and she wouldn't be a responsible parent if she put her daughter in harm's way."

"That's quite an exaggeration, Marjorie. The ruling isn't even final yet."

"And she says St. Mary's is full, with a waiting list! Even non-Catholics are applying there!" She peered out the window and said to no one in particular, "I hope we haven't made a mistake by not sending Eleanor there."

I didn't want to go St. Mary's. But I didn't want to go to that rundown Stonewall either. I wanted to go to Lee.

"Why can't people just go where they want to go? I don't get why everything has to change when *I* get to high school!"

A lump swelled in the back of my throat. I bit my lip to keep from tearing up. I grabbed at the stupid tie Donald was twisting and there was a quick tug-of-war before he let go. I held it flapping out the window like a flag. And he let me.

The phone rang a lot for my parents that week. They went to more meetings. They didn't miss the evening news. When the ruling became final on Friday and forced busing became the law, Father Richard attempted to guide our community into graceful acceptance. My father called him the "sacrificial lamb," thrown to the wolves of angry, spouting parents.

"Father Richard has his heart in the right place," I overheard him tell my mother after one of those meetings.

"But he doesn't understand *Southerners*," she said. "What works in California is not going to work here. People are accustomed to their places, and you can't march in and change that." Father Richard had already toppled from the pedestal where she had put him.

"Marjorie, he's just trying to help folks to see it another way so that we can all do this peacefully. This town has circumvented the federal law for over a decade now. If I had been the judge, I would have made the same decision. It's what the law says."

What the law said, and what my mother believed, were two separate ideals.

※

Sally and I rode our bikes to the pool; she with her bottles of Coppertone and baby oil and I with the QT that promised me a tan. We spread our towels on the white concrete at the diving board end, close enough to catch the spray from the steady succession of cannonballs performed by the younger boys. Being with Sally made me feel better.

"What are you going to wear the first day?" she asked.

"I was thinking about my sleeveless yellow dress with the white collar. What about you?"

"I want to wear something white. You know, your tan always shows up better when you wear white."

Sally's pride in her tanned skin announced itself every time she compared her bronzed arm to my freckled pink one. Her flaxen hair made her tan show up even more while my nondescript dirty blonde did nothing for me.

"You're riding the bus, right?" I asked, flipping to my back. "I mean, I'm kinda nervous about the bus, but I don't want my mom to take me on the first day of *high* school."

"Yeah, I was thinking the same thing." She rubbed baby oil on her arms and flattened herself on the towel. "The bus will be okay because it's probably just picking up all the kids in our neighborhood." She didn't sound worried at all.

"I saw the school with my dad. It's really rundown."

"They'll fix it when white kids start going there."

"And I found out Polly and Lisa are going to St. Mary's!"

"You're kidding me!" Sally propped up on her arms, "Who told you?"

"Her mom told my mom at church." Mother-to-mother

always meant the information wasn't hearsay, and a cloud passed over Sally's face.

"Lisa's mom doesn't think it's safe for Lisa to go to Stonewall. She thinks there will be riots and stuff."

"Are you scared?" Sally asked me.

"Not really. I always thought the colored kids in our school were nice."

"Yeah. But were you ever *friends* with one?"

"Renay and I were kind of friends. It's just I can't see us going home with each other."

"At least if Polly and Lisa aren't there it'll be easier to make the cheerleading squad," Sally said. "Who else do you think is not going to Stonewall?"

"I don't know. Lisa's mom said St. Mary's is full and has a waiting list. So where else would anyone go? I mean the only boys' school is the military one, and can you see Bryce and Peter and that bunch there? No way," I said.

"Then everyone will have to go to Stonewall." Sally straightened her towel and stretched out again. "If everyone goes, it won't be that bad." It wasn't a minute before she jumped up.

"I'm burning up! Let's get in."

We dove off the side of the pool and I angled my body down to the bottom. Gathered on the pool floor were all the leftovers from the summer: nickels and pennies from diving games, straws, bottle tops, the wrapper from a Milky Way bar. I kicked my way to the surface.

"This place has gotten so dirty!" I shook my head to get the wet hair out of my face. Sally wasn't there to hear me. She was on the opposite side of the pool talking to Gary, one of her brother's friends. I swam over and clung to the side to hear the end of their conversation.

"So when are you moving?" Sally asked.

"We've still got to sell our house, so we can get the other one built. But the county rule says you can go to school where you have property, so even though we only have a lot now, if my mom drives us, we can go to school at West River."

"Wow. Do you know anyone there?" Sally asked.

"A guy that works with my dad lives out there and they have kids. We're going to their house for dinner tomorrow night so we can meet them."

"Oh, cool. Well, good luck."

"Yeah. You too."

Sally draped her elbows over the tiled edge and stared into the baby pool. Water beaded up on her arms and her wet pigtails clung to the sides of her face.

"I didn't think about moving," she said. "Gary said there are three houses for sale on his block."

I hadn't thought about that either. The last person who moved out of our neighborhood was a widow. She sold her big house and went to another city to live with her daughter. People with kids only left if the father was transferred.

"Would your parents move?" I asked her.

"I've never heard them talk about it. What about yours?"

"I haven't heard mine say anything either." We watched a kid in the baby pool fall on his bottom and get water splashed in his face. He wailed.

"Ready to go?" I asked. I was tired of the pool and didn't want to see anyone else who might tell me they weren't going to high school with me.

"Yeah. Let's go."

Sally pulled herself up and out of the pool, but I ducked back under the water and swam to the ladder. We peeled our towels off the hot cement and rode our bikes home, the wind drying our chlorine-stiff hair.

Bridge club day meant a cold supper. I never cared for the tuna salad my mother tried to dress up by putting it in the middle of a split tomato, so it was good I wasn't that hungry. Dinner conversation on bridge club nights was dominated by whatever news my mother had learned between dealing and bidding.

"The Garetts have listed their house now. Dorothy was bemoaning the fact they're having to ask five thousand less than they would have a year ago for anyone to even take a look."

"Y'all aren't thinking about moving, are you?" Donald asked.

"Don't worry, son. We're not going to move in your senior year," my father answered.

"If all the white kids are being sent together to a different school, why are people moving?" I asked.

"They're moving because they're afraid of what they don't know," my father said. "There are so few Negro families in the next county the schools there will be almost exclusively white." He took a swallow of his iced tea. "These people are overreacting. If everyone would sit tight, our property value wouldn't plummet, like it's doing. This knee-jerk reaction is making the situation worse."

"Gary Campbell's family is moving too," I said. "He told Sally at the pool today."

My mother put her fork down and cocked her head. My father nodded.

"I'd heard that. They're moving to the other side of Goochland. Those schools aren't nearly as good as what we have." He shook his head, "I don't understand why they would make such a drastic move."

"What we *had*," my mother said, mostly under her breath, but we all heard. My father flashed her a look that meant it would be best for her to say no more.

"Is Nell going to ride the bus the first day?" Donald asked.

"I was thinking Eugene would take her," my mother said.

"I don't want you to take me the first day of high school!"

I said, reminding them all I was sitting at the table and should be part of this decision. "Sally and David are riding. The bus will just pick up in our neighborhood, right?"

"I haven't seen a published route yet," my father said, "but I doubt it will only be the neighborhood kids on the bus."

"I'm going to call Sally's mother and double-check." My mother dabbed her lips with her napkin. "We could take turns driving you," she added as she wiped the condensation off the bottom of her tea glass.

She stood to clear the plates. I joined her and scraped what was left on mine into the trashcan before she could harp about wasting food. Although, I don't think she would have lectured me this night about the starving children in China.

I couldn't sleep. The attic fan roared but there wasn't any cool air to pull in and circulate through our bedrooms. The cicadas were August-loud, like the relentless heat had worked them into a maniacal frenzy. I dozed and sweated and kept flipping my pillow to the cooler side, but couldn't get past the drifting stage to sleep. It must have been the same for Donald because long past the time when the house had gone dark, he came into my room.

"Nell, you awake?"

"Yeah. Too hot to sleep,"

"Can you cover for me?"

"Sure." I sat up and swung my legs over the side of the bed.

My room was above our back porch and on the opposite side of the house from our parents' room. So even though we were on the second floor, it was easy to open the window, step onto the porch roof, and drop into the back yard. Donald had taught me how to do it with bent knees to soften the landing.

He could also climb on the porch railings and hoist himself back up, but I wasn't strong enough to do that.

"I'm going for a smoke," he said. My job as cover was to signal him with an owl hoot if I thought he was in danger of being discovered. It didn't make much sense, but I liked being trusted with the risk.

Donald slid the screen up and wriggled onto the porch roof. "I won't be long."

Usually I closed the screen to keep the mosquitoes out, but after Donald disappeared into the yard, I slipped out too and sat on the porch roof. The asphalt shingles were scratchy on my bare legs when I splayed them out, so I sat with my arms hugging my knees and peered through the tree limbs searching the inky sky. I found the Big Dipper, but only a sliver of moon. The moon landing seemed ages ago, and not so real now that the moon was considerably diminished. The trees surrounding the yard were formless dark shapes, but if I squinted, I thought I could see the burning end of Donald's cigarette next to one of them. I hadn't smoked yet, but since I was going to high school, maybe it was time to try. Sally had.

Donald stayed a long time past when I could see the end of his cigarette. I picked up a magnolia pod that was sitting on the roof and tugged at its red seeds, tossing them into the yard. Puffs of hot breeze blew through my thin baby doll pajamas and I wished the roof was flat and mosquitoes didn't exist so I could sleep there. I didn't hear Donald until his hands grabbed the eaves. He heaved himself onto the roof and startled when he saw me.

"Damn Nell! You scared me!"

"Sorry. I wanted to sit out here."

Donald plopped down beside me. He picked up a magnolia pod and threw it into the night. We heard it hit the roof of the garage.

"Two points!" he said. His white undershirt glowed and smelled of his cigarette.

"You worried about school?" he asked.

"Yeah, kind of. Do you think there could be riots at Stonewall like the ones on the news?"

"Nah. Most people have worse things to worry about—like Vietnam, or Russia blowing up the world. That's what most of the riots are about."

I thought about the air raid drills we practiced at school. I was a half-hearted desk ducker when the siren went off. I didn't want to survive a nuclear attack if my family didn't survive too. I wondered if they practiced those drills at Stonewall.

"Mostly I'm mad I can't go to Lee."

"Yeah, that really stinks."

Donald scooted to lean his back against the house. He threw another magnolia pod, but we didn't hear that one land. Only the cicadas interrupted the night's quiet with their rattling crescendos.

"You know, Lee's not going to be the same either," Donald said.

I wasn't sure if he was worried about that, or if he was trying to make me feel better. Either way, it was nice of him to say. All of a sudden I couldn't keep my eyes open. I stood up, brushed off the little twigs that had stuck to the back of my legs and crawled through the window and into my bed. I was almost asleep when I heard Donald slide the screen back and go to his room. It was so late the cicadas had stopped their frenzied chorus.

Chapter Three

The bus route published in *The Times Dispatch* had our neighborhood picked up first, with an hour on the bus before we arrived at Stonewall. The parents decided Mr. Carpenter would drive Sally, David, and me to school that first week. We would ride the bus home when the route was reversed. I waited on the front porch, in my yellow dress with the white collar, holding a notebook full of blank paper and a brown paper bag with my lunch. When Mr. Carpenter's wood-paneled station wagon swung into the driveway, I slid into the back seat beside Sally.

"You look really tan in that dress, Nell." If she was trying to make me feel confident, it didn't work. Her blonde hair was pulled up from around her face and had just the right height and soft curl. I'd slept with my hair on top of my head, wrapped around a fat empty orange juice can. The idea of straightening my frizzy curl had worked for all of five minutes before my mane expanded and crimped again. At the last minute I brushed it into the same pigtails I'd worn all summer. I looked like I still belonged in junior high, instead of starting my sophomore year of high school.

There was little conversation in the front seat or the back.

And even though the windows were rolled down, there was scant breeze at our traffic-slow pace, the early September day not promising any relief from the leftover summer heat. When the car turned onto Jefferson Street it had taken fifteen anxious minutes to get to school.

Mr. Carpenter pulled the station wagon in behind another car. "Isn't that the Fuller boy?" He nodded to a lanky redheaded kid getting out of the car in front of us.

"Yeah, that's Roger," David said. "That kid is weird. He follows you around but never says anything." David waited until Roger had climbed the steps to the school before he opened his door.

"Thank you for the ride, Mr. Carpenter," I said as I got out.

"Good luck today." He tilted his head to see the front of the school where a crowd of girls was standing. They were so animated in their conversation their gestures could be seen from the car. We heard their laughter as two boys walked up to them. There were no white faces in the group.

"Son, why don't you walk Nell and Sally to their homerooms? You know, be a gentleman." Mr. Carpenter smiled at us, but his eyes were focused on the boisterous group.

"Y'all walk ahead of me," David said. Usually I balked inside when he told us what to do; he was only a year older. But today I didn't mind. Sally and I got into familiar step and walked towards the school. David was so close behind I could hear him breathing. I clutched my notebook against my chest.

"Hey, white girl! You about blinding me in that yellow dress!" I was halfway up the concrete steps before I realized the group was laughing at me.

"Ignore it," Sally whispered. I didn't have the nerve to do anything but ignore it. We quickened our gait and entered the big red doors of Stonewall High School. My forehead was damp and my lip was tender from where my teeth had dug in.

Our eyes had to adjust to the dimness of the front hall. It

27

smelled of old tennis shoes and sweat. Strips of the wood floor were lightened from wear and bare of the polish that always shone from my old school's floors. The yellowish beige walls had patches of white, like someone had forgotten to paint over the repairs. Typed lists of homerooms and their would-be occupants were thumbtacked onto a bulletin board. There was no colorful corrugated trim or any letters traced from a stenciled set that spelled "Welcome to Stonewall High." The three of us stood at the back of a group of students searching for their names, and waited our turn to move closer and find our own. Roger's red head was close to the board, his back to us. The rest of the heads were dark.

When there was room for us, it didn't take long. The students had been grouped alphabetically. When I found the sheet with *Randolph, Eleanor* I also saw some familiar names: *Reed, Rosser, Sampson.* Relieved I would know some kids in my homeroom, I memorized the room number, stepped out of the crowd and waited for Sally and David.

"What's your room number?" David asked.

"111."

"Mine's 116, so we're close," Sally said.

"I'm 212, in case you need to find me or anything." David shoved his hand in his pocket and glanced around. "Guess we should go on." We followed him down the hall; he would have never hung around us this long at Lee.

We passed rows of empty lockers sitting ajar and small groups of students leaning against them. I recognized Renay, who I'd played with in elementary school and who'd been in my homeroom in junior high. Our eyes met and I smiled at her and did a little wave with my fingers. She stared at me, but didn't return my wave or my smile.

"Wasn't that Renay we passed?" I asked Sally.

"Yeah."

"She acted like she had no idea who I was."

Sally shrugged. "Maybe since she's here with her colored

28

friends, she doesn't need the white ones."

A few students were seated in Room 111, scattered in rows facing the front. The desks were the wooden kind with the metal cubby underneath for holding books and the groove on top for keeping pencils from rolling down the incline, not the newer miniature tables with bucket chairs I'd had last year. The open windows faced the blacktop at the back of the school. The crooked blinds appeared to have been drawn up quickly, with the twisted cord left hanging between the slats. A black girl was leaning her head out the window, calling to someone. She ducked as a paper airplane came flying into the room.

None of the acquaintances whose names I'd seen on the homeroom list were there yet. I chose an empty desk in the second row.

"Somebody's already sitting there," a voice said from the back, followed by snickering.

I turned around and saw a group of girls who had pushed several desks together. They were dressed like the models I'd seen in the magazines Sally and I pored over in the library. Short dresses with swirly patterns and big collars, big hoop earrings. I could tell from the way they looked tall, even when seated, that they were used to being in the popular group.

"Why don't you sit in that front row?" one of them said. "That way we can keep an eye on you."

"Not like we going to miss her in that dress!" They burst out laughing.

I tried politely smiling at them. They laughed harder. I took the front row desk and faced the chalkboard. I watched the door, waiting for another white kid to walk through it, or for a teacher to come in and take control. I fumbled with my stuff and pulled out a pencil to keep my hands busy. I let my pocketbook hang from the back of the attached seat and doodled in my notebook, fighting the queasiness in my stomach.

A bell rang and more students paraded into the room. Some came in and found seats together. A few, like me, appeared to know no one else. One white boy sauntered in and I tried to make eye contact with him. But his angry face never looked my way before he slumped into a seat in the back. Finally Laurie Sampson walked in. I motioned to her to take the desk next to mine on the front row and she slid into it. We'd never hung out together before. I didn't dislike her; she just had her friends and I had mine.

When the tardy bell rang there were still half a dozen empty seats in the classroom and no teacher.

"Wonder what Lee is like right now," Laurie said.

"Can't be like this."

"Have you seen anyone else you know?"

"I came with Sally and David Carpenter. And we saw Roger Fuller."

"Did you ride the bus?"

"No. Did you?"

She shook her head. "My dad drove me."

A tall black man with horn-rimmed glasses walked into the classroom. His short-sleeved white shirt was already circled under the arms, but his tie had not been loosened and everything else about him appeared cool and controlled. He stood in front of us holding a stack of papers and conversations hushed.

"Alright, folks. Your homeroom teacher was reassigned to another class, so I'm here today. I'm Mr. Wiley, the Assistant Principal. When I call your name, come get your schedule."

He began reading last names in alphabetical order. One of the girls from the back came up to *Rudolph, Valerie*. She walked the aisle by my desk and knocked my pocketbook to the floor. I hung it back on my seat. She bumped it again on her way back. I pulled the purse by its leather strap over into my lap until all the names were called.

After the schedules were distributed, Mr. Wiley was left with a stack in his hand. Most of the unclaimed papers belonged to names familiar to me since elementary school, white boys and girls who had been with me in one grade or another. I wondered where they were sitting now.

The bell rang and we were released into a sea of students. As I moved with the tide down the hall, my white face and my too bright dress were a beacon that drew the black kids' attention when I would have rather gone unnoticed. The scene was to be repeated six more times that day: I would find my class; I would sit in the front; I would listen to the roll being called and hear the names of friends who were not there.

When I walked into my English class Renay was sitting in the back with two other black girls. There was an empty desk in front of them.

"Hey, Renay." She stopped talking to her friend and squinted her eyes at me.

"Mind if I sit here?"

"It's a free country." She tossed her head back around to her friends. My cheeks heated up as I faced the front, and waited for the bell to ring. The clock on the wall showed 11:05. Four more hours before I would be released.

Sophomores had the same lunch period, and I found Sally and introduced her to Laurie. A girl named Allison was with Sally and we grabbed a table on the far edge of the cafeteria. The room was loud, with trays scraping against tabletops and silverware clanging against plates. The kitchen staff could be heard shouting instructions over a blasting radio. The cafeteria was in the basement and had high, narrow casement windows. They were open, but no breeze could find its way in to stir the stifling air.

"Anyone buying milk?" I asked. Sally glanced across the cafeteria to the milk line on the other side.

"I don't want to be the only white person in that line, do you?"

"No, guess not." I would stand out in my yellow dress and have to walk past all the other tables to get there.

"Water fountain's right outside the cafeteria," Allison said.

So we ate our sandwiches without anything to wash them down and talked about the friends who'd left us to face this school.

"Maybe they're waiting to see how the first day goes," Sally said.

"Yeah," Laurie chimed in, "they haven't withdrawn already or their names wouldn't be on the rolls. Maybe we should call some people and tell them Stonewall isn't that bad and they should try it." Her voice sounded hopeful.

"But it *is* that bad," I said. "What would you say? All the black kids are nice, and can't wait to have some white friends? Even the ones I've known since first grade aren't talking to me!"

Across the room a tray dropped and rattled. A burst of laughter followed.

"Anyone had P.E. yet?" I asked, "I've got it next period."

"Me too." Allison said.

"I had it second period," Sally said. "All you do is sit there and they give you a uniform. But the uniforms are used. First thing I'm doing is wash it in boiling water. No telling who wore that disgusting suit last!"

"Did you see the locker room?" I asked. "I mean, will we have to *shower* with everyone?"

"The teacher didn't say anything about a shower," Sally said. "Bet they don't have working ones."

We finished our sandwiches, potato chips, and Oreos, and moved as a pack to toss our trash and drink from the water fountain. Huddled at the edge of the cafeteria, we waited for the bell to ring.

Allison and I walked to P.E. and sat on the bleachers away

from everyone else. We were the only white girls in the gym. We propped our feet on the bench in front of us and waited for the teacher to call our names and hand us a faded blue gym suit from a pile in a cardboard box. Mine was huge and had a broken snap on the front. Allison's smelled like Donald's basketball clothes.

"Ugh. Where do you think they kept these?" She held it between two fingers like a dead mouse by its tail.

"They were probably sitting in a locker all summer." I rolled mine into a tight ball. "Wish I'd kept my bag from lunch so I wouldn't have to touch it."

"My mom is going to freak out when she sees this thing."

"Mine too."

"I'm pretty sure she won't want me to wear something a colored person's already worn." Allison's mouth contorted in disgust.

Other girls were making fun of the suits too, holding them up and groaning. Some of them were checking the inside tags where names had been written in permanent marker. One girl was walking from group to group asking to see the gym suits. She seemed older and moved her body with authority. I liked her dress and her sandals were exactly like the ones Sally's sister Nancy wore. She didn't skip our group of two.

"Whose you got?" she asked.

"What?"

"Whose suit you got? Read the tag."

"Watkins," Allison said.

"Oh Lord, I don't want that one," the girl jeered.

"Childress?" I read, unsure of the pronunciation.

"That one belongs to me," she said, and took the gym suit out of my hand and tossed hers into my lap. She spun around and strolled to the other end of the bleachers. My new suit said "Cook," and meant no more to me than the first one had.

"Wonder who Watkins was," Allison said, turning her nose up at the suit sitting on top of her books. "Obviously someone nobody liked."

"Guess they didn't like Cook either," I said, rolling up my second suit.

"Am I too late?" The girl standing in front us looked apologetic.

"Too late for what?" I asked.

"Has Janet already asked you to switch suits?"

"Some girl did," Allison said.

"There's a tradition here at Stonewall about inheriting a popular kid's suit. I was trying to get over here to help you bargain with her, cause you're obviously new and wouldn't know about it. Sorry I didn't get here in time."

"Thanks for trying," I said.

"Let me see who you have." We showed her our suits.

"Oh, you'll be okay." She smiled. "It's bad luck if you get certain kids' suits. Cook and Watkins weren't popular or unpopular, kind of like me." She giggled.

Her eyes were kind, and her presence calmed the butterflies that had been in my stomach all day.

"Well, see you around."

I didn't think to ask her name before she was on the other side of the gym.

David, Sally, and I got off the bus at the corner. We walked without much talking, in our own worlds, rocked that day into some foreign country. They peeled off when we reached their front walk.

"See ya tomorrow," Sally said.

She followed David up the walk and they disappeared into their house. They would share experiences at the Carpenter's large supper table, adding to each other's account of the day.

My eyes welled up as I continued on my own. My feet

moved as through mud. No trying out for cheerleading now. No clubs. Would I ever go to a football game at that school? Would one of the handful of white boys I saw today become my boyfriend? The chunk of my life that should be like all the novels I'd read last summer had flipped into an unknown place. But if I gave it words, even if I could find them, it would nail my experience into a permanent spot. I couldn't do that yet. Not the first day.

I took the long way around the corner instead of cutting through the Benson's yard. I wanted to be little again. I wanted it to be summer. I wanted to rewind the year and have the judge make a different decision.

Donald was leaning against the sink drinking a coke when I walked in the back door, still in his khakis and plaid shirt, looking as fresh as he had that morning. His day hadn't altered his appearance.

My mother glanced up from the carrots she was chopping and checked the clock above the stove. "The bus certainly took a long time. Was everything okay?" Her brow wrinkled in concern.

"Everything always takes longer on the first day," I said. I didn't have the energy to reveal the details of my dream-squelching day.

She returned to her chopping. "Did you have any friends in your classes?"

"A few."

"Did you find your way around alright?"

"Yeah."

"Well, good." The little orange circles lined up neatly behind her knife.

"Want a coke?" Donald asked. He sensed I was in a delicate spot, unable to articulate whatever I was feeling. I nodded, willing the tears behind my eyes to stay where they were.

He pulled a wavy green bottle out of the refrigerator and opened it for me. The long swallow of the cold coke tickled and soothed. I'd only had a few sips from the water fountain all day.

"I have your French teacher, Miss Conner. She asked about you."

"Really? She's nice, but she's hard. Wonder why she left Lee?"

"I think the teachers were made to change schools too. Sounded like she really missed Lee."

"Did you get homework?"

"Only from her."

"Lucky you. I got assignments from every teacher."

I faked a sympathetic smile. I wished I'd been given something to do. I left them and went to my room. I took off the yellow dress I'd been so excited to wear and dropped it in the hamper. It was later returned to my closet, washed and ironed, but by the time I had the nerve to wear it again, it would be too tight and too short.

My father's car was in the driveway earlier than usual. I heard their voices in the kitchen talking about me. I tried to act nonchalant as I joined them, back in my summer shorts.

At supper, my father peppered me with questions:

"How was the bus ride?"

"Okay,"

"Any commotion at school?"

"No."

"Were the Davis children there?" I shook my head.

"How about the Maddox girls?"

"I didn't see them." He nodded his head. My answers were confirmation of information he already had.

My mother asked who I ate lunch with. She didn't ask what the black girls said about my dress, or what I had to drink with my lunch, or whether I had gone to the bathroom all day. She wouldn't have thought to ask those questions because they were never relevant questions in my old school. And, for reasons I couldn't identify myself, I didn't want to talk about those things.

I relied on Donald to fill the conversation space. He complained with great fervor that the senior privileges he'd waited so patiently on had been withdrawn. No eating lunch on the lawn, no passes to meet friends for "study groups" in the library, no early dismissals on game days. But he was secure in the familiarity of his immediate world, even if the landscape had shifted. I suspect his animated complaining was intensified in order to give companionship to the lonely and foreign world I had stepped into that day.

My mother dismissed me from doing the dishes. Donald went to his room to do homework. My father settled into his chair in the living room to read the newspaper. I ended up in my room with nothing to do. Usually on the first day of school there were textbooks to cover, notebooks to set up, papers to get signed; organizational tasks that energized me and symbolized all the promise of the year ahead. In junior high we covered our books with inside out grocery bags and decorated them with our embellished magic marker letters and flowers. The Algebra and English textbooks I'd been issued were so old and tattered no one thought it necessary to cover them now. Only Miss Conner had made us copy a supply list for her class: a notebook, dividers, a French dictionary. She was waiting for the textbooks she had requested. We would wait all semester for them.

I rifled through my closet searching for something to wear the next day. The bright colors that dominated my wardrobe would draw attention to my white skin. I stared at my options and chose nothing.

The evening dragged as the day had. I heard the laugh tracks of the television downstairs and the muffled voices of my parents. I listened as Donald made plans with his buddies on the phone. I thought of friends I hadn't seen: Susan, Debby, Kevin, Mark, wondering where they had gone on their first day. I hated the feeling of being left. I took a bath and washed my hair and put on clean pajamas. When I crawled into bed I took my ragged stuffed dog off the shelf to sleep with me. We listened to the crickets through my open window like we used to.

Chapter Four

✳

Sleep evaded me that week. The September air was still sultry and syrupy, sticking to my skin. My tossing and turning made knots of the sheet around my feet. Abandoned by my high school reveries, I had nothing to lull me to sleep. Donald tiptoed into my room during my struggle.

"You awake?" he whispered.

"Yeah."

"I'm going for a smoke."

I was glad for the interruption of the cacophony in my head and the whisk back into a summer habit.

"Can I come?"

Donald hesitated. "You'll get us in trouble."

"Please," I begged. "I can drop down without making noise, and if you give me a leg up, I can get back on the roof."

He raised the screen and sighed. "I suppose you've earned it. Put on your tennis shoes."

I tiptoed to my closet, avoiding the creaky floorboard, and put on my shoes. I straddled the windowsill and followed Donald onto the roof. He dropped down first, his feet meeting the ground with a quiet thud.

"Come on!"

I grabbed hold of the corner of the porch roof and eased myself down. Donald gripped my knees.

"Okay. When I let go kick away from the house. Make sure you bend your knees when you let go." He stepped back and I did as he instructed, but landed too close to our mother's favorite camellia bush. One of its bushy limbs snapped.

"Damn, Nell!" Donald hissed.

"Sorry."

"We'll have to break that limb off and toss it in the back somewhere."

The annoyance in his voice made that familiar little sister intimidation creep back, the one that made me believe I was too young and in the way. He fumbled around in the bush until he found the source of the break and twisted the limb until it broke off. It was large and full of buds.

"We'll be lucky if she doesn't notice this hole."

"Maybe you should leave it on the ground so she'll think an animal did it."

He paused. "You might be right. There's no way Mom won't miss this big of a branch and she'll know a kid did it if it's gone."

Instead of leaving the branch on the ground, Donald stuck the limb back into the camellia bush. It dangled at an awkward angle, its moonlit shadow making it a creepy arm.

"Now she'll think a squirrel jumped off the roof and landed in the bush and broke it."

Donald didn't give me credit for camouflaging my damage, at least not in words, but his tone lost its annoyance. I followed the glow of his moonlit T-shirt as he moved across the yard. The lawn was damp from the sprinkler and our sneakers squeaked as we walked. Once behind the tool shed he pulled out a pack of cigarettes.

"Ever smoked one?"

I shook my head.

"Your friend Laurie has."

"How do you know?"

"I saw her smoking with her sister one time at the Caldwell's." His information was matter-of-fact, like everyone knew this, so I tried to act indifferent. The list of what I didn't know kept getting longer. Donald struck a match against the stucco wall and lit a cigarette.

"Don't inhale too much at first. It'll make you cough." He took a short inhale and blew it out quickly. "Like that," he said, and handed me the cigarette.

I took a quick puff and blew it out. No coughing. He lit his own cigarette. His shoulders relaxed and we sat with our backs against the tool shed. No sprinkler had reached there and the ground was hard and dry.

"So how bad is it?" he asked me.

"The cigarette? I don't think it's bad,"

"No, stupid. School. How bad is Stonewall?"

I drug my heel back and forth in the dirt. "The black kids hate that we're there. Most of the white kids have left for other schools. It's obvious the teachers don't want to be there either. So it's Sally, Laurie, Allison, me, and the goofy kids we didn't like in junior high." Tears brimmed up. "I hate it." I puffed the cigarette and this time I coughed, but Donald didn't fuss at me,

We sat in silence; Donald smoking, and me watching the tip of my cigarette smolder into a short stick with an ember on the end.

"It's not fair what adults do, making decisions that change everything for us, and nothing for them! They're not getting bused. They're not going to Nam." Donald's voice carried the conviction of his words. "Even the colored kids liked the schools better the other way! The ones at Lee are all mad their football team was split up into the white schools."

I hadn't thought about how the black kids might miss the way their schools had been. I could only think about how much I didn't want to go to Stonewall in the morning.

"Maybe they'll see how unhappy we are and change it

back," I said.

"Nell, sometimes you're *still* such a little kid." He inhaled his last drag and crushed his cigarette on the ground. "You might as well learn now, adults don't admit their mistakes. We're stuck." The tears that had pooled up in my eyes spilled out and down my cheeks.

"Give me that." Donald reached for my stump of a cigarette and crushed it with his. He picked up the little pile of butts and put them in the pocket of his shorts. "I flush them," he said as part explanation, part instruction.

We walked back across the yard, and when we reached the porch Donald cupped his hands and I put my foot in them. I struggled, heaving my body up until Donald grabbed hold of the bottoms of my feet and pushed me to where I could leverage myself and pull my legs up under me. I scraped my stomach on the rough shingles, but I didn't care. Donald followed me with the lightness of strength and the benefit of practice. Once we stepped over the windowsill he slid the screen into place and I crawled into bed. I watched his dark figure as he tiptoed across my room.

In every school one particular group finds its way to the social apex. At Stonewall, that clique was black and Renay was the ringleader. They ate in the center of the cafeteria, where their frequent bursts of raucous laughter drew everyone's attention. The white kids ate in the back. Each of us had braved the milk line once, but when we did we were cornered by one of those popular girls the next day, asking for our nickels and dimes. I stopped bringing money so I couldn't be accused of lying when I had none to offer. With no drinking there was little need for the bathroom, where we imagined being shoved between cinderblock and porcelain. Having never witnessed such a thing did not keep my heart from racing or my palms from sweating.

I dreaded fifth-period gym the most. My mother had washed the gym suit I'd been given multiple times in boiling water, after she called every department store in town looking for a replacement. The suit was too big and had a permanent odor of sweat, no matter how hot the water, how strong the detergent, or how long she soaked it in baking soda. Its jumpsuit style prevented rolling over the waist to make it fit, so the crotch of the blue suit was an emery board to my thighs, Like the desks and the textbooks, the gym suit was another example of Stonewall's predestination to operate with only used or outdated supplies.

We played field hockey that fall. Girls with long sticks and no shin guards fighting to drive a hard ball down a field. Girls who were fiercely competitive with girls who cared nothing for the game. Allison had long lean legs and was a fast runner. This talent was a protective shield that kept her safe from the stealthy knocking about that happened on a field with forty girls and one coach. I was clumsy and slow and stayed far away from the ball whenever I could. It wasn't uncommon for a girl from either team to run by me and do a quick slap of their stick against my unprotected shins. My saving grace was the girl who had explained the gym suit tradition to us on the first day. She wasn't much of an athlete either. Even when we were on opposite teams, we found ways to guard the other one. But it wasn't enough to keep my legs from turning mottled shades of blue and purple that then mutated to a putrid yellowish brown. I wore knee socks to cover the embarrassing bruises while the other girls were still wearing their summer sandals. And so did my new friend, Venetia.

Venetia and I were in sixth period Algebra together too, though we never said a word to each other in class. Mr. Jefferson stood at the door every day, demanding our homework as we walked in. Seats were assigned and never changed. Quizzes were frequent and unannounced. It was the only class where I didn't sit in the front row, and the only class where students didn't talk over the teacher. Mr. Jefferson didn't call on students who raised their hands, but always chose someone whose hand was not in the air. If a student answered incorrectly they had to stand until a correct answer was given. Sometimes three or four students would be on their feet, silently praying for a classmate's solution to release them.

Even though students behaved in that class, I was anxious for other reasons: fearful of the teacher, uneasy with the underlying belligerence of the students, terrified of making a mistake. Fear paralyzed me.

"Miss Randolph, what is the value of x in this equation?" Mr. Jefferson's voice boomed. I had no idea; Algebra was full of x's and y's, yet they were never the same. I stared at the unsolved problem on the board and my face radiated heat.

"I don't know, sir."

"Well, I thought for certain from the look on your face you were bored with knowing all the answers." He nodded and I took my indignity. He called on a boy in the back who thankfully gave him the right answer so I could sit down. I trained my face to feign understanding in spite of my anxiety.

When the leaves began to turn I needed a sweater as I waited on the front porch for Mr. Carpenter's station wagon. We'd bought a red cabled cardigan on the shopping trip before school started; one of those lucky occurrences when my mother approved of my choice without my manipulation.

Wearing it lifted my mood on that first chilly morning.

"Love the sweater!" Sally said when I slid into the back seat.

"Yours too!"

Sally was wearing almost the same sweater in light blue. We buttoned the bottom buttons and pulled the white collars of our blouses out at the top, the way Sally's sisters did. Sometimes they draped their sweaters over their shoulders, tying the sleeves in a loose knot around their necks, so I did the same when the day grew warm. Sally walked into the cafeteria wearing hers that way too. I felt a smidge of confidence in dressing the popular way.

"I'll take the trash," I offered our table. Allison, Laurie, and Sally wadded up their brown bags and handed them to me. At the big garbage can I felt a tug on my sweater.

"You think you're cool to wear your clothes backwards, white girl?" She was a head taller than me. Her afro made her a giant. She pushed big square glasses up the wide ridge of her nose with one hand and tossed a milk carton past me with the other. It missed the trashcan.

"I asked you a question." Her hands went to her hips.

"I got hot."

"Well, you look stupid with your sweater like that." Her eyes traveled up and down inspecting the rest of me. I sucked in my lips and attempted nonchalance. I debated whether I should be nice and pick up her milk carton. Instead, I tried to walk past her. She mirrored my steps and blocked me.

"Oh, look at that! Your face the same color as your sweater now!" I was sure she could see the pounding in my chest like she saw the heat of my face. I pivoted. She stepped in front of me, her pungent breath hot on my forehead. A crowd clustered around us, their snickers and snorts with my steps like choreographed laugh tracks.

"Excuse me." My voice sounded like a child's.

I switched directions. A different girl blocked me. I couldn't

45

see a way out. My annoyance accelerated to panic. My friends hidden, the crowd pressing in.

"Excuse me," I said louder, tilting my head like a charging bull, swiveling to move between the girls who encircled me. Someone yanked my sweater. My head lurched. The sleeves choked me before the sweater was jerked off my back. The crowd cheered.

"Okay, break it up!" A tall, willowy black woman marched into the middle of the pack. Her stunning presence silenced the crowd.

"It's almost time for the bell. Get your things and move on."

The girls backed away from me, not meeting the teacher's eyes.

When the crowd disbanded, she followed them into the hall. Allison, Laurie, and Sally rushed over.

"Man, that was scary!" Allison said.

"Do you see my sweater anywhere?"

"I'll bet that girl took it!" Sally said as we scanned the area.

"Go tell that teacher, quick!" Laurie said.

"Here it is."

A girl I didn't know reached into the trashcan and pulled out my sweater. Her nose wrinkled up as she shook the garbage off it. She handed the sweater to me with a sympathetic smile.

"It wasn't in there long enough to get smelly. I'm sure your mom can wash it and it'll be fine." Her kindness arrested my impulse to cry.

"Thank you."

"Don't let Renay's gang get to you. They're not worth biting a hole in your lip."

I licked my lips and tasted blood.

"Thanks again."

She nodded and walked out the cafeteria doors.

I went to get my books. I folded the sweater and put it on

46

top of the stack. When the bell rang and we joined the crowded hall, I noticed Sally had put her sweater back on, even though the school had become an oven.

The color of my skin had provoked a girl I'd never met to bully me. I couldn't understand at the time why my white presence brought such disdain. And it was much later before I recognized the compassion of a black girl to rescue a sweater for a white girl she didn't even know.

Chapter Five

"Eleanor, telephone!"

There were two telephones in our house: the one in my parents' bedroom for private conversations, and the one in the hall for everything else. I ditched my paperback and dashed to my parents' bedroom.

I had devoted a substantial amount of time the year before to that black receiver with its curly tail. It charmed me to the tunes of junior high romance and fashion as I picked at the miniature pompoms on my parents' chenille bedspread. But those evenings had dwindled away. The friends that had been at the other end of the line were gossiping with new friends now; allies forged at one of the newly created private schools.

"Hello!" Click. My mother hung up the downstairs phone.

"Nell, this is Father Richard. How are you?"

My hope bubble burst. "I'm fine, Father."

"How's the new high school? You getting used to it?"

"Uh, yes, Father, I guess so."

"I'm sure it hasn't been easy. I'm proud of your family for moving this community forward by sticking with it." I didn't understand what he was saying, his words on another level, like a sermon.

"Remember when I asked you and Donald about helping me with an idea?"

"Yes, Father."

"I'm trying something new this Saturday I'm very excited about, and would like for you and Donald to come."

"What would you like for us to do, Father?"

"All you have to do is come. We're having a folk Mass. All young people. Guitars, singing, and refreshments after. Five thirty. Can you be there?"

"Ummmm, I guess I can."

"Good. I'll look forward to having you with us. And see if you can bring that brother along, will you?"

"Yes, Father. I'll tell him."

I wouldn't mind having something to do on Saturday, but Donald wouldn't be inclined to waste a weekend evening with his little sister at church. He had taught me, by his aloofness or his warmth, when it was okay for us to hang out and I doubted this would qualify.

"What did Father Richard want?" were the first words out of my mother's mouth after the blessing.

"To invite Donald and me to a folk Mass on Saturday." I liked knowing something she didn't know, especially when it was in her territory. Donald chewed his roast beef and added a spoonful of mashed potatoes.

"What's a folk Mass?" she asked.

"I'm not sure. Father Richard said it would be only young people and lots of singing with guitars and refreshments afterwards."

"Bribe the young with Beatles music and food. Not a bad idea," my father said, chuckling. My mother rolled her eyes at him.

"I told him I'd go. Is that alright?"

"Of course you can go," my mother said. "Why doesn't Donald take you?"

Donald swallowed. "I've got plans. I was going to ask if I

49

could have the car Saturday night."

"Got a date?" My mother's face was hopeful.

"The guys are playing pool at Mike's." My mother would have preferred Donald start dating, but she adored Mike. He was good-looking in the way she liked: fair, clean cut, with narrow, even features. He charmed her by chatting in the kitchen before he went up to Donald's room. His family didn't live in our neighborhood, but he and Donald had been friends since Little League.

"We're having dinner with the Blackwells on Saturday. We can drop you off on our way, Nell." The vision of being dropped off at church on a Saturday night was deflating. I wished Sally were Catholic.

"Donald, you can at least bring Nell home if you can't go with her," my father said. Donald grimaced, but didn't argue. Once my father weighed in on a situation there was rarely any discussion.

"Have fun, honey," my mother said as we pulled up in front of the church.

"Have fun?" I jerked the handle of the car door.

My father flashed a sympathetic half smile, "Maybe they'll have good refreshments."

Two older girls I recognized, but didn't know, were walking up the broad stone steps. I followed them. The familiar sanctuary was changed in the diffused light of early evening. The wood of the pews exuded warmth, instead of severity. In the absence of organ music, the sound of heels on stone invited anticipation.

Father Richard saw us pausing in the back and jogged down the aisle to usher us in.

"So glad you're here! How are you, Stephanie and Julia?

Hello, Nell!"

His greeting had an earnest quality and his sweeping mannerisms contradicted my understanding of priestliness. He wore his clerical collar, but no robe. With his hand on my shoulder he escorted us halfway down the aisle.

"Go on and sit in the front," he instructed, and reeled around to greet more kids.

I tagged along with Stephanie and Julia to where others were scattered in small groups. Older versions of kids who'd been in my First Communion class, coerced by this new priest or arm twisted by their parents to be there. No one talked.

I nestled into the aisle seat and let my eyes wander around the cavernous room. Leftover sun streamed through the stained glass windows and made geometric patterns on the stone aisle. Shafts of light danced in their frames and created prisms when fractured by some small movement outside: a squirrel landing on a tree limb or a puff of breeze. Tiny dust particles floated in the air, invisible until the light defined them. I was mesmerized by these light dances until the sound of music broke the spell.

Two boys with guitars inched down the aisle, singing and playing. Even if the boys were skittish, Father Richard's rich voice behind them urged them on. The tune was catchy and it didn't take long for the teenagers in the pews to add their voices to the trio.

The customary order of Mass was present, but there was nothing else traditional about that service. It was more singing than anything. The liturgy that rolled off our tongues on Sunday was now slipped into music that had its own rhythm. Father Richard didn't deliver a homily, but just a few words praising this new form of worship. Gradually, either from the exuberance of Father Richard, the soothing quality of the music, or the absence of adult parishioners, I was drawn with those around me into the warmth of that sacred space.

When it was over we followed the guitar players out of the sanctuary to the church hall, where I'd played games with my First Communion class, and where church ladies had meetings and bazaars and hosted spaghetti suppers. Stephanie and Julia disappeared. I kept looking for anyone I knew among the kids milling around a long table loaded with bowls of potato chips and trays of brownies.

"Hi!"

A girl with long auburn hair and a freckled nose popped up beside me. She wore big hoop earrings, exactly like ones I had bought. I'd even put them on that afternoon, but my mother declared them "inappropriate" for church and made me change them.

"Aren't you Donald Randolph's little sister?" she asked.

"Yeah. I'm Nell." I'd seen her before. I remembered her mass of red hair.

"I've seen you at Stonewall. I'm Claudia."

"You're at Stonewall? Why aren't you at Lee with Donald?"

"I'm a junior, so I didn't get the option to stay at Lee."

"Do you hate it?"

"It's different," Claudia answered, shrugging her shoulders, "but I don't think I hate it."

We strolled over to the food table and snagged brownies. They were dusted with powdered sugar and left telltale traces on our lips. Father Richard appeared holding a small stack of square white napkins.

"Need one of these?" He laughed. "You can't count on the bachelor priest to think of everything, can you?" He passed some across the table to another group of brownie-eating teenagers.

"That is the best-looking priest I've ever seen," Claudia said as we watched him flit around the room. "Don't you think?"

I'd never thought of priests being good-looking or not good-looking. The comment sounded sacrilegious. But when I viewed him as a regular person, I realized Claudia was right. He moved with the quickness of an athlete and his smile revealed perfect white teeth. He had an abundance of sun-blonde hair that was long enough to touch the top of his clerical collar and his face retained a golden hue while all our hard-earned tans had faded.

"I'll come back just to watch him," Claudia said.

"Do you know when he's having another folk Mass?"

"He told my dad he wants to do this every Saturday night. The best deal is if you come on Saturday you can sleep in on Sunday. I can definitely go for that."

I could go for that, and Donald would too when I told him. I wondered if my mother would.

"Claudia, I've got to go. Donald was supposed to pick me up at six thirty. He's going to be mad at me for having to wait."

"Donald's right there." She nodded her head in the direction behind me. He stood in the doorway scanning the room. Father Richard beat me to him. They were laughing when I reached them.

"Nell, I'm trying to talk this brother of yours into coming to our next folk Mass. I've tried bribing him with the fact he doesn't have to wear a tie, and there's food at the end. What can you add to my bribe?" Now that he'd been deemed good-looking, my face flushed and my words fell over each other.

"Uhhhh, you don't have be here on Saturday if you come on Sunday? I mean, if you come on Saturday, it's okay if you don't come on Sunday. Is that right, Father?"

He nodded. "It is correct you will have fulfilled your Sunday obligation if you come on Saturday evening." He grinned like he had played his trump card. "Think about it. And in the meantime, grab some brownies." Father Richard darted over to another cluster of kids without waiting for a response from Donald.

"Come on, Nell. Let's go."

"You don't want anything to eat?"

"Naw. The guys are waiting for me at Mike's house." I followed him to the car.

"So how was it, really?" Donald asked.

"It was really okay."

I couldn't think of the words to describe the experience. It hadn't felt like church. It had felt better than church. Donald dropped me off at the front walk instead of pulling into the driveway. He did what my father had taught him; he waited in the car until I flicked the front light off and back on to let him know I was in the house safely. That's how I could tell he wasn't mad at me for making him wait; he didn't drive off until he saw our signal.

"You want to go back to folk Mass this week?" Donald asked.

I pulled a Tab out of the fridge and he handed me the bottle opener.

"You want to go?"

He shrugged like that's what he did every Saturday night. "Mike might go too." He took the lid off the ceramic cookie jar and grabbed a handful of Oreos.

"I didn't know he was Catholic," I said. Donald shoved an entire cookie into his mouth and handed me one. He swallowed with a gulp.

"He's not. But Father Richard says that's okay. He just can't take communion."

"When did you talk to Father Richard?" We'd left Mass together on Sunday, and they hadn't spoken then.

"He called last night." Donald appeared unfazed when I studied him. "Nell, he's a priest. It's not like he's the president or someone famous." He nodded towards my Tab. "How can you drink that stuff?"

"I like it." Truth was I had made myself like the soda when all the girls at the pool started drinking Tab. It left an off taste in my mouth, but I'd gotten used to it. Mainly, I liked holding the bottle with the pink label.

"If non-Catholics can go, maybe I can get Sally to go with me."

"Sure, but we'll be doing something after, so I'd drop y'all back home."

"What are you doing?"

"None of your business."

Donald had been that way lately. Nice one minute and secretive or curt the next. I hadn't been able to figure out the trigger to his mood swings. When we were younger his reactions were easy to predict. If he was hungry, or had argued with a friend, he was mean or plain ignored me. Otherwise, he seemed to like having me around, or at least didn't mind. I forged notes for him if he needed to bypass getting parental signatures, and Donald would pay me back by inviting me into his room to listen to records or play "War." When he entered seventh grade, our bond had been cemented by my assistance with his writing assignments.

Donald could not learn to spell. In elementary school my mother tutored him every night on his spelling words, even though the test wasn't until Friday. She gave him practice tests at the kitchen table, and when he missed a word she made him write it correctly five times. Donald concentrated so hard the house became jittery. The hum of the refrigerator synced with his tapping foot, Skipper paced in circles around the kitchen table, and my father turned his newspaper pages in slow motion in the adjacent room. If I were doing my homework at the kitchen table too, I'd slip away to the bathroom or fabricate a question that could only be answered by my father to escape the tension.

My mother never lost her patience with Donald, no matter how many times he misspelled the same word or how frustrated he got at having to do this drill every evening after supper. He managed to do okay on the Friday tests at school, spelling enough words right to render him an average grade from this accelerated study routine. Then the same agonizing task started over on Monday with a new set of words.

There were no spelling tests in junior high; Donald was expected to spell his words correctly on anything he wrote. One night he asked me to read a book report he'd written and even though I was still in fifth grade, all the mistakes on the paper popped out at me.

"Nell, can you help me fix this before I turn it in?"

It was bedtime and his ask was desperate. It made me feel important to help him. I circled the misspellings in pencil and wrote the correct words above them. Donald copied the right words and erased the ones I'd written.

Soon that became our routine, and not one my mother suspected. She thought she had finally drilled all that correctness into Donald's brain by her diligent tutoring and neither one of us found it necessary to tell her any differently.

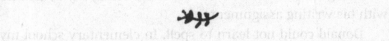

"Come on, Nell!" Donald yelled. I grabbed my sweater and ran down the steps. My mother stood at the bottom with her hands on her hips.

"Folk Mass may be more casual than Sunday morning Mass, but that does *not* mean you can wear pants, Eleanor." Her eyes focused on my purple bell-bottoms so she missed the hoop earrings I'd covered with my hair.

"A lot of girls wore pants last week! Father Richard doesn't care."

"Mom, we'll be late if I have to wait for Nell to change,"

Donald said. "I still have to pick up Mike."

Donald knew how to get around our mother. Being late for church wasn't acceptable to her any more than wearing pants was.

"Don't think for a minute I like it."

We heard the guitars and singing as we walked up the stone steps and into the narthex. The doors stood open to the night air that was quickly cooling what was left of the warm fall day. The earthy smell of spent leaves that littered the walk gave way to the sweet scent of incense. The church didn't feel like the same place where we'd come most Sundays of our lives. There were more kids this time. More girls in pants. Fewer ties. Greater ease.

The same tables of brownies and chips greeted us in the church hall. Donald and Mike broke away from me and headed towards someone Mike recognized.

"You're back!" Claudia gave me a gigantic smile. Her red hair was pulled into a low ponytail that trailed down her back. Her gold hoop earrings dangled freely.

"I've looked for you at Stonewall, but we must have opposite schedules. How's it going?"

"Okay, I guess. I still wish I was at Lee." I tried to think of interesting news to share and could think of nothing. "How about you?"

"Actually, I'm getting kind of used to Stonewall. My teachers are okay. None of them give too much homework. And I've decided to do the fall play. Ever do any acting?"

"My friend's sister used to make up plays and get us to do all the little parts. Does that count?"

Claudia giggled. "Why don't you try out for the fall musical?"

"Oh, I doubt that's enough experience for a high school play. Plus, I haven't done a ton of singing."

"Doesn't matter. If you can carry a tune, you can do the chorus parts." She finished off her brownie and wiped the corners of her mouth. "Any of that white sugar still there?"

"Nope. You got it." I liked Claudia. She didn't make me feel younger or awkward.

"Listen," she said, "this would be the year to get a part. Miss Conner told me they're trying to get a mix of black and white kids in the play, so you'd have a good chance."

"Miss Conner's directing it?"

Claudia nodded. "You know her?"

"I have her for French."

"Then you'll have a better shot at getting a part. Do it!"

We were interrupted by Father Richard standing on a chair and clapping his hands.

"I'm so thrilled to have all of you here! And I want to add something to these Saturday gatherings." His voice oozed excitement. "Anyone heard of the coffeehouses popping up across the country?" A few hands shot into the air. "Anyone ever been in the undercroft of this church?" No hands went up. "Well, I have an idea to start a coffeehouse in the undercroft here, and I'd love for any of you who'd like to be a part of it to join me in creating it."

"What if we don't like coffee?" a guy asked.

Father Richard laughed. "Coffeehouse is a term. It's a place where young people can gather, kind of like this, but in a more comfortable, youthful setting. Kids bring their guitars, or their records, and mostly talk and listen to music. We can have cokes, and hot chocolate, popcorn, whatever you want. It will just give you a place to hang out together where everyone is welcome, Catholic or not."

"That's cool," Claudia said to me. "I'm definitely in for that." It sounded fun to me too.

"So Nell, you have two things now to take your mind off

Lee: the play and the coffeehouse. How 'bout it?"

Excitement stirred in me for the first time since school started.

Chapter Six

"Would you think about trying out?" I pointed to a poster announcing auditions as Sally and I walked into school.

"Are you kidding?"

"There's a girl I met at folk Mass who thinks we should. She's a junior and she's going to do it."

"I stopped considering even cheerleading after the first week at this place." Sally flicked her hair back and sighed. "Are you going to audition?"

"Claudia says they're trying to get a mix of black and white kids, so I'd probably get a part."

"Does Claudia have red hair?" Sally asked.

"Yeah. You know her?"

"She's kind of a friend of David's. She's a little *out there*, isn't she?"

"I don't know. I like her. She's been really nice to me." We stopped at Sally's locker. "If I tried out, would you?"

"Probably not, but I'll think about it." Sally inhaled and forced her breath out like a nervous bull as she jiggled the chrome latch. The locker wouldn't open. "I really hate this place," she said.

Donald was shooting baskets when I got home. Last year he'd been on Lee's team, and in the world before busing he would have been guaranteed a spot as a senior. Sometimes he let me shoot with him at the goal our father had mounted on the garage, and some days he sent me away, telling me he needed to concentrate on his form. This day he tossed the ball to me. I dribbled like he'd taught me, took a shot, and missed. He caught the rebound and passed it back. I made it that time.

"Too bad they don't have a girls' basketball team."

"I'd get clobbered if there was." I missed the next shot.

He seized the rebound, dribbled around the driveway, and shot again.

"You're going to be on the Lee team, aren't you? You're making almost every one."

"Takes more than that to get on the team," Donald answered with another basket. "They've got to balance the team racially, so all our guys won't make it this year."

"But you're a senior."

"Doesn't matter." He threw the ball too hard at the backboard and it came back to him without touching the basket.

"Do you think it would be stupid for me to audition for the play at school? They're doing *Carousel,* the same one Lee did last year." Donald had known several kids that had been in it. "Miss Conner's directing it."

"If she's directing, you have a better shot at getting a part. She's not the most unbiased teacher."

"So? What do you think? Should I try out?" I got his rebound and held the basketball.

"I'd rather watch you in a basketball game, but if you do the play I'll go see it."

I gave him the ball.

"But don't expect it to be like the show you saw at Lee. I haven't found anything that's like it was last year."

We dribbled and passed and shot a few more times, but the day was fading and its warmth had disappeared. Donald handed the ball to me. "I'm going in."

I tried a few more shots but didn't get one in and quit.

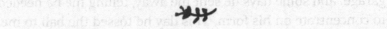

"Now the way this works is there's a vocal audition first. You don't have to sing an entire song, but enough so we can get a feel for your voice."

A statuesque woman stood in front of the stage addressing a small crowd of students scattered in the front half of the auditorium. I recognized her as the teacher who broke up the crowd when my sweater was taken. She was striking in her lavender vest and mini skirt. And her voice was so rich that she had to be a singer. Miss Conner stood to the side, in her neat sweater set and pearls. Miss Conner's wardrobe was extensive. Part of what I looked forward to in her French class was seeing what she wore. She had only repeated an outfit once since school started. But next to this dazzling woman, Miss Conner's style looked boring and stodgy.

"Once we have conducted the singing part of the audition," the teacher continued, "we will ask you to read a short scene and may put you with another student to see how you sound together."

A lanky copper-skinned boy with a short afro came down the side aisle and slipped into a row behind the rest of the students. The wooden seat squeaked when he pulled it down. The teacher paused for an uncomfortable moment, watching him as she wound and unwound her dangling chain necklace.

"And I tell you now if someone comes late to my rehearsal, they are out of my show." She stared unblinking at the latecomer.

"Yes, Mrs. Hayes," he answered, adjusting his glasses.

I sat beside Claudia. My fingers rubbed the indentations in the wooden armrest between us, scarred and scratched from years of student audiences who'd left their marks with pens and paper clips.

"I thought Miss Conner was going to be the director," I whispered to Claudia.

"I did too." Mrs. Hayes rotated her head in our direction.

"Questions?" she asked. We shook our heads.

"May I say something?" Miss Conner asked Mrs. Hayes. She nodded.

"When we cast students in roles, we have to consider all kinds of things: your height, your vocal range, how you blend with the rest of the cast. So if you don't get the part you want, it doesn't mean you weren't good enough. It could mean your unique look wasn't what we needed for that part." She spoke in a sugary tone, as if she were already letting us down easy.

A voice from the back called out. "So does that mean the cast is either all white or all black?"

"Of course not," Miss Conner said.

"How you going to get people to look like they go together if you mix black and white?"

"That's not your concern, Gloria," Mrs. Hayes said, a note of finality in her voice. Miss Conner pushed her hair behind her ears.

"Miss Conner will give you a copy of the script, which includes the music. Choose a song and a scene to practice, and we will start the auditions tomorrow." She locked her gaze on the boy who had come in late. "Right at 3:15."

"Did something happen on the bus?" was my mother's reply to my request for someone to pick me up after school.

"No, nothing happened. I've decided to try out for the school play."

"You have?" She put her fork down. My father raised his

63

eyebrows.

"Yeah. They're doing *Carousel*, you know, the one we saw last year at Lee. Miss Conner's one of the directors."

"How late will you be there?"

"I guess until around five. They didn't say."

"Donald could get you." She nodded at Donald. "Can't you?"

"I've got basketball practice. I probably won't get home 'til five thirty."

"Is Sally auditioning?"

I shook my head.

She cut the round white potatoes on her plate with a knife and fork, slicing them into tiny bites.

"Do you have any other friends trying out?"

"Not any you know. But a friend of Donald's is." Claudia wasn't the type of girl my mother typically liked, but she was white and she knew Donald. That counted for something.

"I guess I'll have to pick you up." She stacked tiny pieces of potato onto her fork. "Getting a part is probably a long shot, so we won't worry about setting up carpooling with her yet." She put the daintily loaded fork in her mouth and chewed.

I hadn't auditioned for anything before. Nancy hadn't given us a choice of our parts in her basement plays, and I rarely had trouble escaping into the imaginary worlds she created. But when I sat on my bed leafing through the script, doubt weighed me down. White, inexperienced, scared. It would be stupid to audition. Claudia called and propped me back up. She had the part of Louise in mind for me: a small role for the youngest cast member. Claudia was so enthusiastic; I couldn't disappoint someone who was being so nice to me.

My mother waited in the station wagon under a streetlamp as

it grew dark. She'd never driven to Stonewall by herself, even in the daylight. When I reached the car she leaned across the front seat and pulled up the knob to unlock the door.

"Why are you so late? I've been sitting here such a long time!" She started the car and steered it away from the curb before I could answer. Her brusqueness jolted me from the tension of the audition to the tension of the car.

"If you even get a part, I'm not sure you can take it." Her hands clenched the steering wheel, and she sighed as the light turned red and she was forced to stop. The drugstore on the corner was the only business with its lights on. Two men stood outside it, smoking.

"Eleanor, lock your door, please." I was sure the men could hear it's emphatic click.

"Why wouldn't I be able to take a part?"

"I don't think it's a good idea for you to be at that school this late." Her foot mashed the gas pedal as soon as the light turned green and the car jerked forward. "It doesn't feel safe, a girl your age in that neighborhood after dark. There was an incident on the news last night about a white girl getting beat up at a Negro school."

"No one's going to beat me up at a play practice."

"You don't know that."

The radio filled the twelve minutes of the ride home; weather and traffic reports, crooning by Perry Como on my mother's station. What gave her safety made me feel trapped. The pork chops we had for supper were dry, and the butter beans had simmered to mush while my mother waited for me. Her silence stifled us and we swallowed our supper so my father could move to his newspaper chair and my brother and I could retreat to our bedrooms. I helped with the dishes first, scraping scattered bits of butter beans and bones into the trash, my acknowledgement of the dinner that was ruined because I decided to audition for a school play.

Results were posted on Friday. A small crowd was gathered around the hall bulletin board when I walked into school with Sally and David.

"Want me to check for you?" Sally asked.

"That's okay. I can handle it." We squeezed between students to see the board. I searched the typed list for my name and found it near the bottom: Nell Randolph...Louise Bigelow.

"Claudia was right! That's the part she said I should go for!"

"Congratulations, Nell!" Sally gave me a sideways hug. "Is that a good part?"

"It's the daughter in the play. She doesn't come on until close to the end, but I'm fine with that. Did you see Claudia's name?" We looked again.

"Here she is," Sally found it first and slid her finger across the page. "She's Carrie."

"That's a pretty big part," I said. "Let me check for one more." Venetia had said she was thinking about trying out, but I hadn't seen her at the audition. Her name was there though. I would know two people in the cast.

"There's a meeting after school today." Sally pointed to the announcement. "How will you get home?"

"I don't know." I dreaded calling my mother. "Maybe Claudia can give you a ride," Sally said as we walked towards her locker.

"Maybe."

"Just so you know, it's really bad riding the bus as the only white sophomore girl."

"Sorry. I'm the only white sophomore in the play, if that makes you feel any better." Sally made a half smirk, banged her locker shut, and walked down the hall.

I scanned the auditorium for Claudia's red hair. I was the only white person in the room.

"Nell, over here!" Venetia pulled down the seat next to her.

"What's your part?" I asked.

"I'm Mrs. Mullin, the cranky old lady," Venetia laughed.

"I'm the young daughter."

"Congratulations on getting a part, Nell!" Claudia appeared behind me and motioned for us to scoot over so she could sit down.

"Thanks! You too! Hey, I have a favor to ask you," I blurted.

"What?"

"Can you give me a ride home?"

"Sure, no problem. My dad's picking me up, and sometimes he's a little late from work. Is that okay?"

"That's fine," I lied. My mother would be mad I hadn't called to tell her where I was.

The meeting wasn't long and was full of rehearsal rules and what would get a person kicked out. Everyone was introduced and I recognized a few students I'd seen in my classes, but there had been nothing remarkable to make me notice them before. If I hadn't been white they probably would have thought the same about me.

After the meeting Claudia and I waited on the school steps. It was unusual for a dad to do the picking up and Claudia hadn't offered an explanation. As the sun sank lower in the sky and the chill of the concrete passed through our coats and our skirts, my anxiety escalated. Maybe my mother was right about being at school so late; maybe the play wasn't a good idea.

"Does your mother ever pick you up?" I asked.

"I don't live with my mother. My parents are divorced and my mom lives in North Carolina."

"Wow. Is that hard?"

"Not really. Dad and I are fine just us." Claudia was nonchalant about this information as if her situation was as normal as anyone else's. But I knew only one other person whose parents were divorced.

"I see her in the summers. She left when I was three, so I don't remember much about her being with us." I had more questions, like who did the cooking and the grocery shopping, but a car pulled up in front of the school.

"Come on. That's him."

I followed Claudia to an old green Mustang. The door creaked when she opened it. She pushed the front seat forward so I could follow her into the back. She leaned up between the seats to give her dad a quick kiss on the cheek. I never greeted my father that way, especially in front of a stranger.

"Hi Dad. This is Nell. I told her we'd give her a ride home."

"Hi Nell. Glad to!"

Claudia and her dad talked all the way to my house. She asked him about work and he asked all about the play and who got what parts, like they were friends. The front porch lights were on when Mr. Douglas pulled into our driveway and I was forced to leave the pleasant conversation and return to the anxiety of explaining myself to my mother.

"Thanks for the ride!"

"Anytime." He sounded like he meant it. Claudia followed me out of the car and got in the front beside her father. They both waved "bye" to me.

My mother wasn't waiting in the kitchen as I'd expected. She and my dad were up in their room getting ready to go out to dinner with friends.

"Is that you, Eleanor?" she called from upstairs.

"Yes!" I yelled back. I stopped in the doorway and peered into their bedroom. My mother was fastening pearls around her neck and my father was watching himself in the mirror as he tied his tie.

"I was beginning to get worried," she said. "Have you been at Sally's?"

"I've been at school. I got a part in the play," I answered as casually as I could.

"What's the play, again?" my father asked.

"*Carousel*, the one we saw at Lee last year."

"Oh, that's right." He finished tying his tie and his reflection smiled at me. "Good for you."

"Who else got a part?" my mother asked.

"A girl named Claudia Douglas. Donald knew her at Lee, remember? She gave me a ride home today."

"Oh, that's nice." My mother folded her lips together and pursed them like a kiss to check her lipstick in the mirror. She glanced at my reflection, picked up a highball glass from the dresser and took a sip. Her fresh lipstick left its imprint. She wiped it away with a manicured thumb.

"Your dad and I are going to dinner with the Crandalls. You can heat up what's left of the spaghetti from the other night." She took another sip. "Donald should be home soon from basketball practice."

"Okay," I said, so relieved she was occupied with her drink and the evening ahead of her.

We rehearsed in the auditorium with its raked 1920s stage and faded velvet curtains. Its wooden seats creaked when they were forced down, and banged when they popped up. We sat in the ones with the worn-out springs to keep Mrs. Hayes's teacher eyes off us; she heard every squeak and clank. Students whispered in small clusters. Claudia, Venetia, and I bonded over Algebra homework and scribbled notes. When they were on stage, I sat alone, separate and conspicuous.

"Hey Louise, mind if I sit here?" He was the latecomer

from the first meeting. "I mean, since I'm your dead father, I thought I should get to know you." He grinned, revealing a gap between his two front teeth.

"Oh, right," I said. In the play the father dies before Louise is born and she never knows him. I uncrossed my legs and slid my arm off the shared armrest. He plopped down.

"I'm Fergy, by the way." He rubbed his chin across a pale line of a scar.

"I'm Louise, I mean, Nell." Fergy laughed. Heat flashed up my neck. Mrs. Hayes stopped her directions on stage and pivoted. Fergy grabbed my math book, pretending to read it. He lowered his voice.

"They're gonna have to use a lot of makeup on you, if you blush that easy." His noticing made me blush even more and Fergy snickered. Mrs. Hayes scanned the seated students again and Fergy adjusted his glasses as he fake read.

"So what do you think about having a black father?" he whispered once her attention was back on stage.

"Um. I haven't really thought about it," I whispered back.

"Girl, I know that's not true!" Fergy was right; it wasn't true. I'd thought a lot about playing the daughter of a black father and a white mother.

"I guess the audience is supposed to pay attention to the characters in the play and not us," I said.

"You think that's gonna happen?"

"I don't know. Maybe?"

"What do your parents think?"

"I haven't told them."

"Now that's something. Why not?"

"I don't know. Guess I'm afraid my mother would make me quit the play." As soon as those words left my mouth I willed them back. Fergy would think my mother was prejudiced.

"But you're not scared to be on stage with a black father?"

"No." I wasn't. Plays were pretend.

"Then, don't you worry about your mama. I'll look out for you." He stood up as Mrs. Hayes called for the next scene and my face gradually lost its heat.

Claudia and I waited every afternoon on the cold concrete steps of the school for her father to pick us up. Their old green Mustang smelled of stale cigarette smoke and never quite got warm. The back seat had a tear in the upholstery I learned to avoid if I was wearing a skirt. Stings from its scratches on cold legs pricked like needles.

I looked forward to riding with Claudia and her dad. Conversation was easy and they never seemed to mind that I was with them. But it became awkward to not return the favor, especially when our house was lit and homey-looking when Mr. Douglas pulled into the driveway. It didn't feel right when my mother would be in the kitchen cooking supper, and Claudia and her dad would have to fix their own meal after they got home.

"Eleanor, is that you?" my mother called when I closed the front door.

"Yes, ma'am."

"Remind me to give you some gas money for your friend." She pulled a meatloaf out of the oven. "She must be going out of her way to bring you home everyday." I hadn't told my mother Claudia was driving, but I also hadn't told her she wasn't. Giving money to her dad would be strange.

"It's actually her dad who is dropping me off."

"Oh." She took the lid off a pot of boiling water and dropped in a square block of frozen broccoli.

"So I should take a turn and drive her home." She picked up a wooden spoon and forced the frozen spears apart. "Where does your friend live?"

"I don't know."

"What time is rehearsal over?"

"Five thirty. Sometimes she keeps us later."

"That's a bad time for the one who has to fix dinner." Her lips tightened around her teeth as she poked at the broccoli.

"Maybe Dad can pick us up."

"He doesn't leave the office until six. I don't want you waiting at that school."

"How about Donald?"

"He'll have practice every day too, if he makes the basketball team, which I'm sure he will." She wiped her hands on her apron. "I'll have to do it. You can call your friend and tell her I'll take her home tomorrow."

I put my books down and started setting the table. I didn't want my mother picking us up any more than she wanted to drive to school to do it.

"I made it!" Donald shouted as he burst through the back door, my father grinning behind him.

"That's wonderful!" my mother kissed his cheek, and backed away with her nose upturned. "Now, why don't you take a quick shower before dinner?"

"Oh, I don't smell, do I, Nell?" He walked over to me and lifted his arm into my face to make sure I got a good whiff.

"Gross, Donald!" I gagged. This playful side of him had been absent for awhile, so even if his sweaty body was offensive, his goofiness drew us into his mood and relaxed the room.

"I'll be back down in five." He bounded up the steps.

"I'm not surprised, but I am relieved," my mother said as she transferred broccoli from the cooking pot to a serving dish.

When Donald returned to the kitchen with wet hair combed back, we sat down to dinner. As we passed serving dishes around the table, Donald entertained us with the nerve-wracking account of the tryouts, embellished with funny anecdotes. He named the boys who'd made the team, but the only name we recognized was Mike's. Willie, DeShawn, and Kelvin were new to us, but would become familiar as the season went on. If I'd had the nerve I could have slipped in my story of playing the white daughter of a black father and everyone could have had a chuckle. It would have been better for me to have gotten that information out there, but for some reason I held back.

⸓⸓

My mother picked us up from school the next day. I worried Mrs. Hayes wouldn't end rehearsal on time, but that didn't happen and Claudia and I walked straight to our waiting station wagon.

"Mom, this is Claudia." We slid into the back seat.

"Hi, Mrs. Randolph. Thanks for picking us up!" Claudia gave my mother her big contagious smile. She got a polite one back.

"Nice to meet you, Claudia. I'm the one who should thank you and your father for bringing Eleanor home so many times." She put the car in drive and inched out into the street. Claudia cocked her head towards me and mouthed, "Eleanor?" I shrugged.

"Where do you live, dear?" My mother asked in her sweet company voice.

"River Hills, right across the bridge."

"Oh." The car crawled. "What do you think is the best way to go this time of day?"

"My dad takes the Marshall Bridge from your house, but from here the downtown bridge may be better."

I could see my mother thinking through a map in her head. She seldom drove outside our neighborhood. If she did my dad would tease about having to leave breadcrumbs so she could find her way home.

73

Claudia leaned over the back of the front seat and gave directions; she was the adult helping the teenager drive. My mother drove below the speed limit, putting her blinker on as soon as Claudia told her a turn was coming, the signal clicking much longer than it should have. Her hands gripped the steering wheel and she dialed the volume of the radio down to a drone as we maneuvered between lanes and across the downtown bridge. At first my mother asked the polite questions about our day and rehearsal, but she abandoned conversation to focus on the oncoming headlights.

We pulled into a narrow street not far from the bridge and Claudia directed my mother to a small house on the right.

"You can let me off here, Mrs. Randolph. The driveway can be tricky when it's dark."

"Are you sure, dear?" My mother regarded the unlit house. "Is no one home?"

"My dad will be home soon," Claudia said as she opened the back door.

"I'll wait until you're in."

"Thanks, but I'll be fine."

I followed Claudia out of the back seat and got in the front, like she did when I rode with her. She pulled a key from her pocketbook, then poked her head back into the car.

"Thanks again for the ride, Mrs. Randolph!"

Claudia walked up the hill of the narrow driveway and we watched her dark shape unlock the front door. She switched on the porch light and waved to us from the stoop, looking like a child from our distance.

"She's seems like a nice girl," my mother said as she maneuvered the car forward and backward a few feet at a time to turn it around. "Now to get home..." her voice trailed off.

She didn't take the Marshall Bridge, which Claudia had said was closer to our house, but retraced our path and went back through downtown. We didn't talk until we were in the familiar outskirts of our neighborhood.

"Does Claudia's mother work?"

"I don't know. Her mother lives in North Carolina."

"Her parents are divorced?" She swiveled her head towards me but I watched the road. I felt her sudden disapproval of my friend.

"Yes."

"What does her father do?"

"I don't know. He's a very nice man." I defended Mr. Douglas, his divorce having condemned him before my mother ever met him.

When we pulled into the driveway my father's car was already there and my mother sighed.

"Dinner will certainly be late tonight."

I didn't have the kind of parents who applauded my successes or had moments of spontaneous affection, so I didn't know to miss it. Donald and I were both skilled at taking the temperature of the room my mother occupied and adjusting our behavior accordingly. Riding in the car with Claudia and her dad shone a tiny spotlight on my mother. For the first time I began questioning my mother's opinions of others, and not always landing on her side.

Chapter Seven

In every class except Algebra, I sat in the front. The popular girls or the smart-alecky boys sat in the back. Kids who felt threatening the first days had lost interest in antagonizing me, and instead, picked on each other. Rough white boys threw insults at the favored black girls. The girls feigned indifference, but there were flashes of fear and anger in their eyes. If anyone tried to defend the girls it was regarded as an invitation to fight. My teachers were a mix of the concerned and the passive, the persevering and the defeatist. Miss Conner was sweet with everyone, trying to keep the peace at any cost. Mrs. Fowler only got involved if a fight actually broke out. She didn't try to hide her annoyance at being transferred to Stonewall and pretended not to hear the racial slurs the white boys were sending across the room. Mr. Jefferson was the exception to this paradigm. He neither gave in to the rowdy kids, nor patronized the timid ones. His sense of urgency for learning allowed no interruptions. And he assigned homework every night.

Each day was like sailing through a storm. Lunch and rehearsal were my safe harbors. Between them, I kept my head down, and myself as inconspicuous as my white face would allow. As intimidating as it sometimes was, sixth period became a different kind of shelter. Mr. Jefferson's control of the classroom protected our learning. Venetia sat in front of me and we became allies in our struggle to conquer Algebra. She was quicker with math than I was, and often whispered explanations of the homework during play practice.

"You seem to have broken through, Nell," Sally said one day, standing by my locker. Venetia had passed us, flashing a grin and telling me she would see me later.

"What do you mean?"

"I mean, you've got friends now that don't care you're white."

"It's the play. When one of your parents is black and the other white, you kind of have to let it go," I joked.

"Have you told your parents?"

"They've never asked what color my stage parents are." My mother wouldn't know what to do with that information. I think my dad would see it in a logical way, like it was a case of assigning parts, which it kind of was.

"Don't you think they should know before they see you on stage?"

"What difference would it make? There's nothing they can do about it." I pulled my history book out of my locker.

"I sure would like to watch your mother's face when she sees you up there! Hey, which night are they going? Maybe I'll come the same night," she snickered.

"Not opening night. Donald has a basketball game." I tried to act indifferent about my parents choosing Donald's game over my play.

"I'll come opening night," Sally said, "and I bet my parents will want to see the play too. We'll be your opening night family." They always treated me like one of them, whether I was sitting on their breakfast room bench or sleeping in their tent. I had no doubt Sally's family would rally around me.

My onstage mother was a white senior named Edith Cohen. She'd been in *Carousel* at Lee the year before, playing the role of Carrie, Claudia's part in our show. Edith hadn't taken the senior option to stay at Lee. When I asked Donald about her, he said she was a homemade hippy and liked to be on the edge of things, like being the first girl to challenge the dress code and wear jeans to school. I'd assumed she would look out for me, since I was white and her daughter in the play. But Edith was oblivious, until she spied me talking to Fergy.

Fergy began stopping by our lunch table. and joking with Allison, Sally, Laurie, and me.

"What's for dessert today, ladies?" He'd reach down and take one of my cookies and pop it into his mouth. "Gotta love me some Oreos!"

Sometimes he brought dessert to our table. The other girls murmured their "no thank you's," but I didn't want to hurt Fergy's feelings, so I munched on the Chips Ahoy cookies, even though I was full.

Black kids and white kids noticed these exchanges. For some, like Venetia, Fergy's friendliness underscored my credibility. For others, like Renay, it provided another reason to distrust me. Edith was on the credibility side.

"Hey Louise! What's your real name?" she asked at rehearsal. Edith was tall and willowy, and traces of cigarette smoke wafted past as she leaned over me.

"Nell." I stopped short of "Randolph"; I didn't want to risk having her associate me with a basketball star from Lee.

"Ever been in a musical before?" she asked, twirling the ties of her peasant blouse.

"I've been in plays, but not a musical."

"I didn't think so." Edith studied my face without catching my eye. "I can see why they cast you as Louise. You have that young, naive aura." She said it in a matter-of-fact way, not as a compliment and not as a criticism.

"I saw you in *Carousel* at Lee last year. You have a really good voice." I wanted to keep the conversation going.

"You did?" She eyed me with more interest. "This role is much more fun for me. And being in love with a black guy adds a lot of color, don't you think?" She chuckled at her play on words. When Mrs. Hayes called her on stage for the next scene I paid closer attention. She and Fergy made a believable couple, if you could see past their color.

Chapter Eight

✿╬✿

The leaves changed, the air cooled, and the days shortened. With the play and the coffeehouse project my days took on a rhythm that created an unexpected sense of normalcy. Claudia and I got closer since she was the link between both worlds. Sally and I began to drift apart. And in those hours in the undercroft Donald became more my equal.

The week of Thanksgiving was balmy. But the boilers had already been switched on at school. The radiators hissed and knocked, making the rooms so hot the teachers opened the windows to let the heated air out as much as let the mild breezes in. November usually brought with it a canned food drive. Homerooms had always decorated boxes with cornucopias or turkeys or Pilgrim hats and set them in the halls for our donations. In junior high there had been an assembly where the chorus sang "Come Ye Thankful People, Come," and the band played "Over the River and Through the Woods," and the winning speeches on the theme "What I am Thankful For" were read. But at Stonewall, Thanksgiving week passed unmarked.

On Thanksgiving morning, we packed up the pies my mother had made and left early to visit my mother's parents in Lynchburg. We rarely spent the night. I have faint memories of Thanksgivings at my other grandparents' house. They'd lived on a small farm in North Carolina before they died, and had the easier names of Nana and Papa. Their old house didn't have untouchables. The bed I slept in there was so soft I would roll to the middle and have to climb my way out. I loved it.

Grandmother and Grandfather had a stiff house, choked with fussy furniture and knickknacks that required careful navigation to make it from one room to the next. I tried to imagine my father picking my mother up for a date at that house. They didn't date long. People might have thought theirs was a whirlwind romance, but I couldn't see it that way. My father had already been to war and was in law school when, as a favor to a friend, he attended a debutante function where he met my mother. Donald thought that since our father was in his thirties he was in a hurry to marry and only saw her charming side.

My mother had one sister, and even though my cousins were not much younger than us, Donald and I had a hard time finding anything in common with them. They didn't like to be outside or leave the living room where the adults were talking. And they didn't give us the respect I thought was our right as the older cousins by following our lead and hanging out somewhere else in the house.

The dining room table was reserved for the adults, which included a few great aunts and uncles. The five grandchildren sat at the breakfast room table. We were polite during the meal, but there were awkward gaps in our table talk when we could hear the conversation from the other room. My Uncle

Charlie's voice was the loudest.

"I can't tolerate these hippies with the peace signs! We fought our war! They need to fight theirs! Now what you people in Richmond should be protesting is for your constitutional right to choose your own schools."

My father did not add to or dispute his monologue.

Charlotte, the oldest of the three cousins, took that as her cue.

"Have you gotten beaten up yet?" she asked me.

"What?"

"Have the colored kids beaten you up?" She put a forkful of food in her mouth and waited for my answer.

"No. No one's gotten beaten up." The sweater incident flashed through my mind.

"There's no way *my* parents would let me go to school with all of those colored kids. They say it's not safe."

"What's not safe is people who think like that," Donald said.

Charlotte ignored him and picked at a piece of food in her braces. "Doesn't Uncle Eugene make enough money to send y'all to private school? I mean he's a lawyer, right?"

"Maybe we don't want to go to any snobby private school," I said.

"You'll get a better education at a private school when it's all white kids," Charlotte said, as if it would be ridiculous to assume otherwise.

"And why is that?" Donald asked.

"It just is. Everybody knows it."

"You're crazy, Charlotte," I said. Donald kicked my shin under the table.

"I'm going to go get seconds. Anybody want anything?" He stood with his plate in his hand.

"Can you bring me a roll?" Charlotte asked.

Donald opened his mouth, but promptly closed it. He went to the dining room where all the Thanksgiving food was on the buffet and returned with his second plate, stacked almost as high as his first had been. There were no rolls on it.

"Wow you eat a lot," one of the boys said.

"It's Thanksgiving. You're supposed to eat a lot!"

Charlotte gaped at Donald's plate.

"I guess you forgot you offered to bring me a roll."

"I didn't forget you asked. You forgot to say 'please'."

Charlotte shoved her chair back, scraping the floor.

"One of the things you learn at private school is when you make an offer to someone, you follow through with it."

Charlotte and her brothers set up a Monopoly game after the Thanksgiving dinner.

"Let's get out of here," Donald said. We walked down the street and once we rounded the corner he pulled out a pack of cigarettes.

"Want one?" I hadn't learned to enjoy smoking, but I wasn't going to refuse an offer from Donald that treated me as an equal.

"I'd like to tie that Charlotte down and make her smoke one of these!" I said.

"She's harmless. Just annoying as hell."

I followed him through some tall weeds to a grouping of rocks. Cigarette butts and beer cans made a pile like a campfire between them.

"How'd you know about this place?"

"I used to go exploring when you and Charlotte played dolls. No one seemed to notice if I wasn't gone too long." He lit a cigarette for me.

"I hated playing dolls with her. We always had to act out the same boring story."

"That's because nothing ever happens in this little backwards town."

"Well, I never thought I'd be defending my high school."

"Stonewall's probably better than living here."

We finished our cigarettes and added them to the

community pile.

"Got any gum?" I asked.

"Nope. But I took a few of those nasty mints Grandmother has in that bowl. Here." He reached into his pocket and pulled out two pieces of the hard candy that had stuck together.

"Gross. They've got lint on them!" I hesitated.

"Beggars can't be choosers," he said, and pried them apart, popping one in his mouth and handing me the other.

We walked back to the house and tolerated the tedious afternoon listening to the men in the living room rant about how the boys who moved to Canada to avoid the draft should be caught and punished. The women stayed in the kitchen. Their conversations, as they washed and dried, were about hairstyles, recipes, and the old neighbor families. The adults showed more tact about the private school issue by avoiding it, but my mother added nothing to the conversation when Aunt Blanche listed all the activities her kids were doing at school. She didn't even mention I had a decent role in the school musical.

Chapter Nine

※

Except for a single light downstairs our house was dark when Claudia's dad dropped me off after dress rehearsal.

"Everything go okay tonight?" my father asked as I eased the front door closed.

"Yes, sir, I think so." He was reading in the living room, waiting for me.

"There were some missed cues and forgotten lines, but the other kids say a rough dress rehearsal means a good opening night."

He nodded his head and closed his book. "And you're okay with us coming to the Saturday show and missing opening night?"

"It'll probably be better the second night," I said.

Having never been in a big show before I didn't understand the significance of an opening night, but it seemed like my parents should have. They should have chosen a singular opening night over another one of Donald's basketball games.

"I'm looking forward to it." He smiled, switched off the lamp, and motioned for me to go ahead of him. My mother stood at the top of the stairs, in her curlers and robe, backlit by the lamp from her bedroom.

"Did rehearsal really have to go this late?"

"Yes, ma'am."

She let out a long forceful sigh before heading back to bed, communicating in that one sound her objection to my lateness, to being in the play, to being friends with a girl from a broken home. I knew seeing the play wouldn't redeem me. She would disapprove of a mixed stage family and not be able to see anything else.

It was too complicated on the day of the show to leave school and come back again for call time, so I stayed with Claudia, Venetia, and Fergy. Most of the students had gone and we were wandering the dingy halls with two hours to kill.

"Anyone else hungry?" Fergy asked.

"I'm starving!" Claudia said.

"Me too," Venetia agreed.

"We can walk over to the drug store and get a root beer float. That'll hold us awhile."

"What drug store?" I asked.

"Williard's. About four blocks from here. Easy walk," Fergy said.

"Works for me," Claudia said.

"I didn't bring any money," I said. My mother would have a fit if she knew I was walking through the neighborhood, but I didn't want to stay at school by myself either.

"I've got money," Venetia said. "I can buy yours."

"I've got money too," Claudia added. She didn't act worried about the walk.

"You think it's safe?" My mother locked her doors and rolled up the car windows in this neighborhood. I'd never seen white people on the streets near the school.

"You got your daddy with you, don't you?" Fergy laughed.

"Yeah, I guess so." I tried to laugh too. We put on our coats and left the strange safety of Stonewall.

We filed past the chain-link fence that surrounded the school and stumbled onto the broken sidewalk. Fergy and Claudia walked ahead of Venetia and me, blind to the seedy row of houses we passed, their weedy yards littered with old tires and rusty metal parts.

"My mother would tan my hide if she knew I was walking in this neighborhood," Venetia muttered under her breath. "I hope Fergy knows where he's going."

I tripped on the raised edges of sidewalk, pushed up by the roots of an ancient tree or a tenacious weed, and Venetia caught me. She stepped more than once on the heel of Claudia's loafers trying to close the gap. The four blocks may as well have been ten.

The bell attached to the door of Williard's jingled to announce our entrance. Fergy led us to the back, past displays for hair products I'd never seen, to a small lunch counter with four empty stools. A fifth was occupied by an older woman, sitting motionless in her hat and coat.

"What do y'all want?" Fergy asked.

"What are you getting?" Claudia asked back.

"I always get a root beer float."

"Sounds good to me," Venetia said.

"Me too," Claudia added.

I nodded in agreement.

"Four root beer floats, please," Fergy said to the older man behind the counter. He surveyed us and began scooping ice cream into a big silver tumbler. The woman sitting at the counter scrutinized our group without swiveling her stool, then turned her head away. She held a coffee cup with both hands and sipped.

"That'll be two dollars, sixty-five cents." The man lined up the root beer floats on the counter and wiped his hands with a towel. Venetia, Claudia, and Fergy pooled their money and handed him a mixture of change.

There was no planning who would take which stool, and I ended up on the end, next to the silent woman. I bumped the pocketbook that was hanging off her arm in my attempt to climb on the stool.

"Oh, excuse me, I'm sorry!" I said, trying to catch her eye. She adjusted her posture and locked her neck in an invisible brace that prevented her from seeing me. The server behind the counter cut his eyes at her, but she wouldn't meet his gaze either. Like a robot, her hand reached for the swinging purse to steady it, then picked up her coffee cup again. She managed a delicate swallow.

I angled my body away from her, but her objection to me settled like a cloud. I listened to my friends' conversation while we sipped our floats. Claudia was oblivious to the two of us being the only white people in the drugstore. She giggled and teased Fergy about his upcoming kissing scene while I flinched every time the bell on the door announced another visitor. When the others finished, I slid off the stool, leaving my glass half full of melted ice cream and dying fizz.

Two classrooms were converted into changing rooms, one for the boys and one for the girls. Paper was taped over the windows, attempting a sense of privacy, and borrowed costumes were rolled in on a hanging rack. Once in costume, the cast waited in the back hall behind the stage. Since my scene wasn't until the second act, I found a tucked away spot where I could watch the backstage version of the show. I'd gotten used to the periphery, being more audience than cast.

"The place is packed!" Venetia was wired when she found me after her first scene. Her deep brown eyes sparkled. "And it's hot with the lights." She fanned her face with both hands.

"Did it make you nervous?"

"A little. But you don't have time to think about it." She adjusted the gray wig on her head. "It's so neat when they clap."

I had to wait for my parents to meet and fall in love, and for my father to get killed in a fight before I came on after intermission as their teenage daughter. In the scene where they fall in love, Fergy and Edith had to kiss. They had only pretended to kiss in rehearsal. Mrs. Hayes had told them it would be more believable if they saved the first kiss for the real thing. Edith hadn't seemed worried about it. I was pretty sure she'd already kissed a lot of boys, but I doubted if she'd kissed a black boy. No one could tell about Fergy.

"Let's get closer," Venetia said. She grabbed my hand and we inched into the wings. We listened for the lines before the kiss. We waited. No one backstage moved. There was a smattering of applause. There were mumblings. Someone booed. The curtain fell.

At Lee, that scene had generated a long applause. People were happy Julie Jordan and Billy Bigelow had fallen in love. In that production all the cast members were white. In this production, a black boy and a white girl stood on a stage in Richmond, Virginia and kissed each other in front of an audience. The crowd didn't know what to do with that.

When Fergy and Edith exited the stage Edith's face was flushed and Fergy's eyes were darting around, as if searching for the enemy. His feet stomped instead of walked. The rest of the cast backed away.

"We knew that reaction was a possibility, didn't we?" Mrs. Hayes said as she pulled Fergy and Edith towards her. Edith nodded but Fergy glared past Mrs. Hayes to a spot on the wall.

"You are still two people in love and you have to convince the audience by your performance that *that* is more important. Do the same great job you've done in rehearsal." She waited for a response she didn't get. "Be so good they forget your color."

We all knew that was impossible. I'd gotten used to Fergy and Edith singing to each other on stage and pretending they were in love. But I knew it was acting. Maybe they'd done such a good job at pretending, the crowd thought it was real.

Intermission lasted fifteen minutes. Cups of lemonade sat on a table in the back hall for us. I was so nervous about my scene I had to go to the bathroom twice. I wondered if I would be booed too, just for walking on stage.

Mrs. Hayes addressed the cast. "I've been watching the auditorium and not everyone has returned after intermission. Usually, that's a sign the show is boring." She regarded each of us with a mixture of kindness and resolve. "But in this case, it's a good sign. I think it means two things: one, your acting is so good it has been convincing, and two, the people who booed are probably the ones who left."

Miss Conner smiled too much, trying to affirm Mrs. Hayes's words. Neither could calm my jitters. But I did my part as rehearsed. We sang *"You'll Never Walk Alone"* and Fergy's voice behind me was strong. We took our bows to weak applause.

Claudia, Venetia, and I emerged from the makeshift dressing room with traces of makeup still on our faces. The back hall was lined with family members of the cast. Claudia's dad handed her a bouquet of droopy flowers. Edith's friends squealed when they saw her. A crowd swarmed Venetia, hugging her and talking over each other in their praises. Two little girls tugged at Venetia's shirt to get her attention. I decided it was time to go.

I sped past the family circles and out the door. Donald, still in his basketball clothes, waited at the curb in the idling station wagon.

"How was it?" he asked as I slid into the front seat.

"Fine."

I didn't feel like talking. The thrill of my first opening night had been tamped down by the ambivalent audience and the awkwardness of not having anyone there to cheer my debut.

"You're coming tomorrow night, right?"

"Yeah."

"Did you win your game?"

"No. And I didn't get much playing time, either. Mom and Dad should have come to your play."

I should have told Donald about Williard's, and the kiss, and the audience booing. He might have recast it into something humorous and lessened my fears. He could have prepped my parents before they saw the show. But those were hard matters for me to talk about, and I was tired.

⁂

The phone was ringing when Donald and I walked in the door and he answered it.

"It's for you." He handed me the black receiver.

"Hey, the play was great, Nell!" Sally's voice said,

"Thanks for coming."

"Sorry we didn't stay to see you afterwards," she paused. "Mom wasn't feeling well."

"When did you leave?" I asked.

"During the bows at the end."

"Oh. Did you see how many people left at intermission?"

"Yeah. That was uncomfortable."

"What did your parents think?" There was a pause.

"They thought they should have cast the couple in the same race, either both black or both white," she said. "It would have avoided getting people all riled up."

"What did you think?"

"I guess they're right. I mean, what's the point of getting everybody mad if you don't have to? Do your parents know about it?"

"No. Not unless someone has told them."

"Are you going to tell them before they go?"

"I don't see the point," I answered. "They might be more upset hearing about it, than seeing it."

"Nell, that's crazy. You know your mom's going to freak out."

"That's another reason not to tell her." By saying those words aloud, I realized I had a solid opinion about the matter. I wanted to defend Mrs. Hayes and Miss Conner for their casting. I wanted to protect Fergy and Edith from people's reactions to them. They weren't a *real* couple, just a stage couple. I couldn't see why it mattered.

I slept late. I was putting a Pop-Tart in the toaster when my father walked into the kitchen, the newspaper in his hand.

"Your *Carousel* made quite the impression last night." He handed me the paper, folded back to the editorial page. I took it to the kitchen table and sat down with my breakfast to read.

Local High School Promotes Immorality

Stonewall High School students presented the popular play, *Carousel*, to a packed auditorium last night. At least it was packed until the white student, playing the leading female role, was kissed by a black student, playing the leading male role. Many in the audience, consisting of both black and white persons, booed and left in protest of such blatant immorality. This event, and the reaction it caused, confirms what this newspaper has been communicating for over a decade: that integration of the races will lead to unrest, sexual immorality, violence, and the degradation of society. Citizens who have kept the schools open by consenting to being bused have been respected for following the law, but can they be respected any longer? Just because the federal government has decided interracial marriage is no longer illegal, does that make it right? We are on a slippery path when we allow a black teenager to kiss a white teenager on a public stage. It is the moral duty of all citizens, white or black, to do everything within their power to stop this behavior in our public schools, whether that means protesting at school board meetings, refusing to allow our children to participate in interracial extracurricular activities, or keeping our children out of school altogether.

"That's crazy," I said. "It's a play. Edith and Fergy aren't getting married!"

He nodded. "What's your role again?"

"I'm their daughter. I have a white mother and a black father in this play."

"Did the atmosphere feel charged to you last night?"

"What do you mean?"

"Did it feel like there was going to be any violence?"

"No. The people who didn't like it left. And there were plenty of people still there."

My mother walked in, a scowl on her face. "Eleanor, I don't think you should go tonight."

"I have to go!"

"I'm afraid something bad might happen, and I don't want you in the middle of it." She crossed her arms in front of her chest.

"I'm not going to let my cast members down by not showing up."

"Are you defying me, young lady?" Her hands moved to her hips.

"Why don't you come? Then you can protect me if you're so worried." I looked to my father for support.

"Let us think about it," he said.

My parents didn't have to ponder long. An hour later the phone rang. Miss Conner told my mother the rest of the performances of *Carousel* had been cancelled by the principal. All those hours of rehearsal for one performance. And my family didn't even see it.

I called three different numbers with the last name "Chiles" in the phone book before someone answered with, "Just a minute," when I asked for Venetia.

"Can you believe they cancelled our show?" I asked her.

"Doesn't surprise me," Venetia said.

"Did you read the editorial in the paper?"

"Yeah. My dad said he was surprised the school got to do the play in the first place. My cousin's school doesn't allow any after school activities at all."

"But if they're busing to integrate, why are they stopping things that are integrated?"

"You don't get it, do you?" I heard irritation in Venetia's voice. "It's the white people who are doing the cancelling. Your parents didn't even come."

"That's because Donald had a game. They were going to come tonight." I'd called Venetia to commiserate. Instead, I was having to defend.

"Too bad they missed it. I gotta go. See you Monday."

I hung up, not understanding what I'd done to merit her anger, except be white. The history that came before us and would follow us couldn't be understood by us. We were teenagers who had become friends the way people became friends. We got along, we laughed at each other's jokes, we watched out for each other in class and in rehearsal. But my white presence reminded Venetia that my people held the power that made the decisions for her people. My white face had made her feel diminished and I didn't know what to do with that.

Chapter Ten

✻✻✻

"Thank goodness you're back on the bus with me," Sally said as we sat down on the raw vinyl seat. "I haven't had anyone to talk to for weeks!" Lines of boisterous students were jostling down the aisle, hitting my shoulder with their books. I slid closer to Sally. I was sad *Carousel* was over and I wasn't hanging out with Claudia, Venetia, and Fergy anymore. The bedlam of the bus unhinged me even more.

"Sorry your parents didn't get to see the play, but are you glad it's over?" she asked.

"Not really. It gave me something to do." I chose not to talk about missing my new friends, or how unfair it was for the principal to cancel our performances, or how Venetia was suddenly so cool to me. I wasn't sure Sally would get it, how I had felt more comfortable with my new friends, more myself with them, than I did with her.

"At least there's Christmas to look forward to," she said. "Are you asking for anything special?"

"I haven't thought about it. What about you?"

"There's a pair of white go-go boots I want *really* badly, but they're *really* expensive, so I don't know if I'll get them."

The bus turned and I saw Williard's through the window.

96

"I went there last week," I pointed to the drug store.

"You did? Why?"

"I walked there with some people from the play and got a root beer float." I was proud of the experience, even if it had been intimidating and unnerving at the time.

"Wow. What was it like?"

"Like any ole drug store." I thought about the woman at the counter who wouldn't acknowledge me but didn't mention her. "It's smaller than People's, but it had an ice cream counter in the back." Sally cocked her head to the side. "Fergy took us there," I added.

"Do you like Fergy?"

"Sure I like Fergy. Don't you?"

"No, I mean do you *like* Fergy? Allison and Laurie have been asking me."

"No, I don't *like* Fergy."

"Do you think you could ever like a black boy that way? I mean, would you ever think about dating someone of another race?"

"Of course not. I mean, there shouldn't be anything wrong with it, but I wouldn't do it."

"I can't imagine kissing a black boy. I think I would totally freak out." Sally shivered. "I thought about that when Edith and Fergy kissed on stage. I get why people left. It didn't seem natural."

I didn't agree with Sally, but I didn't tell her. I was scared to think I might like Fergy, or that other people might think I liked him. I picked at a cuticle on my thumb until it ripped and I had to suck the blood away.

Venetia ignored me. She ran the required laps in the gym with another black girl, not me. She raced to Algebra, instead of walking with me. She never said a mean word; she just didn't talk to me. The normalcy I'd started to feel at Stonewall froze with her iciness. I tried to talk to Sally about it, but she said she knew that would happen because you couldn't trust people like Venetia. When I returned my script to Mrs. Hayes there was something about her presence that made me spill my story, in spite of what Sally had said about not trusting black people. I told Mrs. Hayes that my parents didn't know the racial makeup of my stage family, and the reason they didn't come was because of my brother's game. I told her how Venetia was blaming the cancellation of the show on my parents. She listened without interrupting. The kindness of her eyes made mine water.

"You know, Nell, you and I are a lot alike," she said.

"How?"

"We both are trying to make the best of this busing thing. We're trying to not let skin color be a barrier. That's why Miss Conner and I cast the play the way we did. That's also why there are quite a few people agitated with us."

"But why would Venetia be agitated with me if I'm trying to be her friend?"

"Nell, I'm sure there's a lot you don't know about the black experience. Our experiences have taught us to be wary of most white people. It was white people that shut the play down. Even if your parents weren't part of that, you may have to work a little harder to regain Venetia's trust."

"How do I do that?"

"Keep being friendly. Be patient. Maybe try to talk about what happened another way." She smiled. "Hopefully, I'll be able to cast you both in another play in the spring—if it's allowed." Her smile was replaced by a sigh.

"Thanks, Mrs. Hayes."

She stood up and came from behind her desk to put her hands on my shoulders. "Hang in there, Nell. I know it's been a big change for you to switch schools this year. I'm glad there are kids like you here."

I left her room feeling validated and determined.

It was easier to write than it was to talk to Venetia. I could choose my words instead of stumbling over them. I explained how I never told my parents about the mixed family in the play, and how Fergy could back me up on knowing that. I thanked her for welcoming me into the black school and not minding that I was white. And I went a step further. I invited her to come on Saturdays to help with the coffeehouse. Father Richard had already said he wanted it to be an "open" project, and for us to invite any friends we wanted.

When Venetia showed up in Algebra the next day, her icy demeanor had melted.

"Can Fergy come too?"

"Fergy?"

"Can Fergy come to the coffeehouse too? I don't want to be the only black kid there."

"Sure!"

Mr. Jefferson cleared his throat and silenced us. But when he turned back to the board, Venetia leaned up and whispered.

"Just I can't let my grandmother hear about it. She has a thing about the pope."

I giggled and copied the problem off the board.

Every Saturday a few more kids showed up to help with the coffeehouse. I invited Sally to come a few times, but she was always busy, so I stopped asking. Our small troupe had emptied the dim undercroft of decades of dirt and rodent skeletons, and salvaged what furniture we could. Now, a group of guys worked on constructing a small stage. And the rest of us covered the cinderblock walls with creamy white paint. The excitement of creating something out of nothing also created friends out of strangers. Venetia and Fergy were not just politely welcomed, but accepted into the fold.

"So glad you're all here!" Father Richard stood on a chair and greeted us. He held a bucket of paintbrushes in one hand and a transistor radio in the other. He directed his smile to Fergy and Venetia.

"A couple of things happened this week." He jumped off the chair and started handing out paintbrushes. "Looks like the cinderblock walls soaked up all the paint, so we need to make another go of it. And...we got a donation of old electrical spools." Kids gave him quizzical looks. "We can turn them into tables!" His smile was infectious and everyone clapped.

Father Richard let us vote on the radio station. This affirmed his role as "the cool priest," even if he preferred the legendary Beatles over newcomer Marvin Gaye. Claudia and I made sure Venetia and Fergy were between us as we painted, and it felt like being in the play again. We had a task to share, teasing about paint blots, and easy comfort, even in that cold and musty undercroft.

"Do you have to leave the walls white?" Venetia asked as she dipped her brush in paint.

"I don't know," I said.

"I mean, is it against anything Catholic to use some color?"

Claudia laughed. "You never know—but I'll ask." She found Father Richard.

"I hear you're asking about colors," he said.

"Do we have to keep the walls white?" I asked for Venetia.

"There are no rules about color, if that's what you mean," he smiled. "What's your idea?"

I looked at Venetia.

"Well, I've seen these cool murals. Not really pictures, but swirls of color, like in the paisley shapes. Would that work down here?"

"That's brilliant, Venetia!" Father Richard's eyes twinkled. "Can you draw up a sketch of what you're thinking?"

Venetia nodded. "I'd be happy to, sir."

We never said "sir" to him, but always addressed him as "Father." It sounded funny and he smiled, but didn't correct her.

"We won't be down here again until after Christmas, but if you give your sketch to Nell and make a list of what colors you need, I'll get the supplies so we can get on it after the holidays."

Our priest walked away and Venetia looked stunned that her kernel of an idea could so easily become a reality.

Fergy snickered. "Whoa girl! You gonna have to watch these Catholics or they just might try to make you one!"

"That's not true!" I said. "Father Richard just wants everyone to feel a part of this."

"Nell, don't take it personally. Fergy's just teasing," Venetia said. "Besides, I figure if I just help with this coffeehouse and not go to any of your folk Masses, my grandmother won't have to worry about the pope's influence over me." Her rationalization made me happy because it proved she really wanted to be there.

We picked up our brushes and finished the wall before Fergy and Venetia left and Claudia and I went upstairs for folk Mass. Venetia brought her sketches to school on Monday, filled in with all the colors of the rainbow. I couldn't wait to get started.

Chapter Eleven
✠

I had experienced one white Christmas in my life, and I didn't remember it. There is a black and white picture of me bundled into a snowsuit, held high in my father's arms as if he was getting ready to toss me into the snow. It was taken in front of our house, with Donald standing beside us in a hooded coat and boots up to his knees. The picture is blurry and off-center, but still communicates a certain joy. *Christmas Eve, 1955* is written in my mother's perfect script on the white border beneath the snapshot. Photographic evidence of our lives was done in fits and starts, the result being lots of pictures of the same event and nothing for a year or two. There were lots of pictures of that Christmas snow, most of them of the house in the snow, the magnolia tree in the snow, the unplowed street in the snow. This fuzzy one is the only one that proved we were there too.

On the news the weatherman mentioned the possibility of a snowstorm. It was the only catalyst my mother needed to create the perfect Christmas. She was the Christmas fairy, tying green sprigs of holly with red bows to candlesticks or adding another wrapped present to a growing pile in her bedroom, while she waited for our final day of school when we would get a tree. My father's jobs were always the same: buy the tree, put on the lights, and rig a spotlight to showcase the wreath my mother made for the front door. I don't know why she never came with us to choose the tree. She trusted my father to follow her specific instructions of height and scent, and to check for any gaping holes between the branches.

"Do I have to go?" Donald asked at dinner. "Everybody's going to Mike's tonight."

"Everyone's always going to Mike's. I think it would be nice for you to spend one night with your family," my mother said as she passed the bowl of peas. He put half a spoonful on his plate, obeying the rule that we had to try every dish.

"Why can't we go tomorrow?" he asked.

"It may snow tomorrow, and I don't want to risk not being able to get the tree up." She was unwavering in her opinion of how all matters Christmas should be done.

"Can I go to Mike's after we get the stupid tree?" My mother's face darkened at Donald's word choice. He saw the cloud pass over her face. "I mean, once we get the tree up. Won't there be time for me to do both?" he corrected himself.

"I don't see why not, son," my father weighed in. And with that, the debate was over.

The tree lot was busy and we had to park the station wagon a block away. Donald dashed ahead, determined to get the task done. I walked at my father's pace. The night air stung as it filled my lungs, and even the combination of mittens and putting my hands in my pockets couldn't keep my fingers from tingling.

Donald settled on a tree in the first row, but my father spotted a big gap between its branches. Donald traipsed off to find another. I wanted to amplify the experience, not compress it. I was like my mother that way. I tried to capture the pine scent I knew must be between all those trees, but the frosty air absorbed its trail before it could reach me and I found myself brushing the tree branches and sniffing my mittens in search of it.

"Hey, Nell!" I spun around but didn't see anyone.

"Over here, girl!" I knew that voice. I hurried down the makeshift aisle and found Fergy holding a tree with his gloved hands.

"Hey, Fergy! Gonna get that tree?"

"Nope. Gonna sell this tree, I hope."

"You're working here?"

"Yeah. My uncle's been bringing trees here for a long time and I've been helping since I was big enough to drag one across a field."

"That's cool. I'd love to be around all these trees."

He gave me a puzzled side glance. "It's trees, Nell. Sappy, scratchy trees. We bring the cedars. They're the prickliest on your hands."

"We've never had a cedar." My mother thought cedars were tacky.

"They smell the best."

"Really?"

"Sure. Once you put the lights on 'em they make your house smell good the whole time they're there, not just the first day like the pines." I put my nose to the tree he was holding and inhaled. I found the scent I'd been searching for. Fergy was right.

"I can show you a real good tree if the couple I've been holding this one for ever comes back," he offered.

"That'd be great." My mother would not welcome a cedar tree, but I wanted one now.

"Nell, I've been looking all over for you!" Donald came up behind me. "Come see what you think of this one."

"I'll be right back," I told Fergy. I followed Donald to where my father was holding a tree upright. It was tall enough and full enough for my mother.

"What do you think?" Donald asked. He was waiting for my okay when I put my nose into its branches for a deep whiff.

"It doesn't smell like a Christmas tree."

"What do you mean? You'll smell it when it has lights."

"Mom wants a tree she can smell for more than a day. Why don't we check out a cedar?"

Donald kicked the ground. "Geez, Nell, are you kidding me?"

"Just look at one over here, and let's decide between the two." I didn't want to add to Donald's agony about missing out on time with his friends, but I wanted to consider the tree Fergy had in mind.

I went back to the spot but Fergy was gone. My brother and father followed me mutely down the aisles until I found him.

"Want to see that tree?" he asked.

"Yeah."

Fergy took us to the back of the lot. He pulled a tree out of those leaning against a pickup truck and stomped it on the ground to shake the branches out.

"Nell, Mom's not going to want a cedar," Donald said.

"Smell it!"

"I don't care what it smells like, she's not going to like it and you know what that's going to be like."

"Dad, don't you think she'd be okay with this one?" My father tugged on its branches.

"We had a cedar the first Christmas we were married. If this is the one you want, Nell, I can remind her of that and we'll have to trust in her sentimentality."

"Okay. Fine with me. Let's go," Donald put his hand out to take the tree from Fergy.

"How much?" my father asked, reaching in his back pocket.

"Four dollars, sir." Fergy said. "I'll help you tie it on the car."

"I got it. We brought our own rope." Donald started dragging the tree across the lot in the direction of the car.

"Thank you, Mr. Randolph," Fergy nodded to my father as he accepted the money. "Y'all have a merry Christmas."

"Merry Christmas to you too, son."

I waved to Fergy as I got in step with my father. I liked that he had used the word "son."

❧

"Nell, make sure you get what you need out of your room before your grandparents get here." I was still in my pajamas. My mother was setting the dining room table for Christmas Eve dinner.

"Why can't they stay in Donald's room this time?"

"Your room's larger and they sleep better in the twins. Dad will set up the rollaway in Donald's room for you." The tea kettle whistled and she went through the swinging door to pour boiling water onto red powder to transform it into Jell-O.

"Donald talks in his sleep," I said.

"Make sure you fall asleep before he does." What a silly thing to say, like I had control over when I fell asleep. But it was Christmas Eve, and I wanted it to feel like it was. I halted my argument.

"I hope they get here before it starts snowing." She studied the sky through the window. The weatherman had changed the prediction to rain, but my mother clung to the promise of snow.

"Finished your wrapping?"

"I've still got to wrap Donald's. But he's going to know what it is, even when it's wrapped," I said. "How do you camouflage a record?"

"Still, it looks nice under the tree." She added ice to the dissolved Jell-O and put it in the refrigerator. "I can hardly wait for you to see what you're getting for Christmas!"

I had no idea what they could have gotten me; I'd made only small requests: earrings, a journal, some *Jean Nate* body spray. I didn't trust my mother to pick out clothes or boots or a pocketbook for me. I wasn't even sure what I would have picked out myself. I usually relied on Sally's taste, which was what her sophisticated older sisters were wearing. But now I was drawn to Edith Cohen's style: faded bell-bottom jeans, fringed shirts, big belts.

"Gonna give me any hints?"

"Nope." She was satisfied with her secret. I tried to imagine what cool gift I hadn't thought to ask for. A smidge of Christmas excitement stirred inside me, and I was so happy for its return.

Grandmother and Grandfather arrived that afternoon and we settled into our "happy family" mode. We dressed in our Sunday best and took our places at my mother's festive table, set with her wedding china and silver. In the spirit of Christmas, Grandfather refrained from stoking political discussions with my father, and my mother twittered about the parties that had filled her calendar, delighting my grandmother with magazine perfect pictures of what she had seen and worn and eaten. Donald charmed with his reverential treatment of my grandparents and his sweet, subtle teasing of my mother in her role as our Christmas fairy. They refrained from asking if he'd forgotten where the barbershop was or how I kept warm in my short skirt. No one brought up school or the play or Donald's uncertain college prospects, the heavier subjects of our sometimes dinner conversations. We left early for midnight Mass, tucked into the station wagon, to drive through the neighborhoods of candlelit windows to the backdrop of Christmas carols on the radio.

I loved Christmas Eve Mass. It had a mystical quality that

was absent from other Masses. A divine hush descended on the nighttime church, a holy glow from the votive candles, a heavenly timbre in the music. When I was little there had been the thrill of being allowed to stay up late, to be offered a peek into this sacred world. Even as I grew older I couldn't let go of the belief that a miracle might happen that night.

Guitar music was playing in the sanctuary when we arrived.

"Are we late?" Grandmother whispered as we took our coats off in the vestibule. My father checked his watch.

"Actually we're a little early."

"They must be rehearsing," my mother said.

I recognized the music. The guys from folk Mass were playing their guitars and singing the songs we sang there. I nudged Donald and he winked at me. We said nothing, but watched the reactions as we followed our parents and grandparents into our regular pew. My mother wasn't the only one who shifted uneasily in her seat as she waited for the guitar music to end and her familiar church music to start. Hatted ladies leaned their heads towards their husbands as they, too, wondered about the atypical music. But I didn't want it to end. I had learned to summon up the mystical through its strains and found myself repeating the words to those songs in my head, like a mantra. When the formal Mass began and the liturgical responses were fulfilled by the congregation I was distanced from the sacredness I had found, like a curtain had been drawn and I couldn't figure out how to open it. We left Mass with the ringing of the bells and me still grasping for a sense of the sacred.

"Present time!" my father called out, plugging in the tree. My mother's disappointment with our tree choice had been short lived. Her Christmas mania allowed her to embrace its uniqueness by adding silver and gold reflectors to the big bulbed red and green lights and draping the cedar branches with long strands of tinsel icicles. The tree shimmered and sparkled in the corner of the living room.

"Eleanor, want to open your special gift tonight?" My mother was giddy.

"I think I'll save it for tomorrow and open a small one tonight."

Our family's tradition was to open one present after church. I always wanted to save the best for last. Even when I was little I never wanted Santa to come while we were at Mass; it would have made Christmas end too soon. My decision to wait that year afforded me one more hopeful Christmas Eve. We exchanged the predictable presents of Christmas ornaments and keepsakes and I went to bed with my version of sugar plums dancing in my head, knowing there were still surprises for me in the morning.

When I see the photographs my father took of us on Christmas morning I can tell the ones that were taken before I opened my big gift and the ones that were taken after. I appear older in the latter, even though nothing is changed except the expression on my face. In the early ones my smile is big and broad and animated. In the later ones I still have a Christmas smile, but it is thin and small and forced.

"Eleanor, open the big red one! The one with the gold bow." My mother, still in her robe and slippers, was so excited she couldn't wait any longer. Donald put down his new clock radio and dragged the bulky square package from under the tree. Everyone stopped examining their accumulated piles and watched as he handed it to me.

"Here goes!" I tugged at the gold ribbon until it released from the corners of the box. I tossed it to Donald. I picked at the ends of the paper where the box had tape over tape.

"Dang, Nell. Just rip it!" Donald said.

I tore the paper from the bottom of the package and uncovered a large white box. Sitting on my knees, I opened the lid and lifted the white tissue paper. Inside was a blue and green plaid skirt, a navy V-neck sweater, a white Peter Pan collar blouse, and a pair of coordinating knee socks: the uniform for St. Mary's Catholic School.

"You're in!" my mother squealed. "You get to go to St. Mary's!" Stunned, I stared at the uniform and touched the rough wool. My stomach lurched.

"Oh Eleanor, that's wonderful!" Grandmother said. "You won't have to endure that awful high school anymore!" I kept my head down.

"Whoa," Donald said. "Nell's going to be a Lamb now." Donald's group of friends made fun of the St. Mary's girls, calling them Mary's Lambs and making "baa" sounds if they saw a girl wearing the uniform that was in my lap. The "baa" was more pronounced if the girl didn't happen to be pretty.

"Look up!" my father said with the camera in his hand. I did as he requested and he snapped a picture.

When I study that picture I see the conflict in that girl's face, the confusion in her eyes. My mother was so excited, she missed it. They all saw stunned and overwhelmed and they were right. But they failed to grasp upset and confused. They couldn't have imagined angry.

"What do you think?" my mother insisted. "You're going to have so many more friends now!" She studied me with expectation, but before I could say anything, she rattled on. "I couldn't help but tell my bridge club. I swore them all to secrecy. They said they *know* you'll fit in there. Trudy Hines's daughter Brenda is there and Trudy says she'll be happy to introduce you to all her friends." The gossip about Brenda

Hines was never good. Sally knew her from swim team and said she was snooty and kind of dumb. I was not at all sure Brenda would share her inner circle with me.

"Well, pumpkin?" My father searched my face for assurance.

"Wow. This is so unexpected." I tried to muster a happy voice.

"Go try it on!" my mother said.

At least that was an excuse to get away from everyone's eyes. I carried the box to my room and shut the door. When I shut my eyes the hot tears spilled out from between the lids. Why did I have to change schools again? I didn't want to leave Claudia and Venetia and Fergy. What would Sally do on the bus? I did NOT want to go to a snobby girls' school.

I snatched the uniform out of the box and threw it on the bed. I knew I had to put it on. I buttoned the blouse to the top and tucked the shirttail into the skirt, which was too big and too long. The V-neck sweater bagged under by arms and swallowed my too-flat chest. I didn't recognize myself in the mirror.

"Come on out, Eleanor! We want to see!" my mother called.

"I think it's too big," I said, dragging my feet. "And the skirt's too long."

"It's no problem to take the skirt in at the waist." My mother stuck two fingers underneath the waistband of the skirt and pulled on it. "There's a little room, but you don't want it too tight." She tugged on it again and stepped back. "They have a strict rule about hemlines, you know, so I think the length is fine." The knot in my throat swelled when I visualized wearing such an ugly, ill-fitting outfit every day for the next two-and-a-half years.

"Baaaa..." Donald said from his chair in the corner.

"Stop it!" I ran out of the room and back up the stairs. I didn't mean to slam the door. I jerked the skirt off and flung it back in the box. I yanked the sweater over my head and threw it on the bed. The wadded-up knee socks ended up across the room. I sat cross-legged on my bed until there was a tap on the bedroom door.

"Come on down and join us, Eleanor," my mother said. "Donald didn't mean it, and you're ruining Christmas for the rest of us." They thought I couldn't take a little teasing.

Now that the presents had been opened, my father wadded the torn wrapping paper into an old grocery bag, and my mother and grandmother busied themselves in the kitchen. I found I had nothing to do. It wasn't like when I was little and had toys to play with. I wished myself back to those Christmases. I wished I'd gotten new Barbie dolls with cute clothes that Sally and I could dress and redress as we pretended exciting adventures for them.

"Aren't you going over to the Carpenters' this morning?" my mother asked when I wandered into the kitchen. Every Christmas Sally and I went to inspect each other's presents while we were waiting for our Christmas dinners. I didn't want Sally to see my big present; I couldn't tell her on Christmas Day I wouldn't be going back to school with her. We'd been together since first grade; leaving her now was the biggest betrayal I could think of.

"I don't know. I bet they're still opening presents." My mother pulled a sack of potatoes out of the pantry.

"Mother, I planned on making your scalloped potato recipe. Want to start peeling?"

"Of course. Excuse me, Eleanor," my grandmother reached past me to take an apron off the hook. I left the room to go sit by the Christmas tree.

"Why don't you put some Christmas music on the stereo?"

my mother called from the kitchen.

I was sick of Christmas music. My mother had been playing her favorite Frank Sinatra and Perry Como albums for weeks and their version of Christmas now struck me as sappy and fake. I ignored her request and went back up to my room. I wasn't there long before my father called up the stairs.

"Nell, Sally's here!" I heard their Christmas greetings and Sally's giggle as she recounted some story from her happy house. I came down the steps to see her in a fringed tangerine poncho and the white go-go boots she had so desperately wanted.

"Merry Christmas!" She greeted me with a cheerleader's pep. Seeing her so happy made me even more agitated.

"Cute poncho! And great boots, too." Trying to match her tone of voice was a miserable failure.

"They're exactly what I wanted!" She did an animated twirl and the ends of the poncho lifted up to make her a miniature orange helicopter.

"Let me see what you got!" Sally said and headed towards the Christmas tree without waiting for me. I showed her the small items under the tree and she eyed them with mild curiosity.

"I know this isn't it. Your mom told me last week she had something really special for you."

"When did she tell you that?"

"When I brought my mom's coffee cake over."

"That gift is up in my room."

"What is it? Let me see!" She headed for the stairs.

"You're not going to like it."

"I'm not?" She paused and waited for me to go in front of her. I shook my head.

I closed the door when we got to my room. I opened the box where I'd stuffed the uniform back in and Sally peered in and pulled out the plaid skirt.

"Your mom really thinks you want to wear this?" she

asked. "It's so outdated!"

"Sally! Don't you get it?" I said. "It's the uniform for St. Mary's. My parents have enrolled me in school there. I hate it!"

The hot tears resurfaced. Sally studied the clothing in the box as I whimpered and sniveled. She held up the skirt and examined its length, she picked at the insignia on the sweater. She folded it all back up and put the top on the box. Then she sat down beside me.

"Just because you got in doesn't mean you have to go."

"Oh, they'll make me go," I said between the gasps that happen when you cry too hard. "My mother told her bridge club and they're all conspiring to set me up with their stuck-up daughters." I grabbed a tissue from the bedside table. "I don't want to be friends with stupid Brenda Hines!"

"At least you'll have friends, even if they're not good ones. Who am I going to hang out with now?"

I was distressed about leaving Sally to fend for herself. It wasn't my choice or my fault, but I would be the cause for her suffering every day.

"I'd rather stay at Stonewall and be on that awful bus than go to St. Mary's with all those stuck-up, snobby bitches," I said.

"You're crazy. If I had the chance to go to St. Mary's I'd go."

"Really?"

"Yeah. Really."

"There must be some slots if I got in. Why don't you get your parents to apply?" If I could go there with a friend, maybe it wouldn't be so bad.

"You forget I'm not Catholic."

"They're accepting non-Catholics."

"Yeah, but you pay more if you're not Catholic. And my parents won't put one of us in private school unless all of us can go. I've heard them discussing it." Sally played with the fringe of her poncho. "Besides, my parents think we need to be the ones who stick with it."

"I thought my Dad did too."

"I'll bet your mom freaked about the play. She's probably worried about you getting too friendly with the black kids."

"So now she's going to protect me by surrounding me with nuns?"

"I can never tell what your mom's thinking."

"I know."

That moment on the bed became the dividing line in my friendship with Sally. From that line a wall was built. It was built of hurt feelings and bits of jealousy. Perhaps it was mortared with politeness and restraint. If we could have switched places I would have been happy in Sally's family going to school with my new mixture of white hippies and black friends. Sally would have made more friends at St. Mary's than I would. It didn't make sense.

My mother's Christmas spirit disappeared with my grandparents' departure. Donald spent most of the Christmas break with friends. Sally's family went to her grandparents' house for the week. So I kept myself occupied in my room, nursing my anger and resentment, avoiding my mother. I knew I should tell Claudia and Venetia I wouldn't be coming back to Stonewall, but I dragged my feet. Then Venetia called, asking about painting the undercroft on Saturday, and I had to tell her. My heart raced.

"I've got bad news," I said.

"We can't paint the undercroft?" Venetia asked.

"No, I'm sure that's still a go." I stalled. "Umm...I'm not going back to Stonewall."

"What? You moving?"

"No. My parents are making me go to St. Mary's."

There was an awkward pause, and I rushed to fill it.

"They never asked my opinion! They just enrolled me and gave me one of those ugly uniforms for Christmas! I'd much rather stay at Stonewall than go to that snobby school!" I hoped my indignation came through. I hoped for Venetia's sympathy.

"Huh. I didn't take you for one of those kind of white people."

"I'm not! This wasn't my choice at all!"

"How come they did it? You been complaining about Stonewall?"

"No, I haven't been complaining. I think my mother's still upset about the play." I regretted those words as soon as they left my mouth. I'd tried so hard to convince Venetia that my parents weren't the type to shut down the play. Now whatever trust I'd built was squandered in that one sentence.

"Am I still allowed to come to the coffeehouse?" Venetia asked.

"Of course! Changing schools doesn't change that."

"Does your mom know black kids are coming to your church?"

I hesitated.

"I didn't think so," Venetia said.

"Father Richard's in charge of who comes to the church. Please keep coming, Venetia."

"Are you going Saturday?"

"We're not meeting until after Epiphany."

"Well, you'll have to call me. I don't know when all those Catholic days are."

I started to laugh, but didn't want her to think I was laughing at her.

"I'll call you. Promise!"

We hung up and I called Claudia. I told her about St. Mary's and Venetia's reaction, and how upset I was about everything.

"Just tell your parents you don't want to go. What's so hard about that?" she asked.

"I don't know. My parents aren't the kind you can talk to. They're the kind you obey."

"But they wouldn't want you to be unhappy, right?"

Claudia's logic made sense. Of course parents didn't want their kids to be unhappy. But emotions were not a worthy decision-making gauge for my parents. I presented my case to them, as unemotional as I could muster, but my mother's counter of safety, quality education, and Catholic values overruled my just-made-friends and can't-leave-Sally-alone-on-the-bus arguments. Even my father, who had tried to lead the community by example, was cowed into the decision when my mother reminded him of his vow to raise me as a good Catholic. I would become a student at St. Mary's the day after New Year's.

Chapter Twelve

January's dawn was sluggish, the sun never quite breaking through the drab steel clouds. Cold drizzle stayed suspended in the air, not quite freezing, and not quite falling. It was not a day meant for emerging from under the blankets of a warm bed.

Dressing for school was like donning a costume for another play. My mother had taken in the waist of the plaid skirt, but hadn't shortened the hem. She insisted I would grow into the baggy sweater by the next year and it wouldn't be worth buying a smaller size for two more months of winter.

When I walked into the breakfast room in my St. Mary's uniform Donald examined me with sympathetic eyes.

"You want the Cap'n Crunch?" It was a small gesture, passing my favorite cereal and the pitcher of milk. Since it wasn't in his ordinary repertoire of morning behavior, it became a buttress of support, a wall behind me to shore me up.

My mother missed it in her twittering about the kitchen. She was so excited about the transfer to St. Mary's she couldn't recognize the anxiety Donald was attuned to. My father had already left for work, but he'd called up to my room to tell me to have a *really* good day. He treated my mother's decision to send me to St. Mary's the same way he reacted to all things Catholic. He deferred to her closer connection to the church, something he did not have and felt unsuited to seek. The father who had driven in the rain to show me Stonewall last August had seemingly conceded his convictions about racial equality to the guise of my mother's argument for my religious education.

The drive to my new school was short, but the heavy air that hung over the broad front seat of the station wagon warped and elongated the time. I'd had one week to adjust to the idea of going to St. Mary's and my thoughts remained an angry, nervous jumble.

"I don't understand why you're so nervous. You love folk Mass. I'm sure you will recognize a lot of girls from there."

"I don't know anyone from folk Mass that goes to St. Mary's." I stared out the window and inhaled the cold air. It stung my lungs and smelled of wet wool. My slow exhale created a circle of fog on the glass.

"It can't be any worse than Stonewall. I worried every day you went to that school."

"Worried about what?" She'd seldom asked about my days and had never entered the school, so I had not seen evidence of her worry.

"Worried about your safety!" The car stopped at a red light and she turned to me. "Now I know you'll be safe, and you'll get a good education."

"But you've always talked about how bad the nuns treated you when you went to Catholic school. And now you're sending me!" A lump swelled in my throat and I swallowed hard.

"Nuns are different now, especially the young ones. And there are a lot of younger nuns teaching at St. Mary's." She flicked on the blinker much earlier than needed and its rhythmic click taunted me. "You'll see."

119

I didn't want to see. I didn't want to be a St. Mary's Lamb. I didn't want to wear the uniform. I didn't want to fight my way into a group of snobby girls. I'd rather be with Claudia and Venetia and Fergy. I wanted to wear hoop earrings and peasant blouses, not bulky skirts and knee socks.

We pulled up in front of the school behind other cars where girls were getting out and meeting each other on the sidewalk, strolling together to the big wooden doors.

"You're all registered, but I'll go in with you, if you like." My mother forced a smile, trying to erase the tension in the car.

"No thanks."

"The office is on your right when you enter the school. Sister Bridget will be waiting for you."

I got out of the car and slammed the door. I didn't look back to reassure my mother. I wanted her to worry about me all day, not be relieved she had put me in a safer place.

The nervousness I experienced walking up the landscaped sidewalk was different than what I'd experienced the first day at Stonewall. I'd been scared, but Sally and David had been with me. We'd faced something together. This time I was alone. Even though these girls were white, I didn't feel a connection. The black girls had stared straight at me, had acknowledged my white presence, even if they didn't welcome it. I was invisible walking into St. Mary's. I even waited in the office for the secretary to locate Sister Bridget, who had forgotten I was starting that day.

Homeroom was over and the halls were filled with students on their way to Mass by the time Sister Bridget showed up.

"Ah yes, Eleanor Randolph," she said, studying me as the

secretary handed her some papers. "Welcome to St. Mary's." Her voice had no inflection and warmth was missing from her eyes.

"Hello, Sister." I cast my eyes down as my mother had taught me to do, even though I'd told myself I wouldn't follow her old-fashioned instructions.

"Mass will be starting momentarily. Follow me."

I had to jog to keep up with her accelerated pace. I copied her holy gestures as we entered the chapel and she motioned for me to join a row of girls already kneeling. The girl on the end slid over to make room but didn't acknowledge me. Sister Bridget slipped into the pew behind us.

It was a short Mass. The small chapel was filled with uniformed girls and some lone faith-seeking visitors in the back pews. The girl beside me was older, with large breasts stretching her sweater across her chest. There were holes in her ears where earrings had been, and her lips were shiny with gloss. A spot on her neck had been dabbed with makeup in an attempt to cover it.

When Mass was over, Sister Bridget pulled me aside as we left the chapel and we waited as a parade of girls in their plaid skirts and navy sweaters walked past us. They lowered their heads as they passed Sister Bridget, but I exchanged glances with Lisa, a sometimes friend from junior high, and she gave me a half smile. Polly was right behind her, but she acted as if she didn't see me.

St. Mary's was cleaner than Stonewall and smelled of Turtle Wax instead of sweat. The worn wood floors shone under the yellow glow of antique light fixtures. Polished wooden cabinetry lined the side halls and functioned as student lockers, though none of them bore the combination lock I'd grown accustomed to using. There were icons of the Madonna tucked away in corners and wooden crosses of various sizes visible from any direction. The school had once been a convent; its classrooms created later by knocking down walls between two or three smaller rooms, so many of the classrooms were long and narrow, their shape accentuated by the close rows of student desks. Green slate chalkboards hung at either end. The windows that could have lined the outside wall had instead been sparsely placed and higher to prevent the nuns from being distracted from their prayers by scenes of the secular world. The school had been built as a refuge, but had the veiled bearing of a prison.

"Here we are," Sister Bridget said. We stopped in front of an open classroom door and she motioned for me to go in.

"Sister Bernadette, this is Eleanor Randolph, your new student." She nodded to the Sister, pivoted, and left me standing in front of the class. Sister Bridget's abrupt departure made me feel like I'd done something shameful. I scrolled through my behavior over the past hour but could find nothing that would merit any repentance on my part.

"Welcome to St. Mary's, Eleanor," Sister Bernadette's narrow smile was stretched over protruding teeth. "I regret we have not retrieved a desk for you yet, but you may share with Victoria." She nodded her head towards the back and Victoria raised her hand. "Madeline, will you go borrow a chair from Sister Beatrice?"

After the shuffling of chairs and bodies, I sat next to Victoria and she moved her books to make room for me to balance the edge of my notebook on her desk. Sister Bernadette pulled an Algebra textbook off the bookshelf and handed it to me.

"We are on chapter eight. If you are behind, Victoria will be able to help you." It was the same edition of the math book I had at Stonewall. They used the same old desks Stonewall did too, but no one had carved pictures or bad words on these.

"Where did you move from, Eleanor?" Victoria whispered while we were copying the equations from the board.

"Call me Nell," I whispered back. "I didn't move. I came from Stonewall."

"Ewww. I think that's where I would have gone if I'd been in public school. I'm not sure, though. I don't really know where that is. I've always gone here."

"You've never been in school with boys?"

"No." Victoria didn't seem the kind of girl who would have liked boys. Her round face was marked with red blotches of acne and she wore a wide headband like the ones that had been popular several years back. She breathed through her mouth and I could smell her sour breath. Sharing a desk with her was punishment.

"How do you remember which nun is which?" I whispered. "All the sisters' names start with a "B" and it's hard to tell them apart in their habits."

"Sister Bernadette has buck teeth. Sister Beatrice is the youngest one, and Sister Bridget, well, you just know her," she whispered back with her head bent and tilted slightly my way. Extra talking was not allowed.

"Do you have a question, Eleanor?" Sister Bernadette asked from the front of the room.

"No, Sister," I mumbled.

"It is our practice here that you stand when you ask or answer a question."

I nodded.

"Well?" She stared at me.

I stood. "Yes, Sister."

She nodded and I sat down. The heat crept up my face. It had taken less than two hours for me to hate it here.

When the bell rang, I didn't know where to go. Sister Bridget hadn't given me a schedule. I had to wait for Sister Bernadette to notice me so I could ask her where to go.

"You go to English from here, then to Physical Education. All of the girls in this class have the same schedule. If you go quickly you can catch up with them." Maybe she didn't smile because of the buck teeth, but the way her mouth was pulled over those protruding teeth made her appear angry.

"Excuse me, Sister Bernadette, but which way is the English class?"

"Down the hall, on your left. You'll see it." She began erasing the board. The shameful feeling returned. I couldn't identify what I was doing to make the sisters be so cold.

I followed the group of girls from class to class, trying to act pleasant and open. I knew if I aligned myself with Victoria, I wouldn't make friends with the girls who seemed more fun. Yet those girls gave no indication they needed to widen their circle of friends. I felt sorry for Victoria, but that didn't keep me from feeling sorrier for myself.

St. Mary's didn't have a cafeteria. At lunchtime girls pulled desks together into circles, then retrieved their brown bags from the wooden lockers or picked up a tray from the kitchen. I didn't want to share Victoria's desk but I wasn't invited to join anyone else. I left in search of the bathroom. I spent longer there than needed before I slipped back into the classroom and angled my chair behind the others, balancing my lunch on my lap. There were no nuns present and the girls took their absence as a dare, discussing boys and dates and ways to sneak out of their houses.

I missed the dank smelling classrooms and the rowdy conversations of Stonewall. I wondered what Sally and Allison and Laurie were talking about at their lunch table. Probably how I had deserted them. Probably how snobby I would become. Probably how unfair it was for me to leave them. And Fergy would stop by their table and talk to them even if I wasn't there. He would become friends with them now and think I had deserted him too.

St. Mary's was a safer school than Stonewall. No one pushed me during gym class or "accidentally" knocked my elbows in the hall. I wasn't nervous about going to the bathroom or worried about standing in line to buy milk. My presence didn't provoke anger; it didn't provoke anything.

"How was your day?" my mother asked with smiling expectation as I got in the car.

"Horrible. It's just like I thought: the girls are snooty and the nuns are mean."

"Oh, it can't be that bad." She pulled out of the line of cars. "You'll adjust soon enough."

Each day was a carbon copy of the day before. My mother dropped me off in the early morning cold. I followed the sisters' instructions and did my assignments. I ate my lunch behind the circle of chatting girls, on the sideline of their overt social lives. My mother picked me up when the dismissal bell rang and I went to my room and did my homework, where penmanship counted as much as correct answers. It took less than two weeks to catch up in History. I didn't understand all the chapters in the Biology book, but realized I only had to memorize to get my accustomed A's. I wasn't behind at all in my French class. Sister Joan spoke French like a student. I understood her; it just didn't sound like real French. I waited for Saturdays when I could escape to the church's undercroft and folk Mass. It became the place I was most at home.

Had I never been to Stonewall I would have adjusted to St. Mary's. I could have been part of the chatting circle of girls if they had been my friends from the beginning. I could have been the kind of student the nuns would have loved: engaged, pious, submissive. But even if I had to be on my guard in the halls and bathrooms of Stonewall, I missed the authenticity of Claudia, Venetia, and Fergy, even if I couldn't name it at the time. The girls of St. Mary's were tiresome and boring in comparison and I had to be on my guard in much harder ways than holding tight to my pocketbook.

Saturday finally came. I was so glad to see Claudia and Venetia in the undercroft.

"How's St. Mary's?" Venetia asked.

"Don't ask. It's terrible. The nuns are scarier than Mr. Jefferson."

Venetia laughed.

"Made any friends?" Claudia asked.

"No. Those girls already have their friends and aren't looking for any new ones." I heard my whiny tone and changed the subject.

"Fergy didn't want to come?"

"He had to help his dad today. I think he'll come next week," Venetia said. "I'll be sure to tell him you asked about him," she winked. I tried to ignore her teasing and was grateful for Father Richard's interruption.

"Venetia, these drawings are fantastic! Ready to get them on these sterile walls?"

She smiled her broad smile and took the sketches from his hand. Her designs were intricate and she bore the confidence of a proven artist as I watched her transfer them to the cinderblock. I was proud to be her friend, and a bit self-important to have been the one who invited her. Father Richard watched her process with excitement, looking part angel on top with his priestly collar and glowing face, and part kid on bottom with his bell-bottom jeans and Keds.

"Venetia, this is going to be cool!" he said. "I'm so grateful you've come here and shared your talents with us."

Venetia looked flustered at the attention and paused her sketching.

"And Nell," Father Richard's voice took on a sermon tone, "You're an example of what the church should do: open its doors to everyone, bring them in and make them part of the big circle, whether they're black, white, or purple!"

I hadn't been thinking about the church when I invited Venetia. I was just trying to get her to not be mad at me. But I didn't object to Father Richard having such a lofty opinion.

With the dullness of routine, and the grayness of winter, also came my mother's withdrawal. It seemed as if all her energy had been spent getting me into St. Mary's, and now she had to hibernate to refuel. Yet, memory has provided a way to see patterns, and this detachment of hers was not solely connected to my school situation. Her spirit left us most often in the winters. She did her motherly duties of cooking, cleaning, driving, and shopping. Donald and I were never without what we needed. But she was far away from us. We had our own ways of coping. Donald cajoled and teased and complimented. I became adept at anticipating when the table needed to be set or the clean laundry put away and doing it before I was asked. My rational lawyer father was not a good match for her mercurial ways, and chose a path of mute acceptance. We knew that one day she would snap back and we could go on as before.

When her silence became deafening Donald rotated his time between friends' houses. My newness at St. Mary's and my distance from Stonewall friends left me with Sally's house as my only refuge. The cold January air revived me as I slipped through the hedges, even if it burned my lungs and chapped my lips. Mrs. Carpenter flung open the back door and her arms.

"Nell!" She wrapped her doughy arms around me and squeezed me tighter than I'd been hugged in a long time. "I've missed having you around our house!"

"I've missed y'all too."

"I just took a batch of cookies out of the oven!!"

She lifted a cookie off the baking pan and called for Sally. We stood in the kitchen eating cookies and chatting, with Mrs. Carpenter spearheading the conversation.

"So, how are the nuns treating you?" she asked.

"Okay, I guess. They're really strict, though, and hardly ever smile."

"I've never understood that," she said, shaking her head, "all that talk about the love of God, but you don't see it." She ran water into the dishpan and watched the soap bubbles rise.

"Oh, Nell, I'm sorry, I didn't mean to criticize your faith."

"Oh, that doesn't offend me, Mrs. Carpenter. I wonder the same thing."

She nodded and dropped the mixing bowl into the sudsy water. "You girls don't have to stay here and entertain me." Her attempts to nudge us back together forced Sally to invite me to her room. We hadn't talked since Christmas Day. My hesitation to call or visit displayed its effect in Sally's reticence to let me back in. Our friendship hadn't been tested beyond its childhood disputes, which had been few, and I sensed I was in shaky territory.

I asked her more questions than she asked me. I guess I was more curious about whether I'd left a hole in the fabric of daily life at Stonewall than she was about the new life I had at St. Mary's. I went through the list: Laurie, Allison, Venetia, even Renay, pretending not to know anything about Venetia. Sally was cryptic in her answers, emphasizing in her brevity that my leaving had taken away my right to know what was going on.

"Don't you want to know about Fergy?" Sally asked as she flopped onto the bed.

"Sure. How's Fergy?" I sat on the end of the bed.

"He asks about you every time he stops by our lunch table."

"Really?"

"Yeah. You know he likes you." Sally flipped over to her

stomach, propped herself up on her elbows and watched me.

"No, he doesn't."

"If he liked you, would you like him back?"

"No, he's just a friend." I stretched out on the other bed.

"Allison and Laurie think he likes you too." Sally smirked. "They're both still scared of him—can't even talk to him! You know, black guy, older, real scary." We laughed.

"Maybe I should write Fergy a note, and you can give it to him in front of them," I said as nonchalant as I could. "It'll give them something to really be worried about." Sally and I were our strongest when we joined against someone else. I jumped at the chance to get closer to Sally again. We giggled.

She went to a disheveled desk in the corner that must have belonged to every member of her family before it got to her. She yanked on the drawer and retrieved a piece of notebook paper and a pencil.

"Here." She handed me her Algebra book to write on.

"We've got the same book."

"My class is still on the chapter six. There's no way we're finishing the book by the end of the year." Sally perched beside me. "Where are they at St. Mary's?"

"Chapter ten. I've had to do a lot to catch up."

"Is St. Mary's much harder?"

"No. Now that I'm caught up it's not any harder at all. The assignments are the same every day. It's so boring. There aren't any teachers like Miss Connor or Mr. Jefferson, even though some of the nuns can be as scary as he is."

"Bet they're cranky 'cause they have to wear those long black dresses every day," Sally giggled.

"They're called habits."

"Do they have those things on their heads like in *The Flying Nun*?" Sally snickered. We both loved that TV show.

"I would love for Sister Bernadette to be picked up by the breeze one day, with the wind blowing through her buck teeth." I mimicked her by putting my teeth over my bottom lip.

Sally snorted. I giggled. We egged each other on until we fell back on the bed in a heap, worn out from laughing. We were in sync again.

"So what are you going to write Fergy?"

"What should I write?"

"Don't ask me!" She jumped up and started brushing her hair. I wrote:

Dear Fergy,
I wish I was still at Stonewall. The nuns are so scary!
And I don't think they have any plays here. : (
Nell/Louise

I showed the note to Sally, then folded it into a tight bundle.

"There."

"I'll give it to him at lunch tomorrow."

"I guess I need to go and do all that stupid homework the nuns assigned today."

"If you'd stayed at Stonewall, you wouldn't have stupid homework."

"Yep. I know."

We walked down the steps together and I said goodbye to Mrs. Carpenter and got another one of her doughy-armed squeezes.

"Don't be a stranger, Nell! I want to see you again in this house, real soon!"

I hugged her back. Dark was falling as I walked the short distance home and the cold air made my nose run. I wished they'd invited me for supper.

Chapter Thirteen

We longed for snow. The winter air teased us with its promise, then tricked us with a temperature spike. Kids grumbled and even the nuns had to veil their disappointment. It surprised everyone when thermometers plunged and the high windows of the classrooms turned white. Some mothers showed up with the first flake to rescue their daughters. Some called their husbands from the office to make the treacherous journey. Half of the girls had gone when Sister Bernadette called for Penny and Sylvia, the two most popular girls in the sophomore class, and me. We walked to the front hall together where Donald was waiting. Even though my meticulous father had the snow tires put on a month before, my mother was afraid to drive in snow.

"Who's he?" Sylvia asked when we rounded the corner.

"My brother."

"I didn't know you had a brother," Penny said. "Where does he go to school?"

"He's a senior at Lee." They changed at that moment, asking me what I would do on a snow day, where I lived, and where my neighborhood sledded. They posed coquettish smiles at Donald, and there was some elaborate near falling as they walked in front of us on the sidewalk.

"Bye, Nell!" Sylvia waved to me. "Have fun on your snow day!"

"One of your new friends?" Donald asked.

"Not really," I answered. "I didn't know she even knew my name."

The snowstorm didn't hold back, making up for its lackadaisical arrival. I welcomed the hiatus from my tiresome school routine. I embraced the sense of adventure that stirred the not-too-distant child in me. I relished how the white piles muffled sound and catapulted our family back into a congenial place.

Donald was shoveling the driveway when I woke. My mother was humming as she stirred a pan of hot chocolate. My father was inspecting his old black galoshes.

"Looks like you've got a free pass from school for a few days, pumpkin." My father winked at me and sipped his coffee. "What will you do?"

"Go sledding, I guess."

"If you kids sled in the field behind Mr. Thornton's house, don't cut through his yard." He caught my eye to make sure I understood. "He made it very clear he will consider it trespassing if any of you kids come on his property again."

"Yes, sir."

"I don't know what happened on Halloween. I know you and Donald were not involved. But he's primed to see someone gets in trouble, so make sure it's not you."

"Yes, sir."

We heard the stomping of Donald's feet on the back porch and my mother scurried to meet him at the door.

"Give me your wet things." She took Donald's hat and

gloves and coat and carried them to the basement to put by the furnace.

"You frozen, son?"

"Not really." He rubbed his hands together and blew on them. "Except for my fingers."

"I appreciate you getting the car out."

"No problem."

The only change in my father's winter uniform of an overcoat and felt-brimmed hat were the galoshes he pulled over his leather shoes. As his clumsy footsteps made their way to the cleaned off car he called back, "I'm going to miss this service when you're off on some college campus next year!"

I thought I saw a shadow pass across Donald's face, but it vanished.

"Want to go sledding, Nell?"

Donald and I put on doubles of pants and shirts and triples of socks. Perspiration bubbled on my forehead by the time I got to the hat and scarf stage. When we finally made it outside I welcomed the flying icy crystals, even if they were stinging nettles to my cheeks. Donald pulled our sled as we trudged through the neighborhood towards the big hill behind Mr. Thornton's house. Skipper bounded in front of us. If he could reason, I think he'd decide it was worth it when my mother later banished him to the basement until the ice balls coating his underside melted.

No one called back and forth to make plans. The neighborhood custom was for all the kids to meet on "the hill" on a snow day. Not only was it a perfect sledding spot, but there was a creek at the bottom whose four inches of water could transform into a sheet of slick if it was cold enough. In the absence of ice skates we raced and out-slid each other between its banks until frozen fingers and toes forced us home.

"The hill" soon filled up with neighborhood kids I hadn't seen since summer pool days. Age differences were erased and I took turns sledding with little kids and big kids, friendly acquaintances, and Donald's friends. We mixed it up in a way that never happened at school.

"Where do you think Sally and David are?" I asked Donald as I got behind him on the sled.

"Beats me." He dug his boots into the snow to push off. The sled flew over icy spots, swiveled around other sledders, and bumped over homemade moguls. We raced past Donald's ability to control it.

"Lean over!" Donald yelled. "To the left!"

We plowed into the snow sideways, missing colliding into a giant oak tree by the width of a boot. As we tried to untangle ourselves Skipper's staccato barks were more than excited yelps.

"WATCH OUT!!!!" someone screamed.

Donald scrambled up, but my leg was caught. The sled loaded with kids was unstoppable as it rammed into our wreckage and forced me deeper into the snow. A twist, a flash of pain, a stinging.

Donald hand shoveled snow and yelled commands. "MOVE! DIG! OUTTA MY WAY!"

Donald tugged on my arm. "Can you stand up?" Sharp, searing pain shot up my leg.

"Is she okay?"

The pain was so intense my stomach lurched. Donald pulled me up. Someone brushed snow off my face to the background of jumbled voices and urgent conversation.

"Let's take her to our house; it's closer."

"I don't think she can walk."

"Of course she can't walk! We gotta carry her."

"It'll be quicker to cut through Mr. Thornton's yard."

"We're not supposed to!"

"I don't give a damn!" Donald put my arm around his neck. I threw up in the snow, but I didn't care.

The voices belonged to David, Sally, and Allison. When they got to "the hill" they spotted us going down and had chased after us on their sled.

David and Donald put my arms around their necks and walked on either side of me to the closest house, the Carpenters'. Sally and Allison followed with the sleds and Skipper. There was some yelling back and forth with Mr. Thornton, who was out shoveling his snow. When we got to the house, getting my boot off was excruciating. Mrs. Carpenter wrapped my ankle in ice and my mother walked over.

"Nell needs to go to the emergency room," Mrs. Carpenter told her. "I'm pretty sure there's a break in there." Mrs. Carpenter had been a nurse before she married, so her advice carried weight.

"Eugene is on his way from work. He'll take her."

"We could call an ambulance," Mrs. Carpenter suggested. "Get her some relief faster."

"I don't think we need to do that. Eugene will be here soon."

"I gave her some aspirin, but it will barely help if it's a break."

My father drove us to the hospital. The trip was snail-like on the snowy roads; every jostle and skid accentuated my agony. The antiseptic hospital smell made my head swim and my queasy stomach refused crackers and ginger ale. The afternoon was days long as they x-rayed and set the ankle that was broken in two places. It was dark when we followed the frozen streets home. My mother made a bed of the living room couch for me and propped my leg high on pillows.

"Sally's here!" My mother called from the kitchen.

"Nell, I'm so sorry about your ankle!" Sally burst out." I feel like it's our fault! We were trying to catch up with y'all. We had no idea how fast the sled would go!" She sat down in the wingback chair across from me and unbuttoned her coat.

"I know. We crashed too. That's why I was lying in the snow."

"David said if you and Donald hadn't crashed first we would have hit that big oak tree and there was no telling how bad it would have been." Her legs bounced up and down in agitated rhythm. "Someone might have broken their neck." We sat in silence as I envisioned Sally's dramatic scenario.

"My dad went over there and set up some orange cones so other kids won't go down that close to the trees."

"That's good." More silence. I adjusted the pillow under my foot.

"What are you going to do all day?" she asked as her eyes traveled around my mother's formal living room. "You need a TV in here."

"Mom doesn't like a TV in the living room," I said. "But there's one in the den my dad moved in for the moon landing."

"I'll ask your mom if we can do that." Sally was off to the kitchen and back with my mother before I could respond.

"I'm going to help roll the TV in here," Sally said, her hands on her hips. Being polite to Sally had trumped my mother's dislike of the clunky black and white set sitting in her pretty living room. Together they rolled the TV across the carpet, parking it in front of the fireplace.

"You'll be up in a day or two, but this will work until then," my mother said, wiping her hands on her apron, regarding the set with disdain.

"What do you want to watch?" Sally switched it on. "You need to choose a good channel since you can't get up and change it." She clicked through the three channels and the gray fuzzy screens between them.

"Only soap operas right now," she said. "But I'll leave it on channel six. *Dark Shadows* comes on in half an hour. You can watch creepy Barnabas. That will make you forget about your ankle!" She adjusted the rabbit ears to get a clearer picture. "If you want, I'll stay and watch it with you."

I was achy and didn't feel like company, but I was pleased Sally had come and didn't want her to leave. So I nodded and she stayed, and *Dark Shadows* gave us the chance to sit together and not have to talk. After that, she came every day school was closed to watch with me, even after the TV was reinstated in the den.

It took four days for the schools to reopen, but I didn't go back for two weeks. My mother worried about me getting behind and went to school to get my assignments.

"I don't know what you're talking about when you complain about the nuns. Sister Bernadette was as nice as she could be getting your assignments together for me." She dropped a stack of books on the kitchen table.

"Sure they're nice to the parents!" I sat with my leg propped up on a chair.

"And there were some very friendly girls who asked about you." She tugged at her gloves, finger by finger.

"Who?"

"They didn't tell me their names. They asked if they could come see you."

"What did you tell them?"

"That of course they were welcome to visit!" She put her gloves inside her purse and snapped it shut. "Honestly, Eleanor, you have a wonderful opportunity to make some lovely friends there. I wish you would try harder." Her heels click clacked across the linoleum on her way to hang up her coat.

"What did they look like?"

"They both had long, straight, blonde hair." She reached for her apron and tied it on. "I like uniforms, but it does make people less memorable."

It had to be Penny and Sylvia, showing off how nice and thoughtful they were to the sisters. They would never visit.

But they showed up the next afternoon, fresh from school in their plaid skirts and knee socks.

"Eleanor, your friends are here!" my mother called in her company voice. I heard the muted hum of conversation from my bedroom, greeting the dog and talking to my mother.

"Should I send them up or are you coming down?"

"Coming down!" I didn't want them to see my bedroom: my books, my old dolls, my posters. I wasn't sure my stuff was cool enough for them.

"Hi, Nell!" Penny and Sylvia said in chorus.

"Oh wow, you've gotten that crutch thing down!" Penny added, stooping to scratch Skipper's ears.

"Hi y'all. What are you doing here?"

"They're here to check on you! It's so thoughtful of you girls to come by." My mother beamed at them." Why don't you all visit in the living room. Anyone want a coke?" She never let us drink cokes in the living room.

"Thank you, Mrs. Randolph. That would be so nice!" Penny said.

"Yes ma'am," Sylvia said.

"Eleanor?" my mother cocked her head with raised eyebrows and an overly sweet expression.

"Sure. Thanks, Mom."

Penny and Sylvia walked on either side of me to the living room and sat in the two wingback chairs while I sat on the sofa. It didn't matter that I didn't know what to talk about, because Penny took over the conversation.

"So we heard you tripped and fell in the snow and broke your leg. How awful!"

"That's not what happened. Donald and I flipped over in our sled at the bottom of a hill. And before we could get up, another sled crashed into us. My leg was pinned and twisted underneath so my ankle got broken in two places."

"Did Donald get hurt too?" Sylvia asked.

"No. He tried to pull me out when he saw the other sled

coming but I was too deep in the snow."

"Wow. He must be very brave." Penny sat reverently with her hands clasped in her lap.

My mother appeared, carrying a tray holding three cokes with straws and a plate of cookies. She placed it on the coffee table like servants do in old movies.

Penny's voice switched from dramatic to saccharine. "Thank you, Mrs. Randolph! This is so kind of you!"

"You're very welcome, girls. Let me know if I can bring you anything else." I heard her in the kitchen getting pots out to start dinner, even though it was too early for that. Sylvia picked up the thread of the story.

"Did an ambulance come pick you up?"

"No, Donald and David kind of carried me to a neighbor's house and my dad took me to the hospital."

"Who's David?"

"One of the guys in the neighborhood. His sister's a good friend of mine."

"How much longer are you on crutches?" Penny asked.

"A month."

"Are you going to be at home all that time?"

"No. I can go to school. But they didn't want me using the crutches outside until all the snow and ice are gone."

"Makes sense," Penny said. "You're not missing much. The sisters never do anything different." She reached for a cookie and sat back in the chair.

"If you have to make up work, we can bring you our homework," Sylvia said, flicking her hair over her shoulder, even though it was already there.

"I have the assignments now; Mom picked them up yesterday."

Penny leaned in and said in a softer voice, "No, silly, I mean we can give you ours to copy."

Sylvia giggled.

"Copy?"

"Sure. We do it all the time. I do the homework on the even days, and Sylvia does it on the odd days. We turn it in with our own handwriting so no one knows the difference."

I sipped my coke. "But isn't that cheating?" I'd never cheated before.

"Kinda, I guess," Penny shrugged her shoulders. "But it's just homework. Who cares about homework?"

"I'll bet those stupid nuns don't even check it!" Sylvia said.

I wasn't used to anyone saying, "stupid nuns," even if they thought it. I tilted my head towards the kitchen and listened for the cooking sounds. Penny noticed and scolded her. "Sylvia, don't say that! it's disrespectful."

Sylvia glared at Penny, her mouth agape.

Penny took a sip of her coke and changed the subject. "So when does your brother get home?"

"Depends on if he has practice or not."

"What sport does he play?" Penny asked nonchalantly, taking a bite of cookie.

"Basketball."

Sylvia jumped back into the conversation, not so nonchalantly. "Oh, I just love basketball! Do you go to his games?"

"Sometimes."

"Could we go with you?" She scooted closer to the edge of her seat. "You know, that's what I hate about a girls' school! There aren't any good games to go to! And basketball is so exciting!"

"I'll have to see when the next one is."

Penny tilted her head and raised her eyebrows. "It would be *sooo* neat if we could do that, Nell."

My mother poked her head into the living room, "There's a green car in the driveway."

"That's my mother." Penny stood up to leave.

"Would she like to come in?"

"Oh, no, ma'am," Penny's voice was syrupy when she

140

stretched out her vowels. "She went to the store while we've been here, so I'm sure she needs to get home and put those groceries away. Come on, Sylvia."

My mother retrieved their coats and said all her niceties about how sweet it was for them to visit and how they needed to come back soon. She stood at the front door letting the frosty air in, waving energetically at Penny's mother. I couldn't tell if she waved back or not.

Chapter Fourteen

※

"Nell, can you read this over for me?" Donald stood in the doorway of my room with some papers in his hand, his face crumpled, as if he'd slept in a worried state and it had stuck. His voice was a child's.

"What is it?"

"My college essay. I know it's full of mistakes." He stretched out his hand with the papers. "It has to be postmarked by Saturday." His eyes pled with me, but his voice was resigned.

Donald and I had an established habit of me proofreading his papers. I always left enough mistakes so he wouldn't be accused of cheating. I chose them in spelling or punctuation, never in grammar; mistakes that could be careless errors. But this was different. This college essay would be all the admissions committee would see. If Donald submitted his own work he would be refused admittance. We both knew it.

I put my makeup work to the side. He handed me his essay and sat down on the other twin bed. As I read he stretched out full length, not bothering to take off his shoes. He mimicked a corpse ready to be sealed in a coffin. The laugh tracks from the TV downstairs that were distant a moment before grew louder in our silence.

"How bad is it?" Donald whispered with eyes closed.

"Mainly spelling mistakes," I said. "It's just..."

"It's just what?"

"It doesn't sound like you really want to go there."

"That's because I don't."

"Then why are you applying?"

He raised up on one elbow and cocked his head at me. "Why do you think, Nell?" His voice was sharp and agitated. "I'm eighteen this summer. If I'm not enrolled in college and my number comes up, I'm drafted."

Of course I knew eighteen-year-olds were drafted. We'd watched the news the night they spun the lottery balls and pulled out the numbers that changed young men's lives. But I'd imagined they were drafted from somewhere else: from the farms, or the inner city, or the prisons. I didn't think the war would need someone from my family.

"Can't you tell them you don't believe in the war?" Donald had gone with Father Richard to peace rallies. There had even been songs learned in folk Mass for those marches. "Can't Father Richard write a letter or something?"

"You are so naive sometimes." Donald shook his head. "A letter from a priest is not going to mean squat to the government. I either go to college, go to Vietnam, or go to Canada."

I scratched out words and substituted others. I corrected spellings. I added a sentence here and there. I turned his essay into a persuasive piece of writing the admissions committee couldn't dispute.

"Here." I handed it back to him. "See what you think." He took the marked-up pages, not even reading the first correction. As he left my room he glanced over his shoulder.

"If I get in, how am I going to keep from flunking out?"

Donald didn't wait for an answer. He knew I didn't have one.

Donald had been on an earning money kick since Christmas. He was a little like my mom, focused and manic when he decided on a goal. What was different about his frenzied working this time was that he didn't talk about what he was going to buy or put new posters on his wall for inspiration. His growing savings account was a mystery. My guess was that he was saving up for his own car and one day he'd pull into the driveway and surprise us all. The snowstorm was a gift he didn't squander. He went up and down the block shoveling walks and digging out cars. My father wouldn't let him accept money from Mrs. Crump, the widowed piano teacher, so she gave him candy. We were pretty sure it was leftover from Halloween, but he ate it and gave me the coconut ones he would have thrown out anyway. He took on an extra paper route too, when David got the flu, and got up an hour earlier than his usual five a.m., to get both routes delivered before school. And Father Richard was paying him do odd jobs around the church.

"Nell, if you want to work on the coffeehouse, you'll have to go early. I got some stuff to do for Father Richard," Donald told me on Friday.

"I'll go early," I said. "I'm sick of being in this house."

It took some persuasion tactics to convince my mother I could navigate the undercroft on crutches, but she finally relented when Donald reminded her I needed the practice since I'd be going back to school on Monday.

"Can you believe what your friend Venetia has done?" Father Richard asked when we met in the church basement.

The undercroft had been transformed in my two-week absence. The sterile cinderblock walls now glowed with Venetia's vibrant paisley swirls. The giant electrical spools had been spruced up with wine bottle candles to become tables.

Wooden crates from the milk company circled around them as chairs. It reminded me of the playhouses I used to create for my dolls, turning discarded boxes from shoes and jewelry into tables, chairs, and beds. I was excited at the change, even if I felt erased from the process.

"Opening night's in two weeks, so we'll have to really get at it to finish these walls." Father Richard bounced on his toes as his eyes traveled across the room and back. His jittery excitement was catching, and I was swept up in it again.

Claudia and Venetia showed up with Fergy and we painted and giggled alongside an army of teenagers all afternoon. It didn't seem to matter that we weren't at the same school anymore.

"How's Mr. Jefferson's class?" I asked Venetia.

"I've made it this far and haven't had to stand up yet," she smirked. "I'm going to see if I can make it to the end of the year."

"If I were still in his class I'd be standing a lot. I'm going to be so lost when I go back to class next week. And Sister Bernadette doesn't explain *anything*."

"Why don't you call me? I can help over the phone," Venetia offered.

"Really? That'd be great!"

Claudia glanced at her watch. "My dad's picking us up so we've got to go."

"Why aren't you staying for folk Mass?"

"Venetia can't go."

"Yeah, remember?" she said. "If my grandmother found out I'd gone to Mass, she'd have me in front of our church with people laying hands on me and praying for my soul!"

Just as the snowstorm handed Donald economic opportunities,

it handed me social ones. My broken ankle ushered me into the inner circle at St. Mary's. When I returned to school Penny and Sylvia became my aides, carrying my books between classes and pulling another desk into the ring at lunchtime. Their inclusion gave me a rush of confidence and a feeling of superiority over the Victorias of the school. Penny started calling in the evenings. I was pleased to get her phone calls; my mother was thrilled. When Penny invited me to go home with her, my mother arranged to leave a ladies' tea early so she could pick me up and didn't make me feel guilty about it.

Penny's house was enormous. Her black maid worked there everyday. She made snacks for us and brought them to Penny's room where we were doing homework. I thanked her.

"You don't have to do that, you know," Penny said when the maid left the room. "It's her job. You shouldn't have to thank people for doing their jobs."

When Penny asked for the answers to the French homework, I translated the directions for her. But she wasn't interested in learning French.

"What happens if Sister Joan figures out we shared answers?" I asked.

"It's homework. We check it in class, and she walks the aisles and glances at it."

"She takes it up sometimes."

"She won't be able to prove anything. Stop worrying so much! Stick with me and we won't get in trouble. The sisters love me."

"But how will you pass the test?"

She gave me a shrewd smile. "I have my ways." She took my French answers, but I didn't copy the history homework she offered, reasoning if I did my own work at home, I wouldn't be cheating.

Penny walked with me and carried my books to the car as long as I was on crutches. Donald picked me up on Fridays when he didn't have practice, and Penny was especially indulgent on those days, opening the car door and conversing animatedly with Donald.

"Remember I want to watch you play before the season's over," she said with a coquettish smile. "When's the next game?"

"Tonight. But it's across town. I'm sure you'd rather go to a home game."

"When's the next home game?" She stuck her head through the open door and her blonde hair hung inches from my face. I inhaled her Prell shampoo.

"We play Stonewall next Wednesday."

"Let's go to that game, Nell!" She dropped the books in my lap. "You might even see some of your old friends! Wouldn't that be fun?"

"Sure," I said.

Donald started the car and Penny shut my door.

"Bye!" She waved like we were leaving on a long trip.

"That girl's annoying," Donald said as soon as he pulled out into traffic.

"She's the most popular girl in my class. You should be flattered she likes you."

"I'm not. Why do you think I'd be flattered by the attention of a silly sophomore?" We stopped at the red light and he looked at me. "And she's a fake. You know that, right?"

"Maybe. But it's better than not having friends at all."

A budding boldness came with having friends at St. Mary's and friends at the coffeehouse. Maybe it came from being the center of attention. Maybe it came from not being the minority. With it, I thought I could straddle the two worlds and keep them apart. My first test came when Father Richard asked us to come after school to finish painting. When my mother dropped me off, Venetia, Claudia, and Fergy were already there.

"Whoa...nice outfit, girl!" Fergy said of my St. Mary's skirt and sweater.

"Yep. Good color on you," Claudia giggled. I couldn't think of anything witty to say back. They meant no harm. And I hadn't minded looking like Penny and Sylvia all day. Still, I envied Claudia's bell-bottom jeans and her peasant blouse and peace sign earrings, and I wanted to be her.

"Hey y'all," came out stilted and distant.

"Nice to see you too," Venetia matched my tone.

I tried being cheerier. "So, what should I paint?"

"Why don't you get the blue and paint that swirl next to Fergy's green?" She pointed to a paisley figure.

I grabbed a brush. "Happy to."

Claudia was on the other side of Venetia, painting in hot pink.

"So how are those St. Mary's lambs treating you with that broken ankle?" Fergy asked.

"Actually, most of them ignored me until I broke my ankle." I tried to sound nonchalant. "Now, a couple of them are hanging out with me all the time, but they may just be trying to snag my cute brother."

"I've heard that girls'-school girls are more boy crazy than regular girls." He focused on keeping his brush next to the penciled line.

"Yep."

"How 'bout them nuns?"

"They can be scary."

"Scarier than Fergy?" Claudia asked. She winked at Fergy. "Nell was definitely scared of you at first."

"I was?"

"Yes! Don't you remember when we started the play? You were afraid of me leaving you alone with him." Claudia dabbed paint on the wall.

"Were you scared of me too?" Venetia asked.

"Of course not!" My hands got clammy. I stared at the wall and concentrated on keeping my strokes even.

"I don't remember being scared of Fergy. I was scared of being in the play and scared of standing in the milk line."

Venetia stopped painting and turned towards me. "Were you scared when you went to St. Mary's?"

"I was too mad to be scared."

"So you weren't scared of white girls in those uniforms, but you were scared of black kids like me and Fergy," Venetia said.

"No! That's not it at all!" I plunged my brush into the paint and didn't wipe enough on the side of the jar. A big blob of blue plopped on the floor. I shoved the brush back in the jar and grabbed a rag.

"Why are ya'll ganging up on me?" I heard the tremor in my voice.

Venetia's nostrils flared. Fergy adjusted the glasses on his face. We froze in a staring contest.

Claudia broke the silence. "It's the uniform. It's a reminder you left us, that you chose a different school."

"You know you go to a school without one black face," Venetia said. "They would never allow someone like me at your school."

"It's not MY school! I didn't choose it! My parents made me go!" Tears clouded my eyes and I didn't try to stop them. "I *never* wanted to go, and I don't want to be there now!"

I thrust my paintbrush into the coffee can and walked away from them, wiping my eyes on the sleeve of my fickle sweater.

Fergy walked over. "Tell your parents."

"I have."

"If you really want to come back to Stonewall you can find a way," Venetia said from across the room.

"How?"

"You could protest their integration policy," Claudia said. "I bet they wouldn't let you stay there if you created a stir."

No one was painting now. They'd all walked over to where I was sitting on a spool, wet paintbrushes still in their hands.

"And how would I do that? Stand outside the school in my uniform holding a sign? Sister Bridget would rip that sign away so fast, and I'd be in detention for a month." I picked at a hangnail and sucked the tiny drop of blood off my thumb. "They wouldn't let me out that easy. They'd have to make sure my soul was right first."

I didn't have a choice of whether to go to Donald's game or not; Penny decided she and Sylvia would come to my house and go with us. And my mother quickly changed her opinion about me being able to navigate the bleachers with crutches. I leaned against the kitchen doorway and watched my mother carry out her lipstick ritual in front of the little mirror inside the cabinet door.

"I told you you would find friends at St. Mary's." She blotted her lips with a tissue and puckered to check the color.

I hated it when she got involved. I could have told her they didn't feel like friends, but she wouldn't get it.

She glanced over at me and wrinkled her brow. "Why did you change out of your uniform?"

"I'm not going to wear that uniform to Donald's game!"

"Why for heaven's sake not?" She put the top on her lipstick and placed it back in the cabinet with the half-used tissue. "I thought it was a badge of honor to wear a private school uniform."

"Not for me." The sting of wearing it to paint zapped through me again. The doorbell rang.

"Come in, girls!"

"Hello, Mr. Randolph," Penny said. "My mom had to drop us off early. Hope that's okay."

"Totally fine. I hear Nell coming. She can't sneak up on you with those crutches." They indulged him with their giggles.

"Hello, Penny and Sylvia!" My mother welcomed them with a honeyed tone. She noted their uniforms and gave me a side glance that said, "I was right. You should show off your uniform in public."

They chatted with my mother, using the politeness reserved for impressing adults. My mother complimented their straight hair and Penny told her she could make mine like that.

"I doubt it, Penny," I said. "I've tried giant hot rollers and orange juice cans and all the tricks the magazines say." I grabbed a chunk of my wavy hair as proof nothing worked.

"Let me iron it. We've got time."

"What?"

"Iron it, like clothes."

"Penny does it to my hair," Sylvia said. I studied Sylvia's silken locks hanging straight down her back.

"I guess it's worth a try."

I hobbled to the basement with them behind me and put my head on the ironing board feeling like Anne Boleyn.

"You always have to put a towel between your hair and the iron or you'll fry your hair," Sylvia instructed as Penny ironed. When she finished, my hair went straight down my back like theirs. Its softness felt foreign to me. My mother loved it.

The three of us climbed in the backseat of the station wagon, and my father drove us to Lee. Penny kept the conversation going with my parents until they dropped us off at the gym. The band was playing and the players were warming up on the court.

"There's your brother!" Penny said.

I scanned the bleachers searching for anyone I knew. "Where do you want to sit?" I asked.

"Let's go up there." Sylvia pointed to a spot near the top of the bleachers where a group of boys were sitting.

"I don't think sophomores sit there," I said.

"Who says?"

"It's an unwritten rule."

"We're not sophomores at this school, so it doesn't apply to us." She swiveled her head towards Penny in a way that made her blonde hair fly.

"I don't know if I can make it all the way up," I said.

"Sure you can!" Penny said. "We'll help you! Come on, Sylvia. Get on the other side of Nell." Penny took both of my crutches. "Here, put your arms around our necks."

They practically picked me up to climb to the top of the bleachers. People stared. I concentrated on the steps to avoid eye contact. Penny and Sylvia grew more animated with their helpfulness the higher we went. We stopped at the third bench from the top, in front of a row of upperclass boys, who ignored the excessive hair flinging and boisterous cheering of my companions.

"Nell, Sylvia's got to pee," Penny said about ten minutes into the game. "Where are the bathrooms?"

"Out through those doors and down the hall," I pointed. "The bathroom's on the right. There's going to be a line."

"I know, but when you gotta go, you gotta go!" she giggled. "We'll be back." They stepped around me with a lot of giggling and "excuse me's," and forced the boys behind us to lean back so they could parade in front of them.

The gym was nearly full on our side. Sally's older sister was cheering and I recognized some of her friends in the bleachers. Their plaid skirts and knee socks looked cute and classy and brought back my daydreams from the summer, when I thought high school would be like their world. In a way they were wearing a uniform, but in their favorite colors. Only white kids sat with their group. The black kids were sitting together in another section. They were younger. They would be the future of Lee High School once the white seniors graduated. The gym wouldn't look like this during games next year.

The visitor side had pockets of empty space. I scanned the bleachers row by row to see if I recognized anyone from Stonewall. I hadn't told Sally I was coming, but if she came she would sit on Lee's side, not Stonewall's. Edith wouldn't be the type to go to a basketball game. But Claudia or Venetia might go to a game, or even Fergy. I was looking so intently across the gym I missed what was happening at the end of my row.

"Look at you, girl! Made it all the way to the top with that broken ankle!" Fergy sat beside me and pushed his shoulder into mine as a sort of half hug.

"Hey! How are you?" I was happy to see him.

"Just fine." He glanced around. "If you're thinking 'bout coming back to Stonewall, why are you sitting on this side?" He shook his head like an admonishment.

"Donald plays for Lee."

"I know. I'm just teasing," he grinned. "But why you sitting all alone up here with that straight hair?" he asked.

"Some girls from school came with me, but they're in the bathroom." I paused. "And they ironed my hair to make it straight." I put both my hands behind my neck and flicked it.

"For the record, I like it better the other way." His deep brown eyes kept mine locked for a second longer than was comfortable.

There was an awkward lag in conversation while Fergy watched the game.

"So is Venetia still upset with me?" I asked.

"Naw. She's alright as long as she doesn't have to see you in that uniform that might as well be a white robe with a pointed hat."

I didn't know what he meant, but was afraid to ask. Another awkward lag.

"How's them nuns?"

153

"Mean as snakes."

Fergy laughed. His big deep stage laugh. The boys behind us got quiet. I leaned towards Fergy and lowered my voice.

"And the girls that forced me to bring them have left me to go flirt with some boys, I'm sure. Girls' school is killing them."

We snickered and the dam of uneasiness was broken. We talked like we had during rehearsals. He told me about the teachers, and how he knew Allison and Laurie were a little scared of him when he stopped by the lunch table, and how Renay still hung around his locker, so he knew she still liked him, but he didn't like her.

"Too bad you can't be in the spring play," he said. "Auditions are next week. They made sure there wasn't any kissing in this one," he grinned. "You'll come, won't you?"

"Sure. You're still coming to opening night at the coffeehouse, right?" Before he could answer I saw Penny and Sylvia climbing up to the top of the bleachers. "Here they come."

"Where?"

"Up the right side. The girls with the long blonde hair and the St. Mary's uniforms."

"They're pretty."

"And they already know that, so you don't need to tell them."

"Girl, I never tell a white girl she's pretty when I first meet her. You think I'm crazy?"

We were laughing when they reached our row. They didn't hide their surprised faces.

"Hello." Fergy stood up and nodded to them. "I'm Fergy. Nell and I are friends from Stonewall."

Penny and Sylvia stared.

"I believe I'm in your seats, so it'll be time for me to move on."

I tried to stand to let him pass in front of me and wobbled. Fergy caught hold of my elbow and steadied me.

"See ya around," he whispered as he passed in front of me.

Fergy nodded to Penny and Sylvia like a Southern gentleman and waited at the end of the row until they took their seats. Then he made his way down the bleachers and I lost sight of him in the crowd.

Penny and Sylvia didn't ask one question about Fergy. In their St. Mary's upbringing they probably had never been in the close presence of a black boy who wasn't a bagger at the Safeway or a gas station attendant. They would have never considered being friends with a boy who was black, and that's how Fergy had described us. I didn't talk about Fergy with them either. But that little encounter altered their interactions with me. They still displayed their counterfeit niceness at school, included me in the lunchtime circle, and carried my books for as long as I was on crutches. But the invitations and the weekend plans I thought I wanted never materialized.

Chapter Fifteen

"So what are your plans today, Nell?" my father asked when I moseyed into the kitchen Saturday morning.

"Nothing today, but the coffeehouse opens tonight."

"What do you say we celebrate that with some Krispy Kreme?"

My father was a disciplined man about almost everything. He only drank coffee at breakfast and I never saw him fix more than one martini before dinner, except at Christmas, and then not more than two. He didn't have the spreading waistline of many of my friends' fathers and he still preferred to split his own wood for our fireplace if given the opportunity. He'd played football his first two years of college before a knee injury put him off the team, and still carried the impression of that athletic build in his daily walks. Krispy Kreme doughnuts may have been the only place where his discipline was naught.

"So what will it be, pumpkin? Chocolate iced? Cream filled?"

"Chocolate iced and cream filled."

He ordered my favorite and a dozen glazed. He wouldn't eat the special ones.

"Want coffee?" I'd never had coffee. "They have good

coffee here." He winked at me. "You don't have to drink it if you don't like it, but there's a reason people have coffee with doughnuts."

"Okay."

We sat at the window counter that faced the street on green leather-topped stools that had a little swivel in them, but didn't make a full turn. The memory of root beer floats on those same kind of stools flashed through my mind; it seemed a lifetime ago. My father brought several creamers and a few sugar packets with a stirrer over to the counter.

"I doubt you'll like it black. Add a few creamers and have a taste," he instructed. I did. It was bitter and I made a face.

"If it's too bitter you can put some sugar in it, but if you put in too much it won't give you the coffee taste you need to balance the doughnut." I put in half a sugar packet and another creamer. I didn't like the taste that much but I pretended I did. I wanted to learn to drink coffee.

We sat at the window counter watching the cars, leisurely paced on a Saturday. My father ate in a deliberate way, savoring his favorite combination of airy dough and sweet glaze. It felt cozy and safe, being just the two of us. Safe enough for me to blurt out the idea that been running circles in my head.

"I'm thinking I might be able to go to college a year early. Would that be okay?"

"What makes you want to do that? And how is that possible?"

"If I go to summer school, I can do it. I'm a year ahead in most subjects. I just need English and Government. And it will save you a year's tuition at St. Mary's."

He put his Styrofoam cup down and studied my face.

"What's the rush?"

"I don't really fit in at St. Mary's and it's not going to get any better." When Fergy stood beside Penny and Sylvia in the bleachers, the straddling of my two worlds was over. I knew

I'd been excommunicated from the St. Mary's world.

"What about those girls that went to Donald's game with us? I thought you'd become friends with them."

"They're only hanging out with me so they can flirt with Donald."

A little smile played with the corners of his mouth.

"It's true!"

"I'm only smiling at the power of a good-looking athlete." He sipped his coffee. "I don't think Donald has any idea of the power he has. If he did he'd be asking out a different girl every weekend."

He took another doughnut out of the box. "And I don't understand how my daughter who is so smart and pretty and talented feels like no one likes her."

His voice had a tenderness in it that made my eyes water.

"Your mother wanted you to go to St. Mary's. She's convinced you're getting a better education there. Are you?"

"I don't know," I said. "We're further along in the textbooks, but there's not one nun who's as good a teacher as Miss Conner, or even Mr. Jefferson, as scary as he was."

"Would you want to return to Stonewall?"

"It'd be better than St. Mary's. At least I had some friends there. But I'd rather be in a school that's just normal. Not all white or where you stand out if you're white."

"We've gone about this all wrong," he said, his voice taking on its attorney quality. "*Forcing* two races to change their circumstances will never work." He focused his gaze out the window. "The Negro race deserves the same opportunities as the white race. I just don't know how to help them."

He turned back to me. "And I haven't followed my convictions by allowing you to be pulled out of your assigned school to go to a private school." His brow furrowed and his voice got louder. "Can that boy you knew from the Christmas tree lot afford to go to a private school if he doesn't like his school?"

I tried to picture Fergy at a private school. I'd never considered that he or Venetia might want an option other than Stonewall.

"So you'd be in favor of me going back to Stonewall?"

"It's complicated, Nell. I imagine if this were Donald instead of you, he'd still be at Stonewall, playing on their basketball team and sticking it out until he graduated. But your mother has been so insistent her daughter be in what she considered a safer school I went along with her, as much for her well-being as yours."

"You don't think it's because her bridge club friends are scared of public schools?"

"I'm sure that had something to do with it."

"Once I got used to it, it didn't feel unsafe." I thought about the group of us walking to Williard's. "Once you have some black friends it's different."

The idea of graduating early had been buried in a conversation about integration. I didn't know it then, but my father was having his own professional struggles with the race issue as one of the commissioners for the city's Housing Authority. He wanted everyone to get along, for "mixing" to happen organically. But that couldn't happen as long as the white City Council wanted to keep the races separate and were passing ordinances to make it almost impossible for blacks and whites to live in the same neighborhoods. No one cared to ask what the black Richmonders wanted. Just like I hadn't thought to ask Venetia or Fergy if they were happy at Stonewall.

"Ready?" He stood and picked up the box of remaining doughnuts. "Maybe your mother will allow herself to enjoy one."

We had been poised for opening night of the coffeehouse for weeks. But a few church members weren't convinced of its appropriateness and slowed the whole thing down with what Father Richard labeled "interminable meetings." He charmed the ladies of the church. They responded with mountains of cups and napkins and promises of cookies. He wasn't as successful with the older laymen of the parish. They fretted over the possibility of "long-haired hippies" slinking into the church basement. Sermons about Jesus eating with tax collectors and consorting with "women of ill repute" made them visualize a parade of prostitutes and drug dealers inside the sacred walls. But Father Richard could not be deterred. He invited them to come see for themselves the beauty and community we were creating.

Stepping into the undercroft after folk Mass was like entering one of my childhood made-up adventures. An overzealous church lady had sewn red checked tablecloths to cover the industrial spools. The wine bottle candles contrived an old-world cafe. Stools on the makeshift stage waited for musicians. A donated popcorn popper sat on the cement floor, its chubby orange extension cord too short to reach the snack table. Stacks of favorites from our album collections teetered next to a sturdy record player while Simon & Garfunkel serenaded from it. If I'd had other pursuits, a team to belong to, a talent to pursue, maybe it wouldn't have been such a big deal. But for lack of another, this was my pursuit, these kids were my team. Walking back into this space we had worked so hard to create was a homecoming.

Father Richard planted himself at the open door. His enthusiasm ramped up with each welcome. Some kids were even older than Donald. Most were dressed in jeans and the boys who were carrying guitars on their backs were wearing sandals. I felt young and conspicuous in the blue pants and Pappagallo flats I'd ended up in after changing three times. The hoop earrings my mother thought too "hippy-ish" were insignificant compared to the giant hoops other girls wore. Their arms were loaded with stacks of bracelets too, which made my single charm bracelet look like I'd borrowed it from my mother's jewelry box. These weren't church people and I wondered how Father Richard knew them. He greeted them with an intimacy that excluded me.

"Venetia!" Claudia called. "Over here!"

I was so relieved to see Venetia walk in with another black girl. I grabbed two more crates and squeezed them in by where Claudia and I were sitting.

"Hi! I'm Claudia!" she greeted Venetia's friend with a handshake, like an adult would do.

"Hey, y'all," Venetia said, "this is my cousin, Deloris."

Deloris was taller and darker than Venetia, with a massive afro and a broad toothy smile. Her sparkling eyes were framed with thick, enviable eyelashes. I was stunned by her beauty.

"I'm so glad to see y'all!" My mother's company voice come out of my mouth in my eager attempt to be friendly. Venetia wrinkled up her forehead and grimaced.

"Deloris goes to Madison," Venetia said.

I hadn't heard of Madison until recently when it made the news because of all the fights there. Deloris didn't look like someone who would go to a school like that.

"You've got to see your cousin's artwork." Claudia pointed to the walls. "Venetia designed it all. Groovy, huh?"

"Far out," Deloris said. "Can I go look at it?"

"Sure."

Before they could walk across the room Father Richard hopped up on the miniature stage and whistled to get everyone's attention. Even he had changed into jeans after Mass. As the room quieted, Venetia, Deloris, Claudia and I squeezed in around the spool table. Two older men, with stern faces, leaned against the back wall. Father Richard spoke for a few minutes about how the coffeehouse had come to be and named all the people who had worked on it. He asked Venetia

161

to stand and all the kids applauded her. The men against the wall maintained blank faces. Then Father Richard nodded to two of the guys, and they joined him on the stools with their guitars.

The room quieted as they tuned, the buzz of the guitar strings creating the energy of anticipation. They strummed for a few moments before they sang "If I Had a Hammer." Their mellow voices melted together and warmed the undercroft. A hush encapsulated the room and I got a glimpse of what Father Richard was trying to do in the way the music connected us for a stirring moment. That feeling would be what kept us coming back.

"Did you think I wasn't coming?" a voice said behind me. "'Cause it sure doesn't look like you saved me a seat," I turned to see Fergy's lopsided grin.

"Take mine," Claudia said, "I'm going to get popcorn." Fergy sat down and made a joke to Venetia and Deloris about turning Catholic.

"Have you found the part I painted, Deloris?"

"You painted too? Maybe they're closer to turning you than you think, boy!" They laughed. I was eavesdropping on a private joke, but pretended a laugh too.

"Glad you came, Fergy!" Father Richard had his hand on Fergy's back. "And you brought a friend, I see."

"This is Deloris. She's Venetia's cousin."

"So nice to have you with us, Deloris," Father Richard flashed his movie star smile at her. The hair around his temples was damp and perspiration had formed tiny beads on his upper lip.

"We owe your cousin a debt for all her artistic work. Isn't it amazing?" His eyes were on fire as he locked them consecutively with each pair of eyes around the red checked table.

"You should've seen this room before. It was cold and dark and dreary as a tomb." He smiled at Venetia and nodded to her in a bow of respect. "Venetia's art has made it warm and welcoming and alive."

His speech silenced us, but we agreed by nodding our heads. He moved around our circle and squeezed our shoulders, his zealous touch leaving a warm imprint. Deloris reached her hand across her body and touched the place he had touched.

"Now that is one attractive white man," she said when Father Richard was out of earshot. "No wonder you keep coming here!" She nudged Venetia and they giggled.

Father Richard navigated the room, speaking to everyone, including the two men who were holding up the back wall. They didn't smile at him and they didn't sit in the chairs he brought them. They would not allow themselves to be comfortable while they scrutinized our gathering.

Different combinations of kids put themselves on the modest stage that evening, playing familiar songs on their guitars. Some were good and others were not, but the quality of the music didn't affect the atmosphere of the room. Kids applauded each musical attempt like it was the best performance they'd ever heard, willing with their applause the success of this coffeehouse venture, this place that was by them and for them. I was proud to be part of it. But I felt on the edge of it all, with the influx of all the older kids. Fergy sat with me most of the evening. I thought he was nice to keep me company, but maybe he didn't feel a part of the larger group either.

My weekday life of feigning respect for the nuns' stilted lectures and regurgitating useless facts for homework also kept me from asking questions when I didn't understand. I called Venetia when I got stuck on Algebra homework. I read her an equation over the phone and she solved it in her head. I had no idea how she did it.

"Why don't you come over after school tomorrow?" she asked. "It'd be a lot easier for me to show you how I got the answer than tell you."

I wanted to go to Venetia's house and I didn't want to hurt her feelings by telling her I couldn't. My mother wouldn't say I couldn't go to the home of a Negro, but she would find an excuse not to take me. Venetia gave me directions and I coerced Donald to be my chauffeur. A small price to pay for his college essay.

"Is this it?" Donald asked. We stopped in front of a house matching the address Venetia had given me. I'd expected her to live in a smaller house on a more rundown street. But this was a beautiful red brick two story home framed by boxwoods, with a turret and a stone balcony.

"I guess so."

"I'll wait here 'til you're sure," Donald said.

I walked up the wide stone steps and rang the doorbell. Venetia opened the door and I waved Donald on. We stood in a large foyer with framed paintings and sculptures; a Negro museum. I tried not to stare.

"Come meet my mom." Venetia grabbed my hand and ushered me into the kitchen. Her mother sat at the table surrounded by stacks of papers. She rose and I caught a trace of her perfume. She was lighter than Venetia, honey-colored, and her doe eyes seemed too large for her petite face.

"'Tia's told me a lot about you, Nell. So happy to finally meet you!"

"Thanks for having me, Mrs. Chiles. Venetia's going to help me with some Algebra."

"Guess we're all doing schoolwork this afternoon. I've got to finish grading these tests." She sat down and picked up her red pen. "Never assume your teachers aren't working as hard as you are!" She smiled at me.

I couldn't imagine the sisters spending much time on grading or lesson planning, but I didn't want to talk about my private school. I nodded at Mrs. Chiles in agreement. Venetia grabbed two cokes and I followed her up the stairs to her room. I loved its shade of soft lavender and the big open windows that faced their tidy back yard.

"This is the color I wanted for my room!"

"We painted it last summer. Glad you like it."

We sat on the rug and leaned our backs against her bed while Venetia guided me through problem after problem until I did several on my own that she deemed correct. I laughed as she mimicked Mr. Jefferson, which she waited to do until she was sure I had a handle on the math.

"Are you going to be a teacher like your mom?" I asked her. "You're really good at explaining things."

"Nope. I'm going to be a lawyer like my dad."

If Venetia had lived in my neighborhood we would've been best friends. She was more like me than Sally was. If she'd been French or Swedish everyone would have been impressed with a friendship we had created from our differences. But we were steeped in our racial heritages. It's why I was surprised when she lived in a house that was as nice as mine. It's why I would have never expected her father to be an attorney like mine. I don't know where I learned those expectations, because good manners prevented anyone from saying those things. When I started first grade my grandmother asked me how many colored children were in my class. I didn't know. But somewhere between first grade and high school I'd learned to notice.

Chapter Sixteen

Spring was lethargic in its approach. Then manic when two warm days back-to-back compelled the redbuds, tulip trees, and forsythia to bloom in sync. When the oaks dropped their powdery worms, half of Richmond suffered watery eyes and dripping noses and resented the explosion of color and scent. Donald and my mother were members of that half. My father and I weren't bothered by the yellow cast on every surface, and I helped him sweep off the porches and brush the pollen out of Skipper's fur, trying to lessen the misery of the other two. I longed to open the windows and breathe in spring but my mother forbade it. So our house retained the leftover stuffiness of winter while the rest of the world burst with new life.

I preferred to do my homework on the front porch with Skipper at my feet, even if I had to brush him before he was allowed back in the house. He saw the mailman first, greeting him with leaps and barks, waiting for the head scratching he always received. I accepted the stack of mail, which usually contained nothing for Donald or me, and took it inside.

"Donald, mail for you!" I held the hefty white envelope with the state college insignia in my hand "It's a fat one!" I yelled.

Donald ran down the steps and grabbed the envelope from my hand. My mother called us to come in the den where she was lying down.

"Well, open it!" I said.

Donald tore at the sealed flap.

"I'm in! I got in!" My mother sat up and he handed her the acceptance letter. She barely read it before she reached up to plant a kiss on Donald's cheek.

"I knew you'd get in!"

"Told you!" I said. Donald smiled with relief in his eyes. Or maybe it was gratitude.

"I can't wait until Eugene gets home! He'll be so thrilled!"

"I gotta tell the guys!" Donald bounded up the stairs to use the phone.

"Well, I'm glad that's settled," my mother said. She sneezed, grabbed at the box of tissues in her lap and put her head back down on the fat arm of the couch.

I was glad it was settled too, even if I had an unsettled feeling about Donald's success there. I thought we should have a celebratory dinner with Donald's favorites, but my mother wasn't up to fixing supper that night and instructed my father to take us out.

"How about I take you two to Porter's?" Porter's was my father's favorite steak house, where he often chose to entertain clients.

"I've already made plans with my friends," Donald said.

"Donald, come on!" I coaxed. I loved going to a restaurant.

"Y'all go ahead," Donald said. "Sitting in a dark restaurant and having to use good manners for my family wouldn't really be my way of celebrating."

"Alright, son, but you're missing out on some good food." My father didn't quite cover up his disappointment.

"I can't really taste anything with these allergies, anyway. Maybe later."

"Well, Nell and I will just have to celebrate for you." He looked at me with questioning eyes, and I nodded that I was still up for going.

"I'll change real fast!" I raced up to my room and put on my Easter dress. It was nice to have an activity on a school night that wasn't watching TV or babysitting. Wanda, our waitress, lit up when she recognized my father and predicted his order of a medium rare New York strip, baked potato, and salad. I didn't know the difference between Thousand Island and French dressings and she offered to bring both for me to try. We never ate tossed salad at home; lettuce was for lining a Jell-O plate.

"Which do you like better?" my father asked.

"I think the Thousand Island," I decided.

"It's important to know these things," he said in a serious tone, but with twinkly eyes. "So when you're out on a date you'll know what to order. I can remember how uncomfortable I was when I first took a girl out to a restaurant and had no idea what I was doing."

"What happened?"

"I thought I was ordering veal when I ordered tripe, only to find out I had ordered the lining of a cow's stomach."

"Yuk. Did you eat it?

"Of course, like it was what I'd always wanted."

"How was it?"

"Let's just say I've never ordered it again." He smiled and took a swallow of his whiskey sour. I sipped on my coke. The hostess seated a couple at the table next to us.

"Are there any young men that have caught your eye?" he asked.

"There aren't many to meet at St. Mary's," I smirked.

"Still thinking about graduating early?"

"Yes."

He kept a steady gaze on me, only glancing down to stab a tomato slice with his fork. Sometimes I liked the way he looked at me, like he was appreciating all the details of my face. Maybe it was an attorney characteristic; maybe it was his own special trait. My mother didn't have it. She usually looked past me, preoccupied with something else or anxious to move to the next topic. My father stayed with a subject until he exhausted it.

"What don't you like about St. Mary's?"

"I don't like the girls. I don't like the nuns. And Venetia is having to teach me Algebra because Sister Bernadette can't teach!" I stated a case I didn't think he could dispute.

"What would you gain if you went back to Stonewall?"

"I made friends doing the play, and I'm more comfortable with kids like Venetia and Claudia than the stuck-up girls at St Mary's. Besides, if integration is the right thing to do, why am I in a school with all white kids?"

"We've talked about this, Nell. Your mother is much more comfortable with you being at St. Mary's."

"Would you be comfortable with me going back to Stonewall?" I hadn't thought going back was a possibility until that moment.

"If you were at Stonewall, I wouldn't feel so conflicted about trying to do the right thing by my community."

Wanda delivered our loaded plates. My father loved a good steak. He inhaled its smoky aroma and our conversation switched to lighter subjects while we ate. When Wanda returned and saw my father's empty plate she recited the litany of desserts.

"What do you want, pumpkin?"

"I can get dessert?" I couldn't finish my giant piece of meat. I would be breaking the "eat everything on your plate before you get dessert" rule.

169

"Whatever you want."

"Hot fudge sundae?"

"Make that two." He held two fingers up to Wanda and she smiled.

My father asked about the coffeehouse, and I told him about Venetia and Fergy helping with the painting, and Father Richard's opinion that anyone should be able to come, Catholic or not, black or white.

"That makes more sense to me than a lot of what I've heard from the pulpit. Good for Father Richard."

I told him about Donald taking me to Venetia's house and how I wasn't uncomfortable there. He listened and nodded. Wanda brought our sundaes and his coffee and knew she didn't need to offer cream and sugar.

"Isn't this coffeehouse a way you can keep in touch with your friends from Stonewall?"

"Yeah, but Venetia and Fergy acted differently the day I showed up in my uniform. Like I was against them."

"I'm afraid I don't know a good way to handle that one." He was sensing the predicament I was in and that made me bolder.

"Dad, what do you think about interracial marriage?" I asked. "Kids were talking about it at the coffeehouse."

"And what did your friends say?"

"They don't think the color of your skin should make any difference." I focused on trying to get the right combination of ice cream, fudge, and nuts on my spoon. "Father Richard said he wouldn't have a problem marrying an interracial couple."

"Father Richard probably has enough charisma to pull that off."

"But what do *you* think?" I wanted to know.

"I'm glad it's no longer illegal. In theory, I think a person has the right to marry whoever they want to marry. But in practice, I think it's a lot harder than those who are keen to it are willing to recognize."

170

"Why?"

"Nell, the color of skin may seem like it's only one's outward appearance, but it's an indicator of a person's culture. How you're raised in your own family ways is harder to discern; it's why integration is hard for your mother. Combining cultures is difficult. Not only black and white, but Asian and American, Jewish and Catholic. Shoot, even poor Irish and wealthy French would be a hard combination." He leaned against the back of the booth and tilted his head upwards. "I had some army buddies who married girls they met during the war. Most of them haven't had an easy time of it. And they're the same skin color and miss the judgment that goes with the interracial territory."

"Do you think it'll ever be different?" I asked. He fixed his eyes on me. I pushed my shoulders back.

"Maybe your generation will be able to see it differently. And then maybe your children's generation will be able to accept a mixed community without violence. And then maybe your grandchildren's generation will be able to intermarry without resistance from society. But real change, significant change, takes lifetimes."

We scooped the rest of our ice cream without words; not in an awkward silence, but in a contemplative one. He put his spoon down and smiled at me.

"I'm proud you've started the process, that Venetia and Fergy are your friends."

"So you'd be in favor of me going back to Stonewall?"

"I'll talk to your mother about it. That's all I can promise."

We drove home with the windows down and the scented spring air blowing through them. I relished that fresh breeze and the promise that blew in with it. I wonder if he felt it too or if he was too old to hope for new experiences.

171

✻✻✻

"Remember I'm hosting bridge club today," my mother announced at breakfast, "and your father is entertaining a client, so you two are on your own for supper."

"Who's picking me up from school?" I asked.

"Donald."

"I am?" Donald poured milk over his Wheaties.

"Yes," her irritation dragging out the "s"." "We talked about it the other day." Donald shrugged and put a giant spoonful of cereal in his mouth.

"I declare, Donald, you don't seem to remember anything these days!"

"Don't forget, please," I said. He looked at me and nodded his head. He would remember.

✻✻✻

"Want to get ice cream?" Donald asked when he pulled up to the curb in front of St. Mary's. The afternoon had turned summer hot.

"Yeah, but can we stop by the house so I can take this awful uniform off?"

"Sure. Can't blame you for wanting to do that."

A trio of cars were parked in front of our house.

"Man, I hate it when all those ladies are there!" Donald said as he swung into the side driveway and drove the car to the back.

I slammed the car door. "I'll be quick!"

"I'm coming in too. Gotta change into some shorts."

We heard the tittering of the bridge club ladies before we made it to the back door. The kitchen counters were littered with luncheon plates, most of them holding remnants of the tuna salad inside a wedged tomato my mother had served. There was a tray with a few leftover deviled eggs and the bakery lemon cake impersonating a homemade version by being perched on her china cake platter.

"We need to get out of here before they do and mom wants us to help clean up," Donald said. An outburst of laughter came from the living room.

"Do you think they're still playing?" I asked.

"No. I think they're still drinking," he answered as he held a half full glass of a pink beverage and smelled it. He took a swig and grinned. "So this is what they do while we're at school."

"You're drinking someone's drink and you don't even know whose! That's gross!"

"There's so much alcohol in these things, it will kill any old lady germs." He scanned the kitchen and found another half-drunk glass. "Here. You try."

I hesitated, but he pushed the glass into my hand. I took a sip.

"Drink it, silly!" I swallowed the rest. It was sweet and burned at the same time.

"That is some kind of strong spiked lemonade," Donald said. "I don't remember them having drinks like this before."

"Me either." The swinging door that led to the dining room flew open and Mrs. Harris backed in with two empty glass pitchers in her hands. She startled when she saw us.

"Well hello, Nell and Donald," she said with a broad smile on her face. "Home from school early?"

"No, ma'am," Donald said. "It's four o'clock."

"Oh mercy! I had no idea it was that late!" She put the pitchers down on the counter, adjusted her cat-eye glasses and looked at her watch. "Oh well," she giggled and opened the refrigerator door. Grabbing hold of another jug of the pink beverage she said, "The girls wanted one more round of my special lemonade." She smiled at us and winked. "Donald, would you crack some ice for me?"

"Yes, ma'am." He opened the freezer and took out an ice tray. He jerked the aluminum handle back to free the ice.

"Put it in this one," she said sweetly, holding both hands around the pitcher. "There's only one table left in there." Donald did what she asked. She poured the pink beverage over the ice and took a wooden spoon out of the sink and stirred it.

"There's some left. Would you two like a sip? It's quite refreshing on a hot afternoon." I stole a glance at Donald, not believing Mrs. Harris was offering us her spiked drink.

"Thank you, ma'am," Donald said. "Nell and I were looking for something to cool us off." His eyes darted over to mine and willed me to stay quiet. Donald opened the cabinet and took out two iced tea glasses and put them on the counter. Mrs. Harris filled them three quarters of the way full.

"I've left some room for ice," she said as she picked up the glass pitcher to take back to the living room. "Tastes better that way." Donald played gentleman and held the door open for her and she grinned at him like I had seen dozens of girls do.

"You're such a flirt, Donald Randolph!" I said once the door closed behind her. We heard the women cheer.

"Got us some drinks, didn't it?" he grinned back at me.

"These must not have any alcohol in them," I said.

Donald picked up one of the glasses and took a swallow.

"Wrong. They've got alcohol alright. Vodka, I think."

"You're kidding," I said and picked up the other glass. Donald watched me while I took a sip.

"Let's take these to the back and have a smoke."

"No ice cream?"

"We have been given a gift. Let's enjoy it," he laughed and slipped out the back. I followed him and let the screen door slap behind me.

It was strange to smoke in the daytime. We sat with our backs against the far end of the garage. I was skittish; worried a neighbor might be spying through the hedges.

"Relax. Dad's not coming home for two hours and I haven't heard anyone leave from the bridge club yet. Not that they would notice us after what they've been drinking all afternoon." He took a long drag. I hadn't smoked since the fall. Donald watched me fumble with the cigarette, but he didn't tease me.

"Need another lesson?" I nodded and he took my cigarette and lit it for me. His instructions were simple and slow. It was times like this, when he was kind and patient with me, I loved him best.

"Did you know Dad is thinking about letting me go back to Stonewall?"

"Why do you want to do that?"

"I can't stand St. Mary's. You said yourself those girls were fake, and you were right." I sipped at my spiked lemonade.

"Is Mom going to let you do that?"

"I hope so. I think Dad might tell her it's important for his law firm or something."

Donald took a long drag and tilted his head up to try to blow a smoke ring. "Nell, that doesn't make any sense."

"He told me his firm is defending the city's right to annex the county and get more white kids in the schools. So it's probably kind of important that his kids go to public school." I'd convinced myself that going back to Stonewall would happen because this annexation would pass, my white friends would come back, and I'd have the best of both worlds.

"Father Richard would disagree with you." He took a long gulp of his drink.

"How do you know that?"

"I overheard him talking about it with Venetia at the coffeehouse."

That Donald knew something about my friend I didn't know annoyed me. "What's wrong with making the county part of the city? Dad says it will bring more money in."

"It would also bring in more white votes. Venetia told Father Richard it would overpower the black vote."

I took a baby puff of the cigarette. "Why does that make a difference?"

"Nell, have you been paying attention to anything this year? Black people want different things than white people do, and each side has to get what they want by voting for it."

I still couldn't understand what Donald was saying. Fergy and Venetia and Deloris didn't seem to want different things than me.

"How are the black kids different?"

"They just are. I like DeShawn and the guys on the basketball team, but most of the black kids in my classes are troublemakers. They're disrespectful to the teachers. They want everything done for them—like they're lazy or something. And I know they secretly hate white people."

"Do you like Fergy and Venetia?"

"Yeah. But they're not like the others. And I only know them from the coffeehouse. I bet they're different if they're with their own race."

I jerked a dandelion out of the ground in front of me. "I don't get why people just can't be people. Why did God make different races anyway?"

"Don't ask me. But He did. So there must be a reason."

I was tired of the race talk. I was tired of worrying about whether Venetia and Fergy were really my friends or not. I put out my smoldering cigarette, but kept sipping from the tall iced tea glass. I welcomed the relaxed feeling rippling through my body.

"So, are you excited about going to State?"

"Not really." Donald sounded far away. He threw a rock he'd been rolling around in his hand and it disappeared in the bushes. "Can you keep a secret?"

"Sure."

"Promise you won't tell *anyone*?"

176

I nodded.

"I don't think I'm going to college."

"But you got in!"

He stamped out his cigarette and threw a succession of pebbles into the bushes. "You and I both know I won't be able to do the work. I'll flunk out."

I picked up a stick and drew circles in the dirt. I couldn't reassure him that wouldn't happen. "What'll you do?"

"I don't know yet." He tilted his glass back for the last swallow. "I'll go back as a camp counselor this summer and figure it out."

"When are you going to tell mom and dad?"

"I'm not. That's why it's a secret, Nell." He kicked the dirt. "I've got to act like I'm going. If I'm not registered for college I'll get drafted, and that scares the shit out of me."

Chapter Seventeen

"Dad said I can have friends over Friday night. Want to come?" Claudia's voice was bubbly on the phone, her excitement contagious.

"Of course!" I was sitting on my parents' bedspread, playing with the little chenille pompoms, happily listening to Claudia's plans, grateful to be included.

"I've asked a few kids from the play, and I think Deloris is coming with Venetia." A twinge of resentment surfaced. I twisted a pompom. The spring play. Another point of connection I did not have.

"Fergy wanted me to ask more guys. Do you think Donald would want to come and bring some friends?"

"Sure. I'll ask him." Another twinge, wondering if Claudia would have asked me if she didn't need Donald.

"Want me to help set up? I've got a lot of experience!" I giggled.

"There's not that much to do. It's not like one of your mother's balls or something."

"Balls?"

"Yeah. The way you describe her parties, it sounds like she's hosting something out of Cinderella or entertaining royalty." She laughed. "But you can come early and help me make brownies."

"I'll come right after school." I unwound my hand from the black curly phone cord.

"You can spend the night if you want."

I couldn't wait for Friday.

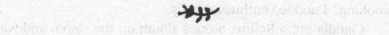

Donald took me to Claudia's, after I made him promise to show up later with some friends. He tried to make me feel like it was an imposition. I said that if he was leaving in a few months, I'd really wish we'd done some fun stuff together. But I didn't need to remind him of his secret. I already noticed the way he was preparing himself for leaving, like sneaking Skipper into his room and asking our mother to make certain favorite dishes; like he was shoring up, packing away the good things, in case he needed them later.

Claudia's house was different from mine and Sally's, and even Venetia's. Its small ranch style felt cozy and claustrophobic at the same time. There was one short hall with two bedrooms off it, one bathroom she shared with her dad, and the living room, which had a TV and an elaborate stereo setup. Claudia led me to a tiny kitchen in the back of the house, the pinkest kitchen I'd ever seen.

"I know," Claudia said. "It's shocking at first. My mom and dad bought this house from an old lady who had a passion for pink. They painted all the other rooms, but I think this one was too complicated." The cabinets were pink, the wallpaper was a giant garden of pink flowers, even the refrigerator was pink. "Dad and I've just gotten used to it."

"Wow," was all I could say.

"It clashes with my hair, though," Claudia giggled.

Claudia's red hair looked exactly like the pictures I'd seen of the "love children" in California. Her hair was kind of like mine, big and untamed, but hers looked softer, not as puffy.

"How do you get your hair to look like that?" I asked. "Mine goes frizzy no matter what I do!"

"I braid it when it's wet, and then I don't brush it."

"You don't brush your hair?"

"Nope. I can do yours like this while the brownies are cooking." I nodded enthusiastically.

Claudia put a Rolling Stones album on the stereo and we mixed up the brownies. She told me all about the Stones concert her dad had taken her to and then she instructed me to put my head under the faucet. I couldn't imagine my father ever going to a concert or my mother ever allowing hair in the kitchen sink. When I mentioned that, Claudia looked confused. She couldn't imagine life without those freedoms. I wondered which one of us was the normal one. She quickly divided my head of hair into dozens of braids.

"Now we let them dry."

"When's everyone showing up?"

"Like seven, seven-thirty. Plenty of time."

We listened to more albums, picked out what Claudia would wear, and she even offered to let me wear one of her peasant blouses. Mr. Douglas showed up with a pizza and we ate together, sitting on the couch. I wondered why it couldn't be this easy at my house. When my hair was dry, Claudia gently undid the braids and ran her fingers through it.

"Cool," Mr. Douglas said.

"Go look in the mirror!" Claudia pushed me up. "But don't brush it. You'll ruin it!"

I went to the bathroom and stared into the mirror. The hair did look cool, falling in zig-zaggy lines beside my face, but like it belonged to someone else. I should have used the hippy hair to become that someone else that night. I wish I could have latched onto the tiny glimmer I saw of a bolder me and not let it be dimmed.

When the doorbell rang, Mr. Douglas stood up, picked up

the empty pizza box and smiled. "I think I'll make myself scarce now. You two have fun."

Venetia and Deloris stood at the bottom of the front concrete steps.

"Come on in!" Claudia motioned to them. Venetia turned and waved to a car at the end of the driveway. Her mom had her head titled down to see us. I waved with the enthusiasm of a cheerleader. I wanted her to know that Venetia was safe with us.

"She wanted to make sure this was your house," Venetia said. Deloris was her poised self, a breezy expression on her face. With her glossy lips and her bell-bottomed white pants she could have been one of the models in my *Seventeen* magazine.

"Whoa!" Deloris grinned. She touched my hair and made an approving nod. "It's not the afro I planned for you, but it's pretty good for a white girl." Claudia winked at me.

"Y'all want to go in the back yard?" Claudia asked.

We followed her through the kitchen, out to a tiny patio and a larger untamed yard. I was used to my mother's orderly azalea gardens, rows of tulips, and the clumps of daffodils that set off her garden bench and birdbath. In Claudia's yard, faint outlines of a formal garden were marked with moss-covered stones and random pink tulips, remnants of another life, like the pink refrigerator inside.

Some kids showed up that I didn't know, and others that I did, but didn't know how to talk to, like Edith. I hung around Venetia and Deloris and we were all glad when Fergy arrived. Claudia enlisted his help to build a bonfire. Mr. Douglas had turned Claudia's childhood sandbox into a kind of fire pit. We gathered up dead branches and sticks that littered the yard.

"I don't think that wet wood's going to burn," Fergy said.

"As long as we find something dry to start it, we can get it going." I was relieved to hear Donald's voice. He'd told me he was bringing DeShawn. Instead he had Mike with him.

"Got any newspapers, Claudia?" Donald asked. Claudia ran inside and brought out a stack.

Mike watched while Fergy and Donald stuffed the paper under and between the wet branches and used up a pack of matches lighting and relighting the fire until the wood finally caught. Everyone applauded.

"I've got stuff for s'mores if y'all want it," Claudia said. I followed her into the kitchen to grab graham crackers and marshmallows.

"Thanks for getting your brother to come," she told me.

"Of course!"

"I guess you can figure out I have kind of a crush on him."

I hadn't figured that out. Everyone liked Donald, but I couldn't see him liking Claudia back.

"Well, if you can snag him, you'll be the first one," I said. I didn't want to discourage her, but I also didn't want Claudia to get her hopes too high.

There were probably a dozen of us sitting on blankets around the sandpit fire. Claudia brought out the guitar she'd gotten for Christmas and Edith strummed it for awhile then passed it to someone else. I was content to be on the edge of the circle, watching this group of black and white kids toasting marshmallows on sticks. Fergy sat next to me and he and Deloris went back and forth with funny stories and impressions and made everyone laugh.

"Would y'all want something more interesting to drink than a coke?" Mike asked. Venetia and Deloris exchanged glances.

"I'm eighteen, y'all. I can buy us some beer."

"Wouldn't your dad get mad?" Venetia asked Claudia.

"He won't care if we don't get crazy," Claudia said.

"We're gonna add some fun to this little party," Mike said as he stood up. "Aren't we, Donald?"

"Sure," Donald said, not sounding sure at all. They walked around the house and we heard them drive off.

In a way, I was glad they were gone. There was a weird line where I wanted my brother around because he improved my social status, but then I didn't, because his presence made me feel too young. I sat down beside Venetia.

"You know, I'm trying to get my parents to let me come back to Stonewall."

"Guess if they annex, you'll be back there."

"Probably."

Her nose wrinkled like she smelled something off, then she changed the subject. "How's your Algebra?"

"Made an A on the last test, thanks to your tutoring."

She nodded. I hadn't been back to Venetia's. I hadn't needed any more help with math. But I hadn't reciprocated and invited her to my house, either. I wanted to, but for some reason I didn't. I wondered if that had hurt her feelings, but I couldn't find the nerve to ask.

Donald and Mike walked back around the house with bags in their arms. Mike pulled out six packs of Miller and lined them up on the patio.

"Hand me a bottle opener," he said to no one in particular. Fergy got up and handed it to him. Mike opened a bottle and let the top rattle onto the slate. "Who's in?"

"I'll take one, thank you very much," Edith said.

Mike opened a second one. "Next?"

Donald took the beer out of Mike's hand.

"I'll take one," Fergy said. Mike popped the top off of another one.

"Me too," Claudia followed.

"I will too," Deloris said.

"Deloris!" Venetia said.

"Oh come on, 'Tia! Don't be such a goody goody!"

"My mother would kill me!" Venetia said.

"Your mother doesn't have to know," Deloris said in a saccharine voice. Mike offered Venetia the opened bottle first, but she shook her head. Deloris took it from him and took a long swallow.

"Alright, Miss Nell, your turn," Mike said as he opened another one. His long pale arm thrust the beer in my face.

I hadn't cared for the taste when my father had let me sample his. My opinion didn't change when I drank it this time. I didn't understand how beer could be so appealing when it tasted so bad. But I sipped it. I watched Venetia and felt bad for her discomfort. She was the only one not drinking. Fergy sensed her uneasiness too, and went over and stood beside her.

"Want me to get you a coke?" he asked her. She nodded.

"Claudia, are there more cokes in the fridge?"

"Yeah, I think so." Fergy walked up the back steps and disappeared into the kitchen.

"Think he'd make a nice boyfriend, Nell?" Mike asked. His kind of teasing could make someone feel appreciated and included or dismissed and ostracized. His tone made me unsteady.

"Leave her alone," Donald said.

Mike and Donald were on their second beer while the rest of us were still on our first. Fergy was entertaining them with a story about some incident at school and they were all cracking up. Even Venetia was snickering. I breathed. Claudia added more wood to the fire.

"Now isn't this cozy?" Mike said, opening another beer. "Should we pair up and make out?"

Deloris laughed but Venetia made a face. Edith already had her arm around a guy I didn't know.

Mike's eyes became slits in his pasty face. "What's wrong, Venetia? Don't think you could make out with a white boy?"

Venetia fixed her gaze past Mike to the blackness of the back yard.

"Hey girl, I'm talking to you," Other conversations stopped." You should look at the person who's talking to you."

Venetia kept her head turned. Mike took a long swallow of

184

his beer. He walked towards her. I bit my lip.

"Girl, don't you know it's rude not to look at who's talking to you?"

Venetia stared at the black trees.

Mike took another step. "Look at me!" His voice was forceful and bitter.

"Leave her alone, man," Fergy said.

"If she wants me to leave her alone, she needs to look at me and tell me herself."

Venetia refused to look at Mike. Her eyes didn't blink. Fergy walked over and stood between her and Mike.

"What do you think you're doing, boy?" Mike spouted. He took a long swig of his beer and tossed the bottle behind him. It shattered, spraying brown glass on the patio. "If you can kiss a white girl, seems only fair I can get me a black one."

Donald stepped around the shards and tugged at Mike's arm." Come on. Let's go."

Mike jerked his arm away. "I'll go when this bitch looks at me and speaks."

Venetia was a statue.

"Come on." Donald said. "I'm leaving and I'm your ride, man."

Mike glared at Venetia. She stared at the back yard. No one moved.

"Shit," Mike said. "I wouldn't want a black one if she was handed to me on a silver platter." He kicked at the broken glass and sauntered towards the street.

Donald's eyes flicked past mine before he followed Mike. We heard the doors slam and the car's engine rev before it left the driveway.

Claudia rushed over to Venetia. "I'm so sorry, Venetia! I never saw that Mike before! He will never be allowed at my house again!"

A long terrible moment passed before Venetia turned her head around. She didn't look at me. She didn't look at Claudia.

All the kids surrounded her and asked if she was okay.

"I'm ready to go home now," she said.

Fergy handed me his unfinished beer. "I'll take you."

I didn't want them to leave. I wanted to make it right. If they'd just stay longer we could get past this and have fun.

"Let's go inside and listen to music," Claudia said. No one responded.

Deloris stood up. "'Bye, Claudia. See ya, Nell." She looped her arm through Venetia's.

"Night," Fergy said. His mouth made a flat line and he avoided my eyes. Venetia never looked at me. She never uttered a word. The three of them walked off the patio and into the lightless yard. Other kids took their exit as a cue and left too. Claudia and I stood by the smoldering fire.

"I don't understand what just happened," I said.

"Remind me not to ask your brother anywhere again," Claudia said bitterly.

"Where's a broom?" I asked.

She went up the back steps and came back with a paper bag and a broom. We shuffled around the patio, picking up trash and sweeping up broken glass and bottle caps. I dumped half-full bottles on the fire to douse it. We were silent as we picked up the remains of the party.

※

I spilled my angst onto pieces of paper torn from a spiral notebook, the raggedy edges leaving tiny white flecks on the floor by my bed. I wrote three almost identical notes to Venetia and Deloris and Fergy apologizing for what happened, and vowing to never have Mike near them again. I couldn't get the notes to sound right; I was either too formal and stilted or too emotional. I erased a hole in the paper and had to start over. I took them with me to folk Mass.

"Have you seen Venetia or Deloris?" I asked Claudia standing by the snack table.

"Did you really think they'd come back here?" Her tone was biting and I felt the blame of the failed party land on my shoulders.

My stomach dropped and my teeth sank into my bottom lip. "I was just trying to get my brother to come," I said, "because you said it would make Fergy more comfortable to have another guy there."

"Why does Donald hang out with a creepy guy like Mike?" Claudia spat back. "I don't get it!"

"I don't know. Mike used to be nice."

She sighed and twisted her mood ring round and round her finger.

"I wrote some notes. Would you take them to school and give them to Venetia?"

"Okay," she shrugged and held her hand out for them. "I wouldn't count on them changing anything, though."

The notes went from my pocket to hers without her even glancing at them as two guys strummed their guitars on stage. Claudia picked up a drink from the table and moved away from me to sit near the front. It didn't feel like she wanted me to follow, so I didn't.

When uncomfortable situations arose in our family, our learned pattern of behavior was to step around the giant boulder of hurt until we created a circular rut of avoidance. Anger stayed under the surface where we trampled its occasional flareups. I was furious with Donald. He was listening to music in his room when I broke the family pattern, burst into his room and asked why he brought Mike to the party.

"Mike's fun at a party. He got your friends beer, didn't he?"

"You said you were going to bring DeShawn."

"Nell, it's weird to ask black kids to a white party. They don't like the same stuff we do."

My anger bubbled up and spewed over. I ranted and raved and stomped and cried about how Venetia and Fergy were my real friends, how the girls at St. Mary's were too snobby to hang out with me, how he had no idea what it was like to change schools twice in one year, and how he and Mike had ruined everything in a single night.

Donald sat cross-legged on his bed and took my fury with his eyes closed.

"Are you finished?" he asked.

I heard my breath escape through my nostrils in pulses like a raging bull.

"Mike gets a little too big for his breeches when he drinks. He didn't mean what he said. If you'll just calm down and ignore it, everyone will get over it. They always do." His voice was sweet and too patronizing.

I stomped over to his record player. My index finger dragged the needle across the spinning album. It's skidding and scratching played through the speakers and Donald's hands clamped over his ears. I marched out of his room. Donald yelled that "if I chose to hang out with the colored kids I better get used to this stuff happening" before he slammed his door.

188

Chapter Eighteen

꧁

"Nell, telephone!" I hopped off my bed where I'd been reading and went into the hall.

"I'll get it up here."

My mother eyed me from the bottom of the stairs.

"It's a young man." Her voice was part teasing and part proud.

"Hello," I listened for the click of the receiver, not trusting her curiosity.

"Hi, Nell. It's Fergy."

"Hi." My mind rattled, picturing how my mother would react if she knew a black boy was on the phone. I faced away from the open bedroom door.

"Thanks for the note."

"You're welcome. Did Venetia and Deloris get theirs?"

"Venetia did. I guess she gave Deloris hers."

"What did she say?"

"She's still mighty upset. She..." he stopped himself.

"She what?"

"She's mad you didn't say anything to Mike or your brother. That you didn't defend her."

I squirmed. My heart whacked my chest.

"She doesn't trust you have her back. She thinks being at a white school is turning you."

"I had a big fight with my brother. I told him what I thought of Mike."

"Yeah, well, she doesn't know that."

"And I hate St. Mary's!"

"But you're still there." Silence. I bit my lip.

"Nell, if you're gonna invite black kids into your white world, you gotta be prepared to face what we face."

"I tried to call Venetia, but she won't come to the phone."

"Are you hearing me? You gotta defend while it's happening, not after."

"I've apologized!"

"Apologies don't mean anything if they're not backed up."

"What can I do now?"

"You got to start from the beginning again."

"So they're not going to come back to the coffeehouse?"

"I don't 'spect so."

"Are you?"

"I'll come, but I don't want to be the only black kid there."

"Bring some friends."

"To tell you the truth, there aren't many of my friends who'd be into that coffeehouse."

"Then I guess I won't see you for awhile."

My mother called up the stairs. "Nell, I need you to come set the table!"

"Coming!" I yelled back, covering the bottom of the receiver.

"I have to go."

"Come see me and Venetia in the play."

The receiver was damp from my sweaty hands. My dry mouth kept me swallowing.

"And in the meantime, you can tell your mom I'm a guy from church. You know she's going to ask. That should make her happy and it's not a lie."

190

"Good idea." That Fergy understood the anxiety about my mother without explanation created a synchronized soft spot of fondness with a pang of sadness. I wished Fergy were white. We hung up and I took my time obeying her call. My father wasn't home yet; setting the table could have waited.

"That boy who called you had nice manners," my mother said as I walked into the kitchen. "Who is he?"

"Oh, a guy from church," I said, trying to act nonchalant.

"You talked for awhile."

"We were talking about the coffeehouse." I lined up each knife and spoon and fork to the sides of the four plates.

"See, I told you you could still meet boys even if you're at a girls' school!" Her path between the stove and the sink clicked with a happy cadence. "And nicer ones too, than at your old school."

I'd been so engrossed in my own life and friend drama I hadn't thought much about Father Richard's plans for Saturday. Folk Mass and the coffeehouse were cancelled for an antiwar march in Washington. We were to meet at the church early and travel in a caravan of cars. Claudia's dad was driving, and one of the older kids from the coffeehouse had a car too. My parents weren't too keen on us going. They were Nixon supporters and thought politics should be played out in the voting booth and not in the street. Father Richard had won them over promising that many priests and churches were involved and it would be more of a community prayer vigil than a protest. They relented and Donald and I were in the church parking lot at eight.

Claudia's car was full. She'd made friends with some of the other kids at the coffeehouse and they were riding with her in her dad's old Mustang. At the time I thought she was still blaming me for ruining her party. Looking back, I don't think she meant to leave me out. She was just that way, always moving on to the next thing, not worrying about what she was leaving behind. Maybe if your mother decides she doesn't want to live with you a person learns to be that way.

"Good morning, Nell. Gonna ride with us? "Mr. Chiles greeted me with a broad smile. I had no idea Venetia's dad would be part of this.

"Thank you, Mr. Chiles. Yes, I'd love to if it's alright with Venetia."

"I'm sure 'Tia's already saved you a spot!" Venetia must not have told him about the party.

I stood beside him trying to think of something to say. Venetia was across the parking lot getting directions from Father Richard. Her lips pinched together when she saw me.

"Here, Daddy." She handed the paper to Mr. Chiles.

"I invited your friend Nell here to ride with us. Who else is coming?"

"Fergy is."

"Still room for one or two more."

Fergy walked across the parking lot with another guy I didn't know. It was looking like I was going to be the only white kid in the car.

"How about Susan?" I asked. Susan was the type of person that blended into the background of any group. She didn't talk much, but was agreeable and pleasant. She didn't have a defined group of friends.

"Sure." Venetia said and jogged over to the group of milling teenagers and picked Susan out of the crowd. It reminded me of choosing teams for kickball.

We made up four carloads. Father Richard called us together to go over the details and pass out poster board and markers.

"Make your signs big and simple. We want people to be able to read them from a distance."

"What do we write?" I asked. I looked around and kids

were already busy sketching big letters and filling them in.

"I'm drawing a peace symbol," Susan said.

Venetia was writing *STOP THE WAR* in big red block letters. She outlined them in black. "The colors of blood and death," she said.

I hadn't thought much about the war. It hadn't touched my life. All these kids seemed to have more emotion about it than I did, and I felt like I was missing the meaning, the depth, the power of the experience. I wanted in on it. I wanted to feel something.

Father Richard whistled for our attention. "While you're working on your posters I want you to think about why we're doing this," he said. "We're going in peace. We're praying for peace. We're walking in peace. The people you will see on the streets with you today are your brothers and sisters. The people we are advocating for on the other side of the world are also your brothers and sisters. The police you will see today are your brothers. The lost ones we grieve for today are your brothers. Let's not go in fear or in anger, but in peace."

I penciled bulbous letters to spell *PEACE*. I filled them in with rainbow colors.

"Nice," Venetia said, nodding at my poster.

I sat in the middle of the back seat between Fergy and his friend Willie. Venetia sat beside her father in the front with Susan, and adjusted the radio dial when we lost a station during the two-hour drive. Her father's blue Buick had plenty of room with its broad seats, so even if I had to splay my legs with the hump in the middle of the floor I didn't have to touch either one of the boys. Our posters rode in the trunk.

Father Richard had given us a meeting spot and a time. The traffic slowed as we got close to D.C., but we found the chosen corner with time to spare. Mr. Chiles knew his way around.

"Y'all ready to do some walking?" Mr. Chiles asked. He opened the trunk. "Best eat something before we get moving."

We grabbed our brown bags and swallowed our lunches, standing on the sidewalk. When everyone met up, we took our posters and joined the stream of people moving down the street.

I'd been to D.C. with my parents once, to the Natural History Museum. We saw the giant elephant and the exhibit on the evolution from ape to man. My mother didn't like that one, saying she didn't want to feel like she descended from a monkey. I remember my father teased her about being afraid of science. The only other time I'd been to the city was on a field trip in the sixth grade, when we went to the Washington Monument and the Capitol. Neither of those times felt like this one.

As we walked, the streets filled up with all kinds of people. Most of them were young, but not all. There were men in suits, families with little kids, church youth groups with the same color T-shirts, and even some nuns. I couldn't imagine the nuns at St. Mary's even discussing the war, much less marching to protest it. Donald and his friends walked ahead of us with Father Richard. Their signs read: *WE WON'T GO* and *LOVE! NOT WAR!*. We walked with our posters held high, until our arms ached. I couldn't see where we were going, but it didn't matter. I felt a rush of belonging as I moved with the tide.

Father Richard found a stopping place near the Washington Monument. He counted to make sure we were all there and we sat on the grassy hill waiting for something to happen. I'd never seen so many people. I'd never seen so many guys with hair past their shoulders. It felt like I'd been dropped into another world as I listened to strumming guitars and inhaled traces of incense, and what I learned later was pot. Certain people had megaphones and started chants and songs. Father Richard took hold of one and did a mini-sermon on peace. People swayed during his open-eyed prayer with their fingers making peace signs in the air.

It was late afternoon by the time we edged towards the reflecting pool with the swelling crowd. The sun stayed behind the clouds and the spring air turned chilly. I wished I'd worn a jacket. Susan walked arm in arm with Venetia and me, bridging our gap, oblivious to the thin layer of ice between us. I hoped that what we were a part of at that moment was more powerful than the altercation at the party. I wanted to use this shared experience to erase the other.

Hippies squeezed between the tight crowd, passing out black armbands and flowers. We took them.

"I get the flowers," I said to Venetia, "But what is this for?" I held up the armband.

"Put it on," she said. "It's a sign of mourning the dead soldiers."

It always seemed like Venetia had inside knowledge of culture I wasn't privy to. Maybe her dad told her stuff. Maybe she actually read the newspaper. Maybe she was just smarter. I wanted to be like her.

Father Richard had brought a transistor radio with him, so even if we were too far away to hear the bands and the speeches, we could hear them from the newscast on his radio. When Peter, Paul and Mary sang about Johnny having to follow his captain's call I started to understand, but just a little. There was more melancholy in their tune than I wanted to feel.

A willowy young woman wove her way through our group. She stopped in front of me and grasped my hand. Hemp bracelets crowded her thin arm. Long dark hair draped her face like a pair of curtains. Her eyes caught mine in a fiery gaze.

"Don't forget his name," she said.

"Whose name?" I asked.

"This young soldier's." She pressed a strip of paper into my hand and I read *Otis E. Booker, 1967*, written with a backward slant in red ink.

"Say it." Her eyes pleaded with mine.

"Otis E. Booker, 1967."

She nodded. "It's been three years since they killed him." She dropped her gaze and moved on. I wondered how she'd picked me. I slipped the paper into the pocket of my jeans, his name already memorized.

The sun was sinking when we walked the long blocks back to the car, our posters damp and curled, our conversations sparse. The excitement of being part of something significant had morphed into a deep sadness. I replayed movie clips in my head that I'd seen on the news. Flag draped caskets. Burning villages. Vietnamese children crying. All accompanied by the whirring drone of a helicopter. Donald would turn eighteen in a few months. Fergy would come of age next year. It all felt so hopeless.

Chapter Nineteen

❦

Time dragged its feet as the days got longer and the sunshine warmer. The nuns seemed to have tired of the school year as much as we had. They passed out assignments, written in faded purple mimeographed script on paper that had yellowed around the edges, pretending they had not scrounged them from a dusty file. Their uninteresting sentences, composed so we could decompose and diagram them, were about the advantages of Hawaii becoming a state, or the dream that someday man might land on the moon. I wondered if they weren't allowed to watch TV and didn't know that had already happened. I wondered if their sheltered lives protected them from the news that spring of Vietnam and the tragedy of Kent State.

There were other antiwar protests, but after the students at Kent State were killed, my parents wouldn't let me go with Father Richard to them. Venetia and Fergy still went, and I heard Deloris joined them. I became an outsider at my own church when I went to the coffeehouse, where kids knew songs I'd never heard and conversations centered around the next protest. The activism scared my mother who was even more determined to keep me sequestered in a private school.

I'd always made sure my grades were exemplary, but now I couldn't force myself to sit down and do the mundane homework. Instead, I piddled away the afternoons making macrame belts and reading *The Outsiders* and *Lord of the Flies* instead of the assigned *Paradise Lost* and *Sinners in the Hands of an Angry God*. I blamed my stalled life on Mike, and on Donald for bringing him to the party, and on my parents for being so strict. When Fergy invited me to the spring play at Stonewall, I decided to go without their permission.

There weren't many people milling around when our station wagon pulled up in front of the school. It looked more rundown than I remembered, without the green grass or blooming shrubs that lined the walks of St. Mary's.

"You okay?" Donald asked.

"Yeah."

Two black girls with big afros and big voices walked past the car.

"You sure you have a ride home?"

"I'll call you if Claudia's dad can't take me. And remember, you took me to Claudia's house, if Mom and Dad ask."

Donald nodded. We were bonded in our deception.

The halls still smelled like old tennis shoes mixed with a leftover hint of school lunch. The bulletin boards held thumbtacked lists of honor roll students and posters pushing the upcoming prom. I stopped at the table set up in front of the auditorium and paid my fifty cents for a ticket. More people were seated in the auditorium than I expected and most of the aisle seats were taken. I chose a row by deciding who to ask to stand up to let me squeeze by them. I scanned the audience and saw no one I recognized and put all my attention on the thin playbill.

"Nell?" Claudia's dad stood beside me. "Saving this seat?"

"Hi, Mr. Douglas! It's all yours!"

"How have you been? Haven't seen you in awhile!"

"Okay, I guess. I miss doing this." I held up my playbill. He nodded as if my sentiments were logical, without the assumption I should feel so lucky to go to a private school, like most adults implied.

He crossed an ankle over his knee revealing all the scuffs on his loafers and a heel that was worn down on one side. His corduroy jacket was out of sync with the season and the bottom edge of his jeans was frayed from a hem that dragged the ground. My father wouldn't have kept wearing clothes in that condition and only wore jeans on Saturdays. I wondered if Claudia's mom would have insisted on remedying his appearance if they'd still been married.

The auditorium wasn't packed the way it was with *Carousel*. The play was not one with memorable lines or scenes or flamboyant characters. What was apparent from my creaky auditorium seat was the invisible bond that tied these actors together. I saw the hours of rehearsal, the backstage conversations, the walks to Williard's for root beer floats. I couldn't see the characters for the actors.

When Mr. Douglas and I filed out of the auditorium, a small crowd was waiting for the cast members to reappear from backstage. Deloris was standing with Venetia's parents. I hadn't seen her since the party.

"You don't have to hang with me if you want to see your friends," Mr. Douglas said.

"Thanks. But I'm not sure they want to see me."

"You mean after what happened at the party?"

"You know about that?"

"Yeah."

"Wow. You and Claudia are more like friends than father and daughter."

"I guess that's what happens when it's just us." He nodded his head towards Deloris. "Go seize the moment."

"I'm afraid to."

"Pretend you're a character on the stage and play the role. Sometimes it's easier to make a move when there's an audience." He was pushing me out of the nest. I didn't want Mr. Douglas to think I couldn't muster the courage so I crossed the hall and tapped Deloris on the arm.

"Hey, Deloris."

She spun around and glared at me for an edgy moment. My heart raced.

"Why you here?"

"I wanted to see the play. They did a great job."

"Yeah."

"It made me miss being here, and miss doing a play with them."

"Uh-huh." Deloris reeled back around. I felt the redness climb up my neck.

"Did you get my note?" I asked the back of her head.

"Yeah."

"I meant what I said." I waited for her to answer, but she didn't. "I'm sorry about all that stuff Mike said and I wish I'd stood up to him at the party. I never invited him."

When there was no response I walked back to Mr. Douglas. The actors were coming through the double doors.

"Nice job, kiddo!" Mr. Douglas greeted Claudia with a big hug.

"Thanks, Dad!"

"I forgot flowers," he said with downturned lips and a shrug.

"That's okay," she smiled. "Hi, Nell."

"You were great!" I gave her a quick hug.

"Thanks."

"It made me miss being with y'all."

She nodded. "Aren't you going to go see Fergy and Venetia?"

I bit my lip. "I tried to talk to Deloris, but it's clear she doesn't want me around."

"Want me to tell them you're here?" I gave her a grateful smile and Claudia grabbed Fergy out of the crowd.

"Hey. I didn't know if you would make it or not."

"Y'all were great!"

"My role wasn't as good as playing your dead father, but it was still fun."

He reached out and shook Mr. Douglas's hand. I was proud of his manners and his confidence, even though I had nothing to do with either.

"Claudia, are you going out with us?" Fergy asked.

"Sure! Has anyone decided where we're going?"

"Pizza at Shakey's. Want to go, Nell?"

"Isn't it just for the cast?" I asked.

"Let's say, cast and alumni," he answered.

"Think it's okay with Venetia?" I asked. After our day together at the march, Venetia had gone back to her closed ways with me. What I had interpreted as forgiveness that day had been a brief moratorium out of respect for the soldiers dying in Vietnam. I didn't want to do anything else that would push her further away.

"I'll take care of Venetia. Come on, it'll be fun!"

Claudia's dad offered to drop us off at Shakey's and pick us up later. What would have been a complicated manipulation of negotiating a ride in my house was not a big deal with him. When I slid into the back seat of his old green Mustang I felt at home. I didn't mind the torn seat and the cigarette smell. I didn't care if I wasn't part of the conversation; I was content in being witness to it.

"What time should I pick you girls up?" Mr. Douglas asked as he pulled into Shakey's parking lot.

"I don't know. Hour? Hour and a half?" Claudia said.

"Got it. Y'all have fun!"

"Claudia," I said as we walked up the sidewalk, "I appreciate you asking me to come."

"I didn't, Fergy did."

I stiffened.

"But it's fine," she smiled. She grabbed her mass of auburn

hair like she was going to put it in a ponytail, then let it fall down her back. "I'm glad to have you around."

I stuck close to Claudia. We joined some of the cast already seated at a long table in the back. Venetia came in and I motioned for her to sit by me, but she chose the seat on the other side of Claudia. They talked about where they messed up and what had gone on backstage. I fiddled with my silverware. When Fergy arrived he took the chair next to mine, organized the pizza order for the table, and kept everyone laughing with his impressions of Miss Conner and Mrs. Hayes.

"Do Mr. Jefferson!" someone called out, and Fergy did a perfect imitation of my old math teacher. The table roared. The manager came over and asked us to be quieter.

Fergy whispered, "Yas, sir."

As we giggled the manager put his hands on his hips and his red pudgy face bobbled as his squinty eyes traveled around the table. His eyebrows scrunched into a confused furrow when he came to Claudia and me, the only white kids.

"I'm warning you," he said, when he had finished his visual tour of the table. "If other customers complain, I'll have to ask you to leave."

Our pizzas came and the chatter was more unobtrusive while we ate.

"Bet you've never been kicked out of a restaurant before, have you Nell?" Fergy said.

"No. Have you?"

"I've not been allowed in one before."

"Why?"

"Because I'm black, silly!" He winked at me and put his arm around the back of my chair.

"But that's illegal," I said.

"Doesn't mean people don't do it." His smile disappeared.

"I'm sorry," I said. Venetia stole a look at me. I wondered if she hadn't been allowed in a restaurant before. The sick feeling in my stomach resurged when I thought of the cruel words Mike had said to her.

"I'm going to the bathroom," I told Claudia.

"Hello, Nell," a voice said as I wove through tables. Penny, Sylvia, and two boys I didn't know were sitting in a booth. "I thought that was you over there," Penny said. She and Sylvia were wearing the frosted lipstick they weren't allowed to wear to school and their hair had been curled and sprayed into a different style.

"Hi," I said. "How are y'all?"

"Just fine," Sylvia answered. "I thought that was you, but couldn't figure out why you were with so many colored kids." Her mouth puckered like she'd tasted something sour.

"I'm with some friends from my old school. I saw their play tonight."

"Oh," Penny said as she leaned up to get a good look at our table. "Is that the boyfriend from the basketball game sitting next to you?"

"Uh...Fergy's just a friend." I bit my lip.

"What's Fergy's last name?" Sylvia asked.

"Sutton." I became flustered with their questions, rushed into giving answers, then wishing I hadn't. "I've got to go to the bathroom. I'll see y'all Monday."

I stayed in the bathroom washing my hands over and over. I slunk back between the tables farthest from their booth, keeping my head down. Our group was settling the bill when I got back. I took out my wallet but Fergy stopped me.

"You're my guest tonight, Nell."

"Thanks, Fergy, but you don't have to pay for me."

"It's already done." He put his arm around my shoulder and gave it a squeeze. I panicked. I shrugged my shoulders as if to toss Fergy's arm off me.

"You okay?" he asked.

"I don't want those girls from school to see us."

"You embarrassed?" Venetia said. It was the first time she'd spoken directly to me the whole evening.

"Of course not."

Claudia stood up and nodded her head towards the door. "My dad's here." She pushed her chair in. "See y'all Monday!"

I was so flustered my goodbyes were rushed niceties that must have felt fake to this table of black kids. I'd ruined my opportunity to regain some trust. I was agitated that I'd allowed the distraction of Penny and Sylvia to curb my actions. And I was distressed that I had no idea when I'd see any of them again.

Chapter Twenty

※

"Eleanor, Sister Bridget needs to see you." Sister Bernadette put the note on her desk, returned to the board, and picked up her chalk. I stood up to go to the office.

"Take your books with you, in the event the bell rings before you return."

The big clock above the board showed a half hour left of class. I couldn't imagine what would take that long, but I gathered my books as instructed and left. The polished floors gleamed in the empty halls as I walked past open doors catching snippets of lectures on American history and English literature. With the promise of summer ahead, school was bearable. In truth, I didn't mind this part of St. Mary's, the part that felt like learning. Girls said the nicer nuns taught the juniors and seniors. Maybe St. Mary's wouldn't be so bad if I stayed.

I recognized my mother's navy pumps before I could see the rest of her.

"Come in, Eleanor," Sister Bridget said. There was no hint of warmth in her voice. I walked in her office and saw my mother perched on the edge of a wooden desk chair. Her gloved hands rested over the purse in her lap; folded, as if she were in prayer. She didn't look at me.

"Leave your books with Sister Margaret, then close the door."

I did as Sister Bridget said and waited for permission to sit down. She didn't give it. My mind raced, searching for the reason I'd been summoned and why my mother was sitting here.

"It has come to my attention that there has been a serious infraction," Sister Bridget said.

"An infraction?"

"You have been seen displaying affection with a Negro boy."

"What?" My heart was beating so fast I was sure they could see it through my white blouse.

"You were seen on Friday evening in a local restaurant holding hands with and hugging a Negro boy. Our policies here forbid St. Mary's girls from dating boys of another race, which includes any public display of affection, or private display, for that matter."

"But that's not true!" My palms were clammy and my voice came out shaky.

"Are you disputing me, Eleanor?" Sister Bridget picked up a paper and blinked several times. "It has been reported by more than one person."

"Forgive me, Sister Bridget, but there must be a misunderstanding." I looked to my mother for support but she stared at her praying hands.

"We take this infraction very seriously, Eleanor. Our school rules are put in place to honor our Lord Jesus Christ and any disobedience is not only to our school but to Him. I have asked your mother here in order to take you home until we have reviewed the situation and come to a final decision as to your future here."

"I'm being suspended?"

"We do not call it that here. You are being granted time to

contemplate your sins and to come into a place of repentance, as we are granted time to prayerfully consider your place here at St. Mary's." She stood up and my mother followed suit.

"Good day to you both."

I followed my mother out of Sister Bridget's office. Sister Margaret handed me my books. My mother put on the white sunglasses that hid half of her face. No one spoke. The yeasty smell of rolls baking in the kitchen filled the air as we walked out the main door.

"None of that is true!" I slammed the car door. "You can ask Claudia!"

"I don't need to ask Claudia anything. You lied to us about where you went. You went to a part of town where I've asked you not to go. And now you're maintaining relationships that are detrimental to your future. I don't want to hear another word out of you."

My mother said no more on the drive home or for the rest of the day. I stayed in my room. I wanted to be outside, to ride my bike somewhere, to live at Sally's house. I played the events of Friday night through my head over and over like a movie. This was because of Penny and Sylvia. They were out with boys, probably doing much worse things than I'd ever done, but I was the one who got in trouble. Sister Bridget willed me to feel shame. My whirly mix of emotions included anger and confusion, but not shame.

"Nell, supper's ready," my father tapped on my closed door. I cringed at facing him. Even if I couldn't find my sin, his presence chastened me. I joined the meal of fried chicken and rice and green beans: Donald's favorite. I was hungry, so I ate. Two helpings of rice and a slice of pound cake with ice cream as well. I wondered if my mother expected me to have no appetite, to manifest my shame and repentance that way. The dinner conversation was a lopsided one between Donald and my father.

"Did Lee's baseball team win yesterday?"

"Got any grass cutting jobs lined up?"

All questions from my father requiring one-word answers. I wasn't sure if Donald's reticence to engage was in solidarity with me or if he was in his own moody world and didn't feel like talking. Over the years of my mother's sporadic periods of silence my father had honed his ability to let her be alone when surrounded by us. He knew one day she would speak again, so he attempted to keep up civility with polite conversation while he waited. The difference in this meal was I was silent too and it offset our learned pattern of communicating through my mother's nonverbal disposition. I would have answered a question if he or Donald had asked me one, but they didn't. If one of my parents had yelled at me it would have broken the dam and I could have fought back, but that was not their way.

"Need a smoke?" Donald whispered. It must have been past midnight, but I was nowhere close to sleep.

"Yes," I whispered back.

"Thought so." He went to my open window and raised the screen. I followed him onto the porch roof and we dropped into the damp grass. The air had not retained the warmth of the May day and I wished I'd worn my sweatshirt. We walked without talking to the backside of the garage. He pulled out two cigarettes, handed me one and lit it for me.

"What the hell happened, Nell?"

"Do you even care?" I snapped at him.

He puffed his cigarette, taking my anger.

"The cast went to Shakey's for pizza after the play and they asked me to go. We were at a big table in the back and Fergy was sitting beside me. He put his arm around me *once,* but honestly, that was it!" I tried to puff the cigarette with my trembling lips.

"I went to the bathroom and passed the booth where Penny and Sylvia were sitting with their boyfriends. I guess they spied on me. They're the ones who went to Sister Bridget!" Tears of anger and frustration filled my eyes.

Donald looked at me while I spoke. He and Sister Bridget were the only ones who had looked at me. He took a long drag and tilted his head to blow. He inhaled once more, then dropped the last bit of cigarette. His foot ground it until there was a patch of uprooted grass and dirt surrounding the butt.

"Why do you want to hang out with those kids?"

I dropped my barely smoked cigarette onto the ground too and stepped on it.

"I don't know. The play made us friends. The girls at St. Mary's already have the friends they want, and I'm not one of them." I covered the butt with dirt. "Why do you like to hang out with Mike?"

He ignored my question." What happened to Sally?"

"What do you mean?"

"Why don't you hang out with her like you always have?"

"Sally doesn't get me anymore."

He nodded like he understood.

"What am I going to do?"

"I don't think you're the one who's going to decide. If St. Mary's lets you come back, I guess that's where you'll go. And if not, your only option is Stonewall." He gave me a weak smile. "Or you could run away to Canada with me."

"Are you thinking about doing that?"

"I'm thinking about everything."

We stayed behind the garage for a long time, not saying much more, sitting in the wet grass until the moon was high. I was wet and cold and sleepy by the time we walked back across the yard. I fell into a dreamless sleep and did not wake until the sun was bright and the late spring air blew a fragrance of the budding magnolias through my open window. Donald had gone to school, my father had gone to work, and my mother had gone who knows where. I was alone in the house and I had no place to go.

I didn't call Sally or even Claudia. I called Venetia.

"I think I've been kicked out of St. Mary's."

She listened as I told her how Penny and Sylvia twisted what they saw at the pizza place and tattled to Sister Bridget, who called my mother.

"So the nuns are suspending you because they think you've got a thing going with Fergy?"

"Yeah." It sounded so racist the way she said it. I didn't want her sympathy. I wanted her to see how I was now on the side of the persecuted. Her side.

"And you lied to your parents about where you were going?"

"Not exactly. I just didn't tell them."

"Are your parents punishing you?" she asked.

"Yeah, if you count my mother's silent treatment."

"Girl, there wouldn't be any silent treatment in my house! There would be yelling and grounding and maybe even some spanking." She laughed. It'd been a long time since I'd heard Venetia's laugh.

"It'd be easier if they'd punish me. This way it drags on. My mother will be furious with me forever."

"You gotta put up the wall."

"The wall?"

"Yep. You gotta pretend your mother doesn't exist right now."

Emboldened by the distance of a telephone line I blurted, "Is that what you've been doing with me?"

"Course it is. That's what I've been taught to do. I can't go mouthing off at all the white people that make me angry. I'd make it worse for myself."

"Is the wall down now?" Venetia didn't hurry to answer.

"Nell, you gotta know I didn't get mad at you cause you're white. I got mad cause I thought you were my friend, but you didn't act like you were. It was like you all a sudden got embarrassed to have a black girl as your friend. If I'm your friend, I'm your friend all the time, not just when it suits your social circle."

I had heard a sermon.

It was three days before my parents received a call from Sister Bridget. Three silent days. Two of those nights Donald had plans with his friends and my father had dinner meetings with clients so neither was home for supper. My mother fixed me a plate, but didn't eat with me. My father came to my room to hear my side of the story. He listened without interrupting. At the end of my story he asked attorney like questions: Where were you sitting? What did Fergy do? What did you do? What could Penny and Sylvia have seen? My face flushed when I told him Fergy put his arm around me, but his expression didn't change. Perhaps he was preparing an argument to defend me to Sister Bridget. Perhaps he was satisfying his own mind. In the end it didn't matter. St. Mary's decided not to extend an invitation for me to return.

If Sister Bridget had talked with my father instead of my mother I believe he would have put up a fight, not because he thought St. Mary's was such a great place, but because of the principle of the thing. In my mother's trained reverence for the nuns, she thanked Sister Bridget for her gracious response to my indiscretion, hung up the phone, clipped the earring back on her left ear, and finally spoke to me.

"I guess you've gotten what you wanted now." Her voice was restrained; detached and measured, pronouncing all of the t's her southern accent usually elided over. She repeated to me what Sister Bridget had said like a monologue performed on a stage.

"Since we are almost at the end of the academic year we have decided to issue Eleanor a report card based on her present grades which will indicate she has passed all classes to advance to the eleventh grade. This will allow her to attend another school without academic repercussions of this unfortunate situation."

My mother fixed a cold stare on me. "She told me we should be grateful they will not put the word 'expelled' on your permanent record. That we should consider it an act of forgiveness."

She didn't wait for a response. Her heels clicked across the kitchen floor. They stopped and she called back to me.

"Even Father Richard couldn't get you out of this!"

So she had gone to ask for his intervention. I could have told her that wouldn't have helped. Sister Bridget wouldn't speak against a priest, of course, but she stiffened when Father Richard's name was mentioned. The class he'd wanted to teach at St. Mary's had been put on hold due to "scheduling conflicts" and Sister Bridget had refused requests from the school choir members to perform any of the songs that were sung in folk Mass. A favor for Father Richard would have been dismissed by her.

My mother left the house and didn't return until late afternoon. She dumped a small armload of books and notebooks on my bed and handed me my report card from St. Mary's. The envelope was still sealed.

"You didn't read my report card?"

"No, I did not. I fail to see what difference whatever is on there can make now. You have taken a wonderful opportunity and thrown it away with your selfish, inappropriate behavior." She turned to leave.

"How was what happened selfish?" I called after her.

"Just asking that question shows how selfish it was!" She spun back around with fiery anger. Her mouth trembled. Her eyes were wide and wild. Her fine neck splotched with red.

"Have you even considered what this has done to my situation? You haven't just ruined your own life, you have permanently damaged mine! How can I go to my bridge club and face these women who helped get you into St. Mary's? Even the people who don't know what happened will wonder why you're back in public school! And how am I to explain that? Tell them my daughter likes to be with Negro boys? Guess you didn't think about those repercussions, did you, Eleanor?"

"You never even asked what I wanted before you put me in that stuck up school! You're the one who's selfish! You care more about your bridge club friends than you do about me!"

I said it. I had broken the family code. It was the first and last time I ever yelled at my mother. Her stunned expression changed to contempt before she marched out of my room.

None of it made sense. For a religious school to profess God's love and forgiveness, then to promote no-mixing rules didn't make sense. For Penny and Sylvia to tell lies and still gain the sisters' favor didn't make sense. For my mother to care more about what her bridge club thought than how her daughter felt didn't make sense. There was nothing fair about what happened. I would have to put up Venetia's wall and pretend those who hurt me didn't exist. But it wasn't until years later that I drew a comparison of my encounter with one personal inequity to the long history of injustices the Venetias of the world had endured.

Chapter
Twenty-One

✗✗✗

I made myself invisible the last two weeks of the school year. Fergy called once. He wondered if I blamed him. I didn't. Neither of us referred to the moment I shrugged his arm off me, but that sudden shift of my shoulder dug a hole beneath our footing. We weren't sorry I'd been kicked out. Still, he wasn't comfortable calling and his mother didn't approve of girls calling him. Our communication slowed to a trickle.

My mother washed her hands of me and threw herself into planning Donald's graduation party. She set her hopes high for this celebration of her only son. Her mania seemed doubly fueled by my failure, as if saving any blessings for me would be pointless; all of her had to be poured into Donald. It was already summer hot by early June and she fretted over all the weather possibilities for the afternoon party.

"I'm thinking we should make it an ice cream party. What do you think, Donald?" she asked as we passed around the meatloaf and macaroni and cheese, a meal not in sync with the sweltering evening.

"I don't care, Mom. Whatever you want." Donald had kept his distance from the planning since the beginning, no matter how much my mother tempted him with details she thought would entice him.

"I wish you would show some interest in this," she said, while dishing peas to a particular spot on her plate. "This party is all for you, you know." My father hid a smile that said the opposite beneath his bowed head. "And I'm certainly glad I sent the invitations as early as I did. Beverly Ripple told me they were planning on having Mary Beth's party at the same time until they got our invitation."

"You invited the Ripples?" Donald asked.

"Of course I invited the Ripples! You and Mary Beth have been classmates since first grade!"

"Yeah, but we've never been friends!"

"I don't know why not. Mary Beth is a very nice girl." She poked at scattered peas. "And she's going to State too. It would be nice for you two to share rides back and forth."

I stole a glance at Donald, but he avoided my eyes. He started to speak but stopped himself and took a bite of meatloaf instead.

"Son," my father cleared his throat, "have you thought about the other summer job?" My father's law partner had offered Donald a job in the office for the summer.

"Yeah, but I've told camp I'll do the full six weeks as counselor. Plus the training week." My father watched him as Donald continued to put forkfuls of our supper in his mouth.

"I think it would be a better choice for you to do some work in an office. You've had the camp experience quite a few summers now."

"I know, Dad, but this is my first opportunity to be a full counselor, and I'll have a lot of responsibility with that, which would also be good for me."

"Eugene, I think Donald is entitled to one last summer of camp." My mother almost always took Donald's side. "He will be in an office soon enough." My father nodded his head, but I don't think it was in agreement. It was the nod of knowing further debate would be futile.

"I expect for you to call Mr. Williams and tell him your decision tomorrow."

"Can't you tell him? You see him everyday."

"Yes, I could tell him. But it's not my job to give him your answer." He pushed his chair away from the table. "You may not be working in an office, but you will conduct yourself in the appropriate way in these matters." He stood up and put his napkin beside his plate. "Thank you for dinner, Marjorie. I'm going to pass on dessert tonight."

He left the room and the three of us went silent. Donald stood up, picked up his plate, and deposited it by the sink with such a clatter I thought it was in pieces. He stomped up the stairs and slammed his door.

"I hate it when they argue," my mother said. She gathered up dishes and started scraping and rinsing them. I cleared the table of the food we had left to turn cold and serve as leftovers some other day.

My father and Donald had hardly argued. My father had disagreed with Donald's choice and let him know. There were no raised voices, no predictions of what would happen to him, no strong emotions displayed. Usually my mother was the one who changed the temperament of a room. And when she did, we tiptoed around her until life went back to normal, which it eventually did. My father's way of making a point was not so mercurial. His presence and his manner of not arguing made you sense in your gut his way was the right way. The perception of disappointing him was a strong deterrent to disagreeing with him, and if you did, the emotional consequences of your choice lingered, and in some cases, never left.

The day of Donald's graduation dawned with a violent

thunderstorm, and the graduation exercises were moved from the football field to the gym. We dressed up to sit packed on bleachers, inhaling the stale air of decades of basketball games and pep rallies. Sweat trickled down my back. I wondered how my mother could stand wearing her hose and pumps, but the only sign she suffered from the heat was a little glistening above her lips.

I spotted Sally's family across the gym and as usual, I envied the sheer number of them. Both sets of grandparents and all four siblings were there to celebrate Nancy. They looked like the big happy Catholic family; we did not. We were a pitiful representation for Donald. My grandparents decided at the last minute not to make the trip from Lynchburg. Apparently my grandmother had a cold.

Everyone knew this was the last year the graduating class of Lee High School would look this way. There were still more white graduates than black, even if the band that played for them was more black than white. There was a long list of retiring teachers in the program. When they stood to be honored it was clear not all of them were old enough to be calling leaving "retirement."

I daydreamed of being in the Class of 1970, of being in clubs and plays, of playing field hockey without my shins turning purple, of having teachers who smiled, of having boys who teased good-naturedly in my classes, of having a diploma from Lee High School. I envisioned Claudia and Sally and Fergy and Venetia with me here. Why hadn't the adults left our school alone? Was Stonewall any better for the black kids by sending a few white kids there? I yearned to be the one graduating and getting away from it all.

The skies had cleared by the time the graduates marched out of the gym, and my mother was giddy with relief. She rushed the picture taking and congratulations with high-speed energy in order to get us home and assign the party tasks.

"Donald, we need all the chairs wiped off outside," she

delegated, before Donald had removed his graduation gown. "And I want to use your cap as part of a centerpiece," she continued, taking the mortarboard out of his hands. "Nell, you can get the tablecloths on and the trays out." We fell into her rhythm as we always did and we were ready when the first stream of guests arrived.

Father Richard lingered at the table where I was serving ice cream until other guests had moved on. "I'm sorry I couldn't have been of more help in your situation, Nell."

"That's okay. I don't think Sister Bridget liked me from the beginning."

"Guess we're members of the same club, then." He offered his compassionate smile, making me grateful to be in his club.

"My father thinks there are so many girls on the waiting list now she was more than ready to fill my spot."

"Could be true." He dipped a spoonful of ice cream. "Will you go back to Stonewall?"

"Yes."

"Are you okay with that?"

I nodded. "My mom asked me not to tell anyone what happened, so no one knows yet." Another guest came up and Father Richard disappeared into the crowd while I served and smiled and conversed as I'd been taught to do.

It was a nicer party than the holiday ones. Maybe because there wasn't a precedent of how it should be done. Maybe because it really didn't matter to me. I watched Donald switch on his charm and answer the college questions about roommates and majors and fraternities. He'd done his research and had tutored me in his answers in case I was asked about his future plans. No one would suspect he wouldn't be attending. I almost convinced myself he'd changed his mind and would be falling in step with these predictable plans for his future. The sun had come out and the storm had cleared the oppressive air. Everyone was there to celebrate him and my parents were so proud.

But the subtle changes that had seeped into our family ways that pivotal year became profound in the early days of summer. We had become less of a family and more like four people who slept in the same house. Donald went out every night between graduation and camp. My father had a big case consuming most evenings and my mother was fanning her anticipatory grief of Donald's leaving by shopping for his college room in the daytime and retreating to her sewing room in the evenings. There were no plans for a beach trip; it couldn't be fit in between Donald's camp and State's orientation.

Donald expressed no opinion about the color of his bedspread or the number of his towels. A year ago he would have teased my mother about her shopping obsession or conceded and gone with her to make her happy. But now he barely acknowledged her efforts. She added to the pile in the corner of his room almost daily, determined he wouldn't even need to buy a tube of toothpaste his first semester. I was the one who initiated our last conversation on the roof the night before he left for camp.

"Donald," I whispered into the dark of his room. "Are you asleep?"

"No."

"Want to smoke?"

"Not really."

"Will you come out on the roof with me?" I waited.

"Okay." He threw the sheet off and the moonlight caught his white T-shirt in its path and made him glow. He lingered on the side of the bed and I thought he was changing his mind. But he followed me down the hall, tiptoeing around the creaky parts of the hardwood floors. We crawled out the window and sat on the asphalt shingles. A chorus of katydids and the faint scent of honeysuckle welcomed us. But what usually made my heart leap at the promises of summer couldn't reach me on this night. As Donald methodically stacked prickly gum tree balls into a pile the unsettled feelings in me grew.

"Are you going through with it?" I asked. He threw a gumball into the night.

"Yeah, I guess I am," he said. "I don't see another option."

"You could try college. You don't know you won't be able to do the work. It might be a whole different way of grading and stuff."

"Nell, you know I hate to read. I hate to write. And math confuses me. I can't go to college."

"What are you going to do?"

"Father Richard has a friend in Canada he's setting me up with."

"You've talked to Father Richard?"

"Yeah."

"Why didn't you tell me?" Even though I was glad he'd confided in Father Richard, I felt excluded. Donald could have entrusted that information to me.

"If I told you stuff and Mom and Dad suspected anything, they would ask you. Father Richard thought it'd be better if you didn't have to hide anything from them."

"So after you leave tomorrow, when will I see you? Will you come home for Christmas?"

"Nell, don't you get it? I can't come home for Christmas! I can't come home until this damn war is over."

"How will I know how you're doing?"

"If I go to Father Richard's friend, he'll know."

"Does Mike know what you're doing?"

"Hell no. Mike wouldn't get it."

"What are you going to do about money?"

"I get paid this summer at camp. I'll use that to travel and get a job when I get where I'm going."

"I don't think I can stand being in this house when you're gone."

"You'll get back with your friends at Stonewall and you'll be fine."

I envisioned Christmas without Donald coming home and began to cry. Not silent tears but choking ones that made my body shake. He scooted closer to me and put his arm around my shoulder. It was awkward at first; we weren't the type of brother and sister who showed affection. But I curled into his body and he let me cry until my tears were spent.

"It'll be okay. We gotta grow up sometime."

"But why does *everything* have to change all at once?"

"I don't know." He dropped his arm from my shoulders but he didn't scoot away from me. "You gotta promise me something."

"What?"

"You can't tell Mom and Dad anything. Not even after I don't come home. You've got to pretend you don't know where I've gone. And you can't ever tell them Father Richard helped me."

"Okay," I said. "But can I write you letters and send them through Father Richard?"

"I guess so. But don't count on long letters back."

"Send postcards."

"Deal." He threw a magnolia pod and we heard it hit the garage.

"Two points!"

Donald left early the next morning. My father said goodbye to him before he went to the office and my mother fixed him a big breakfast before Bobby, another counselor, picked him up. I watched as Donald threw his duffle bag into the trunk, wondering how he'd fit everything for the rest of his life into that single bag. I tried to act casual as we said our goodbyes, fighting the voice in my head that was saying "this may be the last time you see him." There were little things that probably escaped my mother's eyes: the way he smothered his face into Skipper's furry head and whispered in his ear, the way he packed up all the rest of my mother's biscuits to take with him, the way he avoided my mother's eyes when she said her goodbye.

"See ya, sis," were the words he said to me before he left for anywhere. The phrase was the same as every other time, but his eyes held the intensity of all we had said on the roof less than eight hours before and some of what we had left unsaid, including a caution on my trembling lips. When the car backed out of the driveway and onto his adventure I ran up to my room, closed the door, and buried my face in the pillow to muffle the sound of my sobs.

Chapter
Twenty-Two

An entire summer in that house was a daunting prospect. I'd signed up for summer school, but it wouldn't start for several weeks. My mother hadn't queried me about how I would spend my time, nor had she offered her usual suggestions for projects or babysitting customers. We politely avoided each other around the house. Sally's family was on an extended camping trip to Maine to celebrate Nancy's graduation, so I rode my bike to the library or the pool by myself whenever I couldn't stand it anymore.

Father Richard came to my rescue by offering me a job as a counselor in a day camp. It was a volunteer job, and only for the two weeks before summer school started, but it was something. He'd enlisted Claudia and Deloris too. Venetia was typing and filing at her father's law office and Fergy had a real job working at Williard's. I worried about being the third wheel with Claudia and Deloris, but my exit from St. Mary's reinstated me into their small band.

A mixture of ages and races from the poorer parts of town attended the camp. The youngest ones were reticent and shy the first few days but soon greeted us with hugs. The older ones weren't so demonstrative, but most were happy and full of energy. Each morning we boarded an old school bus that had been repainted light blue, and bounced and bumped along for thirty minutes to an abandoned farm owned by a church member. We had free run of the place; even the old farmhouse was open to us. There were bits and pieces of furniture still in it: a sagging couch, a rocking chair with one broken rocker, some framed paint-by-number pictures on the walls. I liked its old wooden floors and huge windows that we opened up to let the breezes in.

There were no breezes on this June day. There were no clouds in the white sky. The air smelled of heat and of the grasses that had dried on the cut field; their brittle ends pricking our shins when we sat in in our camp circles. By noon, the heat had stolen the energy and the enthusiasm of campers and counselors alike.

"We need to get everyone out of the sun," Father Richard said, as he led us into the farmhouse. "We're picnicking inside today." He directed the kids to find spots on the floor to eat their bagged lunches and we passed out cups of Kool-Aid. No one felt like doing anything after lunch, but something had to be done with thirty kids who were hot and lethargic and grumpy.

"I wish there was a lake out here." Father Richard surveyed the restless group of campers. "You all hold down the fort. Play *Bear Hunt* or *Simon Says* while I check out an idea."

He left us alone and Claudia went from *Bear Hunt* to telling ghost stories. She did all the voices in the story, as if she were on stage. Her red hair was pulled away from her sun-freckled face into two thick braids. Beaded chokers circled her neck. I rolled the tiny beads between my fingers of the single strand around my neck and decided I wanted to make more and wear them all at the same time, like Claudia.

"That girl's even got me scared!" Deloris whispered to me.

"Yeah, I bet some of these kids will have nightmares tonight."

Father Richard had slipped back into the room and was listening to the story too. Deloris nodded her head towards him and whispered in my ear. "You think he look better with the collar or without?" I poked her with my elbow and she giggled.

Claudia finished her eerie story and none of the children made a sound. Father Richard broke the spell with a clap of his hands.

"Who wants to get wet?" The kids cheered.

We followed him outside where he organized a giant game of *Red Rover*. Every time someone was called across he sprayed them with the hose he'd found. We played water games for the rest of the day.

The campers were a subdued bunch by the time they climbed into the bus. Father Richard had soaked the counselors at the end of the games so we sat in our damp shorts all the way back to town, too tired to lead the usual songs. Deloris sat in front of me with a young camper's blonde head asleep on her shoulder. A little golden-skinned girl with a dozen braids had her head in my lap. I liked the symmetry of the picture we made.

"Why are you going to summer school?" I asked Deloris.

"I got to if I want to graduate on time. I didn't do so hot in U.S. History, so I gotta take it over." She sighed. "Don't you even think I'm lookin' forward to that."

"That's what I have to take to graduate early."

"You taking it at Lee?"

"Yeah."

"Me too. Guess it's the only school with air conditioning."

"It'll be easier since you're taking it the second time."

"Hmph. I hate memorizing dates."

"Maybe we can study together and I could help you."

Deloris glared at me. "I'm not dumb." She adjusted her shoulders and the little blonde head leaning against her slid down to her lap.

"The problem last year was the teacher didn't teach anything. Over half the class failed! I think that sorry white excuse of a teacher was mad at being placed at our school. She took it out on us and they let her get away with it." She shook her head at the injustice.

"Since summer school's at Lee, maybe it will be a Lee teacher."

"How come they keep all the good teachers at Lee?"

I didn't have an answer for her. I leaned my head against the partially open window and let it bounce with the bus. Being in class at Lee with Deloris could be fun; at least I'd know somebody.

Twelve of us had been together every day for three weeks learning the history of our country. Miss Lewis had a different activity every day—debates, role-playing, *Jeopardy* games—the four hours had flown. Most of the students had already failed the course once and Miss Lewis had told us she did not allow anyone to fail her class. She hounded, she drilled, she tutored. But she didn't bore us.

"When did slavery end in this country?" Miss Lewis paced in front of the room as she talked. She moved with a lightness that was incongruent to her size. If she wanted an answer from you, her watery blue eyes did not allow you to escape her gaze.

"1861," came an answer from the back.

Miss Lewis shook her head.

"1865," another student answered.

She shook her head again.

"Juneteenth," Deloris said.

"Juneteenth?" Miss Lewis looked puzzled.

"Yeah. That's when slavery really ended." Deloris's eyes

solicited the room for agreement. The black kids nodded their heads.

"I've never heard of Juneteenth." Miss Lewis's voice revealed curiosity, not criticism.

"The slaves found out they were free on June 19th, 1865. That's when slavery ended."

Miss Lewis hesitated. "I was aiming for the date of the Emancipation Proclamation, which was January 1st, 1863."

"That might've been when the President said they was free, but they weren't free 'til they knew it. They didn't find out for two and a half years." Deloris spoke with authority, and Miss Lewis didn't challenge her.

"Thank you for sharing that, Deloris. I'm going to do some research on that."

"They don't put stuff like that in no history book," said a boy in the back who hardly ever spoke.

"There are other ways to research history: old newspapers, biographies, letters, documents like that." Miss Lewis scanned the room. "If any of you has anything at home that tells more about Juneteenth, would you share it with me?" The boy in the back nodded.

It had been uncomfortable to discuss slavery. Even the textbook skimmed over the topic with one paragraph about the cotton plantations and how labor was needed to run them, and another on how the slaves were fed and housed and taken care of. My image of slavery was a *Gone with the Wind* picture, where Mammy and Prissy chose to stay because they liked their life the way it was.

"Alright, let's move the desks, and take a break. You'll have thirty minutes to work on your timelines when you come back in."

Deloris and I were in a timeline group with a quirky curly-headed boy named Rudy. He was small for his age and his narrow face was spotted with acne. With his glasses and braces he was a real-life caricature of the misfit teenager. I doubt Deloris or I would have ever talked to him if we'd encountered him somewhere else. But he was smart and witty and made us laugh until he had endeared himself to us.

Our long-term assignment was to create a timeline of American history using symbols. Deloris and Rudy were good at thinking up the symbols. Rudy was the best artist so he drew them. Deloris and I filled them in, cut them out, and assembled the timeline. Rudy suggested a Confederate flag as a symbol for the Civil War.

"I'm not coloring any Confederate flag," Deloris said. "It'd be like dancing with the devil."

"How about cotton?" I asked Rudy while Deloris doodled.

"How 'bout this?" The paper she held up displayed a set of shackles. "That's the truest symbol there is for the Civil War." Her voice carried a tone of resignation, not anger. Rudy and I squirmed in our knowledge that she was right.

"Want me to cut it out?" I asked.

"Nope. This one's all mine."

I wanted to know if Deloris's great-great-grandparents had been slaves but I didn't want to ask. I peppered my parents with questions about our family history at dinner that night.

"My people didn't own any slaves," my father said. "Actually, the percentage of people who had slaves was quite small. Most people weren't that wealthy."

"I believe my great-grandmother grew up on a plantation that had slaves," my mother said, a hint of pride in her voice. "They owned a lot of land that had to be cared for."

My stomach dropped. I saw the shackles Deloris had sketched.

"Doesn't that bother you?" I asked my mother.

"Why should it bother me?" Her head tilted like a dog's does when it hears a funny sound. "My people are from an aristocratic line. They owned slaves because that's what people did then. And I'm sure they treated them well and provided for them in a generous way."

She kept eating, but I lost my appetite. I'd been trying so hard to prove being white shouldn't matter to my black friends. But if Deloris knew this fact about my family, it would matter.

Chapter Twenty-Three

"Why don't you and Deloris come by the drugstore after summer school tomorrow? I'm working until two, and I can fix y'all the best ice cream floats you've ever had!"

"Okay. I've got to figure out how to get there."

Fergy and I had gotten into the habit of talking on the phone. It was a little bit like talking to Donald, except I only felt comfortable talking to him when I was in the house by myself.

"What difference does it make now?" he asked when I told him I heard the car in the driveway. "You've already been kicked out of school. What else can happen if you talk to a black boy on the phone?"

"I don't know. I guess nothing. It just makes me nervous and then I don't feel like talking."

We hung up and I tried to figure out a way to get to Williard's. I called Deloris.

"Ride the bus, stupid," she said. "Don't you white people know how to ride a bus?" She snickered.

"I've ridden the bus before," I half-laughed with her, "but I don't know which one to get."

"Want me to go with you?"

"Yes. Fergy invited you too."

"Uh-huh. He knew you would need some help from me." I envisioned her head nodding on the other end of the line. "Anything to help the star-crossed lovers."

"It's not like that! We're just friends."

"The hell it ain't, girl! Apparently, I can see what you two can't!" She laughed her big laugh. "See ya tomorrow!"

I'd gotten used to Deloris's teasing and didn't let it bother me. I liked that she didn't pretend with me, but said what she was thinking. But I still held that Fergy and I were just friends. Period.

Deloris and I caught the city bus two blocks from Lee. It wasn't crowded, but we shared a seat. As we got closer to Williard's and the Stonewall neighborhood, only black people were boarding. By the time our stop came, there was one other white person left on the bus. I was glad Deloris was with me.

"Girl, if I had a chance to go to Lee, I'd take it. Why you coming back to Stonewall?"

"Remember, I can't go to Lee. That used to be my school, but they bused me to Stonewall."

"Why couldn't they have bused me to Lee? They ain't never going to be able to fix Madison up enough to even come close to Lee."

Her face and her voice hardened. "You have no idea what it's like to always be in the bad school. I coulda been smarter in school if I'd been in a nice one. How we ever s'posed to get ahead when we always got to start behind? I mean, if I'd had a school where the water's never cut off and didn't have to share old outdated books, maybe I'd have been smart enough to be thinkin' bout college too."

What she was saying made sense. I'd had it easy compared to her.

"I'm sorry. I know it's not fair."

Her big smile returned. "I don't blame you." Her smile disappeared. "But there's some ole white men responsible. I

231

blame them."

I was uncomfortable thinking about Deloris as a little kid in a school with the water cut off. I didn't even know that could happen. I changed the subject. "I like your bracelet. Is it new?"

She lifted her arm and tilted it so I could read the name inscribed on the silver cuff around her wrist.

"PVT Reginald V. Johnson," I read. "Who's that?"

"He's a soldier sitting in a prison in Vietnam somewhere. I'm gonna wear this 'til he comes home."

"Do you know him?"

"No. But I got a brother and two cousins over there and I want them to get home before there's a bracelet with their names on it."

She watched out the window. "Here's our stop."

We got off and waited on the traffic to slow. The exhaust fumes from the bus engulfed us. Squiggly heat waves radiated off the concrete.

"Lord, it's hot!" Deloris said. "I can't wait for that ice cream float!" We crossed the street and started walking down the block.

"Isn't Williard's the other way?" I asked.

"Girl, you may be smart, but you got no sense of direction!" She laughed and pointed. "There it is!"

I was so disoriented. "I wouldn't have gotten here without you."

"You damn right, girl!" We giggled as we pushed the door to the drugstore open and its bell jingled.

Fergy was getting items off a high shelf as an elderly woman pointed to what she wanted. He saw us, flashed a grin and a head nod, and turned his attention back to his customer. Deloris and I wandered the aisles. The same products lined the shelves that were in every drugstore: remedies for headaches and stomach bugs and colds. And there were entire shelves of the specific hair products for afros or for straightening hair that weren't in the drugstore in my neighborhood.

"Wonder what would happen if we put some of this in your hair?" Deloris asked as she picked up a bottle of Afro Sheen.

"I have no idea," I answered, afraid she would want me to try it.

"Don't worry," she laughed. Deloris could read my face even when I thought I had no expression. "I don't have enough money to throw away to find out!"

"Hey y'all!" Fergy said, calling down the aisle. "Ready for me to practice my great float making skills on you?"

We went to the back of the store and sat on two stools at the short counter. There was one other man there, drinking coffee and smoking a cigarette. He nodded at us and I smiled back. We drank our floats and told stories from camp and summer school and laughed at Fergy's descriptions of peculiar customers long past when our tall glasses were empty. I forgot where I was as I relaxed into the tales, until the manager came over.

"Fergy, your shift is over. I won't be paying you for any extra. Y'all best be movin' on so the seats be free for the next busy time." He wore a scowl on his face and didn't acknowledge Deloris or me.

"Yes, sir," Fergy answered. He took our empty glasses and wiped the counter.

"Let's go, girls." The tone of Fergy's voice made it sound like we'd done something wrong. We followed him out of the store.

"What's wrong with your boss?" Deloris asked when we were on the sidewalk.

"Nothing," Fergy answered. "There're some regulars that come in every day about this time. I guess he wants the seats free for them."

"Fergy, we didn't pay!" I said. "We should go back in and pay!"

"I'll take care of that," he said.

"But maybe that's why he's mad at us. We don't want to

233

get you in trouble."

"That's not why he's mad. I'll take care of it." I thought there was a silent exchange between Fergy and Deloris, but I wasn't sure.

"I got to get myself home," Deloris said. "I promised I'd watch my little cousins today, so they'll be waiting on me. Thanks for the float, Fergy."

She walked back to the bus stop where we got off and Fergy and I were left standing on the sidewalk.

"Want to go do something?" he asked.

"Like what?"

"I don't know, see a movie?"

I checked my watch. Two thirty. "If I'm not home by suppertime I get the inquisition."

"So we got a couple of hours."

"Where's a movie theater?"

"Near here?" Fergy shook his head. "There's one further downtown that way," he pointed, "but I wouldn't take you to that one."

"Why not?"

"It's not very nice."

We started walking without a destination. The white sun was beating down and the oven-like air was stifling. We passed a furniture store with big handwritten sale signs in the windows. A shoe store and a hair salon had their doors propped open. The shoe store man stood in the doorway fanning himself.

"Why don't they have their air conditioning running on a day like this?" I asked.

"Not everybody has air conditioning."

I wished I hadn't asked. We were walking in step with each other but not close enough to touch. A woman passed us and I smiled at her. She didn't smile back.

"It feels like people are staring at us," I said.

"They are," Fergy laughed. "Not many white girls come

234

this way."

"I feel conspicuous."

"I'd feel the same way in your neighborhood."

"It's so stupid, isn't it? Why does the color of your skin have to matter?" We'd had this conversation before. I liked the way Fergy could talk about it; most people couldn't. But our conversation never got past the questions.

"We're not far from my house. Want to meet my mother?" he asked.

"Sure." But I wasn't at all sure.

We turned at the corner and walked down a street of small, neat houses; not brick or stucco, like the houses in my neighborhood, but wood, painted in light shades of blues, greens, and yellows. The sidewalks were cracked where old tree roots had popped up the cement. The shade of those trees was a welcome relief. We walked for a block without talking. I checked my watch again.

"Fergy, how am I going to get home?" I was having a hard time getting a full breath.

"If there's a car available I'll drive you, and if not, I'll put you on the bus."

"But I don't know which bus!" I was wishing I hadn't come. I didn't belong in this strange neighborhood, not knowing how to get home, not sure if Fergy's mother would approve of me. I was wishing for the flinty familiarity of my oppressive house.

"I'll make sure you're on the right bus." Fergy caught my elbow as I tripped on a crack in the sidewalk. "I'll ride with you if you're nervous." The gesture comforted and scared me at the same time. He let go. "Here we are."

I looked up at a narrow white house with sky blue shutters. It had two stories and a porch that went across the front. Two folding aluminum lawn chairs sat beside each other on the porch. They were the kind with the straps of plaid fabric woven under and over each other, like the ones we kept in our trunk for picnics. One of the chairs was overfilled with a gray-headed woman. Her socks were rolled down past her swollen ankles where bedroom slippers were perched on her feet. There was something odd about the way she cocked her head when we climbed the concrete steps to the porch.

"That you, Fergy?" she asked.

"Yes, Grandma. It's me with a friend."

"I thought I heard somebody with you," she smiled. Her eyes were half-closed and I realized there was no sight in them. She was pulling some kind of beans out of the brown bag beside her and popping the shells off.

"Butter beans! Yay!" Fergy said and leaned over and gave her a kiss on the cheek.

"Yessiree," she said. "Your daddy brung 'em up from the country this morning. "They feel mighty fresh, so they're gonna be some sweet ones." She tilted her head up and smiled. "Gonna introduce me to your friend here?"

"Grandma, this is my friend Nell." Fergy pushed me gently towards her.

"Nice to meet you," I said.

"Lean down, child, so my hands can see you." I leaned towards her and her hands reached to find my face. They were rough hands, but they moved with tenderness, skimming my features and outlining my lips. They touched the top of my head and ran through my hair. "You not a Negro, are you, child?"

"No, ma'am, I'm not."

"That's nice. That's real nice you and Fergy is friends." She bobbed her head up and down and pressed her lips together like she was keeping something in. "You gonna stay and eat some of these butter beans with us?"

"Oh, I don't know if I can stay that long. But I do like butter beans," I said.

"Then you a smart girl!" We laughed.

Fergy opened the screen door and motioned for me to go in. The laugh track of a television show greeted us as the screen door slapped behind us.

"Fergy!" Two little girls jumped up from the floor and ran over to Fergy, and he tickled them and chased them around the room. When they were out of breath they stopped and stared at me.

"Who's that?" one of them asked.

"This is Nell," Fergy said. "Nell, these are my cousins, Cora and Lena."

"Nice to meet you, Cora and Lena." Cora took hold of one of my hands and one of Fergy's hands.

"Come watch TV with us." She pulled us over to where they'd been sitting on the floor. "It's almost time for *Superman.*" I sat on the floor between them and we leaned our backs against the sofa.

"You know, you can sit on the sofa," Fergy said.

"This is fine." I liked sitting between the two girls. They leaned on me like the camp kids and Lena popped her thumb in her mouth. Little by little her head slid down and ended up in my lap. Fergy was sitting in the rocking chair when his mother came into the room holding a full brown grocery bag in each arm. He jumped up and took one of the bags from her.

"Thanks, Fergy. My hands have gone all numb holding onto these."

"I could have gone to the store, Mama."

"I waited, but you weren't home at your usual time."

"Oh yeah," he nodded his head my way and I stood up. "Mama, this is Nell. We walked over when I got off."

"Where's your bike?" she asked.

"At the drugstore," Fergy answered.

Mrs. Sutton wrinkled her brow and frowned at him.

"It's locked up safe, Mama."

She turned to me. "Hello, Nell."

"Hi, Mrs. Sutton. Nice to meet you." She nodded at me, but I couldn't read her face.

"I need to get these groceries put away and start supper.

You're welcome to eat at our table this evening, Nell. It's our family dinner night."

"Thank you, Mrs. Sutton. I'd like to but I need to get home soon." She nodded again and walked to the kitchen. Fergy followed her with the other bag and didn't return for a few minutes.

"You sure you don't want to stay? It's our best meal of the week."

"I'd like to, but I think my mother would flip."

"Can you call and ask?"

"You want me to?"

"Sure. My daddy will be home and I can use the car to take you home instead of you riding the bus." He pointed to the black phone sitting on the table by the window.

The heat of the afternoon had settled in the room and there was no breeze coming through the open windows. I felt the wetness under my armpits. My hands were clammy as my index finger dragged the hollow circles of the dial around to call my own number. My finger slipped and I had to push the button to disconnect and start over. I told my mother I'd been invited to eat dinner with a friend from summer school, which wasn't true, but it made sense to her and she said "fine." My father had a client dinner so she was probably as happy to eat alone as with me.

There were so many people at the Sutton table it felt like Thanksgiving. Besides Fergy's parents and grandmother were Fergy's aunt, Fergy's older sister and her husband, and another sister who came in towards the end of the meal, in hospital blue scrubs. The plates were a mixture of styles as were the silverware and glasses. There was some ham, but the meal was mostly vegetables: corn on the cob, yellow squash with onions, butter beans, tomatoes, and little white peas that were new to me. I'd never had vegetables taste so sweet and fresh before. They didn't have rolls, but cornbread, and for dessert we ate the best banana pudding I'd ever tasted. It was a little like eating with Sally's big family, except louder, with people talking over each other. No one paid much attention to me; I probably wasn't their first white guest. But I'd never be able to return the favor.

After supper we caught lightning bugs and put them in an old mayonnaise jar with holes poked in the top. Cora and Lena worried about them and kept opening the jar and letting them fly away. I was on their side.

"My parents think it'll be better if my mom takes you home instead of me," Fergy told me as we sat on the front steps.

"Really?" I could already feel the discomfort of that.

"Yeah. They don't want me to drive you by myself to your neighborhood."

"Fergy, no one will care."

"Still, my mom's going to drive you."

"Are you coming?"

"Yeah. And then she's going to drop me by the drugstore to get my bike."

I sat in the front seat with Mrs. Sutton and Fergy sat in the back. The car was wide and even when Fergy leaned up he didn't fill the space between us. The seats were still warm from the heat of the day, and the balmy evening air blew through the open windows. It wasn't dark yet, but the streetlights were coming on as we went through town. Fergy told a funny story about his grandma and Cora and Lena and we laughed. Once we were on the main streets I gave directions to my house. It didn't take long to get to my neighborhood, and when we did Mrs. Sutton rolled up her window almost to the top. Fergy did the same with the windows in the back.

"Nell, would you mind rolling up your window, please?" Mrs. Sutton asked.

I did as she asked. The air in the car grew suffocating. Beads of sweat popped up above my lip. Fergy sat back and no one talked anymore. A siren sounded in the distance and Mrs. Sutton flinched. I felt the shaking of Fergy's jittery knee through the seat. Mrs. Sutton stopped on the street in front of my house instead of pulling into the driveway. My house looked like a mansion from that viewpoint. It made me self-conscious and flustered.

"Mrs. Sutton, I enjoyed dinner so much. It was so good. Thank you so much." My use of all of the "so's" made my compliments insincere to my ears.

"You're welcome." Her face was unreadable.

Fergy got out of the back and opened my door.

"Thanks for coming to my house."

"Thanks for asking me." This formal exchange didn't match the fun of the evening.

They drove away and I walked up the driveway and around to the back door.

"I'm home!" I called as I closed the door behind me. I heard the faint sound of a TV and went to the den, where the door was closed to keep in the cool air from the window unit. I cracked the door open to see my mother sitting on the little sofa with her legs curled up under her, holding a highball glass. She peered up at me in a delayed way.

"Have fun?"

"Yes."

"That's nice." She turned her attention back to the TV and I closed the door and went to my room.

Chapter Twenty-Four

✻✻✻

The rest of summer passed the ways summers did in Richmond, with a lethargic nod to the heat and humidity that determined the pace people walked and the speed ice melted in a glass. I invited Deloris to come home with me one afternoon on a day I knew my mother wouldn't be there. We were awkward with each other when we were in my house; she was more guarded and reserved and I overplayed the welcoming host. I would've gone to her house if she'd asked me, but she didn't.

The pool was not as crowded as the summers before. People had moved and membership had dropped. Even the lifeguards they hired were from somewhere else, and not the teenagers who had aspired to sitting in the tall chairs above the pool ever since they learned to swim there. I went a few times with Sally, but it didn't have that carefree summer feel about it. The splashing sounds were isolated bursts rather than the cacophony of the slap of the diving board, the calls of "Marco Polo," and the smacks of the group cannonballs.

I thought Sally would be excited I was returning to Stonewall, but her response was tepid, as if she was going to hold the St. Mary's stint as a tally mark against me. Mr. and

241

Mrs. Carpenter were the same as they'd always been, and I experienced the warmth of their supper table once or twice that summer. But if Sally and I were alone she didn't initiate conversation or ask me about being a camp counselor or summer school or anything. Allison was the one she took on their family camping trips that summer.

When it came time for Donald's return from camp I'd convinced myself he would show up, realizing the Canada plan was too far-fetched, like when he and Mike had tried to dig a tunnel to connect all the houses in our neighborhood. My mother picked up her flurry of shopping, and the pile of what she thought he needed for State grew higher. One day she spent the entire morning using a laundry pen to write his name on the sheets and towels and clothing she'd purchased. My mother was frying chicken when Bobby's old Falcon pulled up in front of our house.

"He's here!" my father called from the living room where he was reading the paper. I'd just set the table for four and followed my parents to the front porch. Bobby got out of the car alone and walked around to the front steps.

"Hello, Bobby," my father said. "Did you lose a passenger?" My father chuckled, but Bobby didn't laugh with him.

"Where's Donald?" my mother asked, pressing her hand against her chest. "Is he alright?"

"Yes, ma'am. Donald's fine." He handed an envelope to my father. "He asked me to give you this."

"When's he getting here?" my mother asked.

"It's all in the letter, Mrs. Randolph." He nodded his head to my parents, turned around, and walked back to his car.

"Wait!" my mother said. "Is Donald in trouble?"

"I don't think so. He said the letter explains it. I don't know anything else."

Bobby got in his car and drove away. My stunned parents stared as his car sped down the street.

"Open the letter, Eugene!"

My father studied the envelope, then turned and walked into the house. We followed him into the living room where he eased onto the sofa, as if it pained him to move. My mother sat next to him, her hands rubbing down the front of her apron, rolling invisible dough. I sat across from them, on the edge of the wing-back chair, my heart racing in my chest. My father slit open the letter as carefully as he opened the bills. He unfolded a piece of notebook paper, scanning its contents before he read the letter aloud.

Dear Mom and Dad and Nell,

I've decided not to go to college. I don't think I would do very well at State and it would be a waste of your money. I don't want to die either so I'm going to find a job in a place that is safe from the draft. Don't worry. I have some nice friends who are helping me out.

Love,

Donald

P.S. Give Skipper a long ear scratch from me since he can't read this letter.

"Oh Eugene! He can't do that!" She took the letter to read for herself. "He can't be far. We'll have to go get him!"

"And where do you suggest we go, Marjorie?" my father snapped.

"Maybe he's still at camp."

My father walked to the window and stared at the yard. "I don't understand how Donald thinks he'd be able to pull off such a stupid stunt!" The anger in my father's voice was matched by the balled fists his hands made. My mother walked up behind him.

"Can't we please try to go find him? Drive to camp and ask some questions?"

"Marjorie, he's not at camp. He could be anywhere by now."

Skipper had snuck in and was leaning on my legs. I concentrated on scratching his ears as Donald had asked, trying to hide my lack of surprise. My mother grabbed my father's arm.

"Aren't you worried about him at all?"

"Of course I'm worried!" He slumped back onto the sofa and looked into the empty fireplace.

"Donald's a resourceful boy. I'm not worried about his safety or his ability to find a job. He's not lazy." He looked at me. "I don't think he could have gotten mixed up with drugs. Do you, Nell?"

"No, sir."

He paced back to the window. "What I'm worried about is he's breaking the law by dodging the draft. I don't know if Donald has any idea how this stunt could alter the rest of his life."

I'd seen my father be sad before, when my grandfather died, when our other dog was hit by a car. I'd seen him be concerned like he was when we saw Stonewall for the first time together or when he was wrestling with a difficult case. I'd seen his face in pain before when he had appendicitis and had to have emergency surgery. His face now was a mixture of all of those: concern, pain, sadness, and something else—angst. I'd never seen him look like that before.

"We need to eat," my mother announced.

Donald's favorite meal stayed mostly untouched on our plates. I fed Skipper a few bites of chicken under the table and neither parent bothered to correct me.

"Do we have a last name or a phone number for this Bobby that Donald got a ride with?" my father asked.

"I think it started with a T," my mother said.

"I'm going to call the camp director tonight and see what I can find out."

"Oh, Eugene, that's an excellent idea. We have a week before he leaves for State. That should be time enough to get it all straight." My mother adopted the belief Donald would be home in a few days and everything would go on as planned.

I cleared the table and did the dishes and listened to the one-sided phone conversations my father initiated. It was late before he stopped making calls, and the only fact he learned was Bobby had dropped Donald off at the bus station in Roanoke. Bobby either didn't know what bus he got on, or had sworn not to tell, and he didn't. A strip of light leaked from under my parents' bedroom door until way past midnight. I'm sure they didn't sleep, even after the lamp was switched off. I couldn't find the moon from my window, so I crawled onto the roof. As I stared into the dark I wondered if Donald was watching the same stars from his bus window as he traveled north.

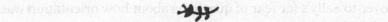

We were used to Donald being gone so our patterns of moving around each other should have been familiar to us. But not knowing where he was or what was happening to him made the interactions between us silent and awkward. My father stayed at the office longer; my mother was either out of the house or in the little den. I didn't hear her sewing machine, but she planted herself in there with it. If I was alone in the house Skipper and I would go into Donald's room and sit on his bed. Most of the decor of Donald's room was my mother's doing. The orange and brown stripes of his curtains made the room shrink. His matching bedspread was chosen for its ability to camouflage dirt. But it was my father who'd put up the shelves that held the models of cars and airplanes Donald used to put together. He let me help him once, but I got confused with the pictures of how to do it and gave up. I wonder if that's how Donald felt about words on a page. There were clues in his room that he wouldn't be coming back. His

Simon & Garfunkel album was missing as was the baseball signed by Atlanta Braves players from a game he'd gone to with our father.

The day circled on the calendar, for when Donald would leave for State, passed in slow motion. My parents moved from silence to an unresolved argument about whose parenting fault Donald's decision was. My father argued this couldn't have happened if Donald had worked in his office instead of being a camp counselor and my mother's rebuttal was this was a reaction to how hard my father was on Donald. I could have eased their pain if I'd explained his fear of flunking out because of his inability to learn like others, but that would have betrayed Donald's trust and thrown an unwelcome spotlight on me. They kept quiet about Donald's decision and I was asked to do the same, so I felt quarantined, unable to even go over to Sally's for fear of questions about how orientation was going for Donald at State.

School was to start on Monday. The three of us attended Mass together on Sunday. Father Richard greeted us as we left church.

"Mr. and Mrs. Randolph, so glad to have you with us today!" He spoke warmly to my parents, shaking my father's hand with energy, and using both of his hands to cover my mother's as he met her eyes. I knew he was searching her face for what she had learned about Donald. Her stoic presence revealed nothing. He nodded at me when he took my hand.

"So you start back at Stonewall tomorrow."

"Yes, Father."

"Are you excited?"

"A little bit. And nervous."

"My prayers will be with you." He leaned in towards me and whispered in my ear. "I have news from Donald. All is well."

"Thank you, Father."

I wanted to ask all kinds of questions, but this was not the time. My parents waited for me at the bottom of the stone steps and we went home to a cold lunch of ham, biscuits, and potato salad.

"Will you be riding the bus tomorrow?" my mother asked.

"I'll ride it home, like last year. Mr. Carpenter is driving us in the mornings."

"I'll need to take a turn driving you all to school," my father said.

"I don't think you have to. Mr. Carpenter is used to dropping Sally and David off every day. I can walk to their house in the mornings, and he won't even have to stop here to pick me up, so it won't be any different than what he's used to."

"Your father will help with the driving. We won't take advantage of the Carpenters' generosity."

"You can tell them I will drive next week," my father said.

The rest of the conversation was sparse. My mother had no comments to make about the ladies she'd seen at church or Father Richard's sermon. My father didn't talk about the weather. And no one talked about Donald. I had to wait until folk Mass on Saturday to find out what Father Richard knew of his whereabouts. And there was a week back at Stonewall before then.

"You excited about coming back?" Venetia asked on the phone.

"Of course!"

"What are you wearing tomorrow?"

"I don't know. What should I wear?"

"Jeans and a T-shirt. No yellow dresses," Venetia giggled.

"Don't worry. I've never worn that dress again." I tried to share her humor, but the memory of last year's first day at Stonewall stung. I didn't even know Venetia then, but the yellow dress had earned a legendary spot in the inside jokes once Fergy admitted seeing a white girl in a bright yellow dress that day.

"I'll meet you in the front hall by the big bulletin board and we can compare schedules. Hopefully we'll have the same lunch," Venetia said.

I hung up the phone and went to my room to pick out clothes for the next day. There had been no real school shopping this year. My mother had a distaste for jeans and refused to think they were appropriate school wear, so her passive rebellion was not to buy them for me. I'd gone shopping with Claudia and bought a cheap pair of bell-bottom jeans and a peasant shirt with my babysitting money. My mother hadn't asked what was in the bag I brought home and I didn't offer to model my new clothes for her. I planned to braid my wet hair to recreate the style Claudia had taught me. I envisioned Stonewall had become like the Coke commercial, with all the different colors of people singing happily together. Now that I would join them I wanted to look like them.

But Stonewall hadn't become anything different in my absence. The halls were still dingy and stale. The bulletin boards were colorless and borderless. The floors remained unpolished. The textbooks that were distributed were old and battered. There were even fewer white kids in my classes than had been there the year before. With the exception of my small band of friends, no one seemed to notice I'd been gone and come back.

The schedule I took off the bulletin board had me taking U.S. History, even though the credit from summer school should have transferred. I went to the office to stand in line for the guidance counselor. The only person in the office I recognized was the redheaded Roger Fuller. I remembered the way the carload of us avoided him last year when we thought we had the luxury of being choosy about friends. He nodded at me with a vacant expression, and turned to face the front of the line.

"You're correct, Eleanor. We do have a letter here with your credit for U.S. History." Mrs. Burrows, the guidance counselor, was an older black woman whose oversized breasts nearly rested on the desk in front of her. Her straightened glossy hair, when compared to the afros the younger staff wore, revealed her age more than her face did. The open window couldn't rid her office of the stuffiness that hung in the air, even this early in the morning, and her face was shiny from the heat.

"What do you want to take in its place?" She was leafing through a manila file with my name on the tab.

"I went to summer school so I could graduate early. I was supposed to be taking twelfth grade English and French IV, but neither are on my schedule."

"French IV isn't on there because Miss Conner left and we haven't found someone yet who can teach that level."

"Miss Conner's gone?" I'd looked forward to being in her class again. I'd planned on being in the play she would direct.

"Eleanor, most of the students who are in your situation," she paused and I wondered if my situation meant white or a person with extra credits. "They are going to school half days and working in the afternoons. Are you planning on going to college early?"

I nodded. What else would I do? I hadn't thought that far.

She thumbed through the file again. "You're already a year ahead in math. If we substitute Government for US History and you're willing to take eleventh and twelfth grade English at the same time, you'll be on target to graduate in June."

"That's what I want to do."

"Let me see if those classes fit your schedule." She opened a giant notebook on her desk, licked her finger, and flipped through the pages. The bell rang and student chatter and the clanging of lockers meant I had missed all of first period.

"Here." She handed me a schedule, rearranged with red ink. "Let me write you a pass. There's a strict policy this year about students in the halls during class time." She scribbled another note to allow me into second period.

249

"Thank you, Mrs. Burrows." I stood to leave.

"Eleanor, may I ask you a question?" She stood up from behind her desk and her large presence filled the room. I nodded. "Most white students are leaving Stonewall. Why did you come back?" I could have told her St. Mary's wouldn't allow me back, but that was only part of the truth.

"I liked Stonewall better than St. Mary's," I said. That was the other part. She wrinkled her brow and studied me. Then she nodded, but she never smiled.

"Have a good year, Eleanor."

I left her office to find my next class.

Chapter Twenty-Five

Between summer school and the day Donald didn't come home I got my driver's license. I didn't like driving much. Meeting cars when there wasn't a median made my grip on the steering wheel tighten. My mother's wide-paneled station wagon was jumpy, accelerating too quickly and stopping too abruptly. Donald had taken me driving out in the counties the previous spring and been uncritical of my clumsy attempts at the wheel. He was a patient teacher. My father had ridden with me when Donald was at camp, enough for me to take the driving test. I drove with my mother one time, but neither one of us wanted to do it again. She pushed her foot into the floorboard hitting her imaginary brake, and made faint gasping sounds every time I made a turn. Even with a license proving my ability to drive it was a long time before I could back out of the driveway without panicking, but gradually the freedom it allowed me trumped my fear.

I drove myself to folk Mass, anxious to hear what Father Richard knew about Donald. My mind wandered through the service. I listened to the songs and stared at the windows, willing the late afternoon sun to transport me to a peaceful place. But the guitars that so mesmerized me in those first folk

251

Masses had become prosaic.

When the kids left the sanctuary for the coffeehouse, I lingered, hoping for a private conversation with Father Richard. The cavernous room was empty when he made his way back down the aisle.

"Nell! I almost missed seeing you there." He gave me a generous smile.

He approached the altar, did a quick bow of his head, and began undressing the communion table.

"Want to help?"

"I thought only altar boys could help."

"I think the heart is more important than the gender." I walked the few steps up to the altar and bowed my head as he had. He worked efficiently drinking the rest of the communion wine and covering the bread. He motioned to me to pick up the ends of the cloth to help fold it.

"I take it you're here to ask about your brother."

"Yes, Father."

"I heard from my friend he arrived safely in Canada. And yesterday I got a postcard from Donald. It's in my study. When I finish here I'll share it with you."

I went around to the back of the church and waited in the hall for Father Richard to complete his priestly duties.

"You can go on in, Nell. The door isn't locked."

There were piles of papers and books and the white coffee cups from the church kitchen cluttering the surface of his desk. He picked up a postcard from the top of a pile and handed it to me. It had a picture of a cathedral on the front.

Dear Father Richard,
Please let Nell know I'm fine.
Your friends are nice. I think I've found a job. Thanks
for all your help.

Donald

I ran my fingers across the words he'd written. I wanted to know more than I could figure out between the lines.

"Can I write to him?"

"Of course."

"Where do I send it?"

"I'll mail it to my friend. The fewer names and addresses out there, the safer Donald will be. He shouldn't have sent me a picture postcard that would give clues to where he is." I read the tiny print with the name of the cathedral and town as Father Richard took the card out of my hand. I'd never heard of it.

"I don't understand. How come I can't know where he is?"

"I've heard of agents searching for draft dodgers by activating alerts in post offices. Mail for any suspected name or address can be confiscated. False letters are sent luring the dodgers home with a pretense of some family emergency, and when the boys return to the States, they're arrested. No doubt when Donald didn't show up at State an alert was placed on his name. If someone from the government hasn't visited your house yet, they will soon. You won't have to lie if you don't know where he is."

My heart rate quickened.

"Will he have to stay in Canada until the war is over?" I asked.

"Possibly longer."

"Why longer?"

"Some laws will have to change or pardons issued for the boys who decided to leave the country before they can come back." He picked up two of the coffee cups from his desk. "Or they'll be arrested when they're back on American soil."

"Did Donald know that when he left?"

"He did." Father Richard picked up another cup. "Nell, can you help me get these into the kitchen? I know Miss Allen disapproves of my untidiness when she comes in here on Monday mornings, and I'm trying to gain more of her respect and less of her disfavor." I picked up cups, some of them half full of cold coffee.

"May I have the postcard?" I asked, my hands holding multiple cups by their handles. "I won't show it to anyone."

"Let's wait until things settle down. I'll keep it in a safe place for you." The clunky cups rattled against each other as he slid Donald's card into the middle of one of the piles on his desk.

"Miss Allen may look *under* piles, but she never disturbs a pile. "He smiled.

I got a part in the fall play. It had a smaller cast and was directed by a teacher who didn't act like she cared much about doing it. Fergy kept his job from the summer, so he didn't even audition. Claudia and Venetia got parts too, but we couldn't get it to bring the excitement or create the camaraderie Miss Conner and Mrs. Hayes had. It was a blip in our semester, instead of the main event like the year before. At least I had Mrs. Hayes as my teacher for both my English classes. She lectured without notes and introduced books I'd never heard of before. She always looked like she had just stepped out of a fashion magazine, and reminded me of a grown-up Deloris.

Venetia ran for student government president. Claudia and I made signs and gave out buttons and got the white kids to vote for her, although there were so few left at Stonewall Venetia would have won whether they voted for her or not.

I saw less of Fergy that fall, instead of more. Our class schedules had us crossing paths once during the day, which became a quick "hello" in the halls. Even if I didn't want to admit it, I missed his flirtatious teasing. Sometimes, he rode his bike to the coffeehouse and we sat together, but he was working at Williard's as much as he could, saving money for college. My father would pay for my college. Even my babysitting money didn't have to be saved for anything important and that made me feel different from him, like I should apologize for not having to work for what I got. Fergy was the one person who knew the whole story about Donald going to Canada. I'd told him on the phone one night soon after Donald didn't come home, and Fergy had listened without interrupting and didn't try to tell me everything would be okay with a fake happy voice. But his favorite uncle was serving in Vietnam and Donald's choice to move to Canada added to the differences tallying up between us.

I wrote letters to Donald and slipped them to Father Richard. He put them in another envelope and mailed them to his friend, who took them to Donald. I was never sure how long the process took. After seeing the mess that was Father Richard's desk I didn't quite trust that he got them in the mail in a timely manner.

When Donald wrote back, his letters were short and stilted, like the ones he had to write as a young camper, outlining his activities like bullet points in a to-do list. He'd gotten a job busing tables in a restaurant at night and would be shoveling walks and driveways for his landlord when the snow came, which he'd been told would be a steady job all winter. I thought about the winter coat hanging in his closet and wanted to mail it to him. One time he wrote a line about missing our mother's cooking, and in every short letter he told me to give Skipper a good belly rub for him. Those were the only hints he gave of missing home. The hole he left in our lives seemed bigger than any loss he felt.

I kept Donald's few letters from my parents. I sensed their pain in not knowing and yet Father Richard kept reminding me the more people who knew, the less safe Donald was. But no government men showed up at our house and my father managed to negotiate a deferred enrollment for Donald at State. It felt safe enough to tell them when Donald saved me from having to make the decision: he enclosed a letter to my parents in the envelope with mine. My mother was already in bed when I got home from the coffeehouse the Saturday night before Thanksgiving. My father was reading by a lone lamp in the living room. I handed him Donald's letter.

"What's this?" he asked, putting his book aside. I didn't need to answer; he recognized the handwriting and ripped open the envelope. His eyes tracked across the lines, reading Donald's words with haste, and then a second time before he broke away from the page. I sat across from him, perched on the sofa.

"Have you known his whereabouts all this time?" His voice had the edge of anger. Skipper, who'd been curled up at his feet, got up and walked over to me and leaned against my leg.

"Not the whole time," I answered. "I still don't know where he is. Father Richard gives me his letters when they come to him through a friend of his."

"So Father Richard knows where he is?"

"I guess so."

"And Donald has been writing to you and you've chosen to not share that information?" His eyes bored into me and I couldn't maintain the gaze. I looked down to see blood from the hangnail I'd been tugging at on my thumb.

"Father Richard thought it would be dangerous for Donald if you knew where he was."

"Dangerous for me to know the whereabouts of my son?"

"He said if government officials came asking about Donald, it was best if you could honestly say you knew nothing."

My father stood up, folded the letter and put it back into the torn envelope.

"Donald cannot be arrested as long as he's in Canada, so there's no danger in me knowing his location. And he can't be drafted as long as he's enrolled at the university, which he is. Father Richard needs to stick to preaching and leave me to interpret the law."

He left the room and climbed the stairs. I heard the bedroom door close. I sat for a while, still in my coat, scratching the spot behind Skipper's ears, and wondering how I'd gotten it so wrong. My father knew a way to protect Donald. I should have known that. I should have handed over Donald's first letter to him. But I'd promised Donald I wouldn't. There had been no way to not betray someone in my family.

The smell of bacon frying woke me up.

"Nell, I'd appreciate it if you would go to Mass with us this morning," my father said as I walked into the kitchen in my pajamas. He was drinking coffee and reading the paper while my mother stood at the stove, already dressed for church with an apron covering her emerald knit dress.

"Even though I went yesterday?" His expression stopped any more argument from me.

"I'd like for Father Richard to see us together and be reminded we are a family."

"Are you going to talk to him about Donald?"

"I am." His look softened. "Nell, I understand you thought you were doing the best thing for Donald." I nodded my head, relieved that whatever disappointment he had with me had dissipated. He folded his newspaper and put it on the table.

"My aggravation is with Father Richard," he continued. "He has become involved in a situation that is beyond his expertise. And frankly, he has taken advantage of his realm of influence, and has stepped a little too far into this family."

My mother placed plates of scrambled eggs, bacon, and toast in front of us. She still had pin curls set on each side of her face. She always complained her hair wouldn't curl in the winter so she coaxed it with Dippity-Do, bobby pins, and

AquaNet.

"I hope we can get Donald home by Christmas," she said, sitting down at her place at the table. She seemed older that morning. Maybe it was the dark circles under her eyes. Maybe it was the winter paleness. Maybe I hadn't really looked at her in months and just hadn't noticed.

"I plan on being straight with Father Richard. He will either make time for me after Mass or I will set up an appointment with him first thing in the morning. I won't tolerate any more secrets."

We were the last parishioners to file out of the sanctuary. I listened to Father Richard's amiable voice as he greeted the congregants ahead of us. I was as nervous as my father was determined. He motioned for my mother and me to walk in front of him.

"Nell, I'm impressed you're at Mass this morning! Nice to see you all together." He took both of my hands and locked his eyes with mine, as was his habit. I couldn't think of anything to say.

"And how are you, Mr. and Mrs. Randolph?" I started to walk down the stone steps to the sidewalk but my father grasped my elbow as a way of telling me to stay where I was.

"Father Richard, we are relieved and also terribly concerned this morning," my father answered. He caught Father Richard's gaze and didn't release it. "We've heard from our son and now understand you have been instrumental in his decision to forgo his college career and move in with some friend of yours in Canada."

Father Richard adjusted his shoulders and stood taller.

"It is true he's staying with friends of mine in Canada. However, he made the decision on his own to not attend State."

"Pray, Father, how could he make that decision if there wasn't an alternative offered to him?" My father had every appearance of the attorney he was as he kept our priest bound to his gaze. My mother inched herself towards me, away from the two of them.

"Mr. Randolph, this is a multilayered situation that requires thoughtful consideration. This is hardly the time or the place for us to have this conversation."

"We're not having a debate on what decision Donald should have made," my father continued in a matter-of-fact voice that exposed the edge of anger. "What I need to know is where Donald is, how I can get in touch with him today, and why you have become so involved in this critical situation."

"Mr. Randolph, I am obligated by Donald's trust to my silence in this matter."

"Father Richard, I don't believe Donald was seeking asylum in the church, which would be the reason you are citing. He has chosen to contact us, so it would be best if you would share what you know."

"Donald has spoken to me in confidence, and it is my duty to honor that."

"I don't believe you understand the law in this matter. I have arranged deferred enrollment at State, so Donald can return without fear of arrest."

Father Richard was quiet for a moment.

"I will pray on the matter, Mr. and Mrs. Randolph."

"You pray on it and I'll be at your office at 8 a.m. tomorrow morning for the information I need." Only then did my father release the priest from his gaze. He nodded to me and the three of us walked to the car and rode home in silence.

The priest handed my father an address scribbled on a scrap of paper when they met Monday morning. But the phone number beneath it was written in my father's precise hand.

"This was all I needed to find my son," he said when he presented it at the dinner table, "and I had to use my attorney skills to get it."

"Did you talk to Donald?" I asked.

"I did."

"What did he say?"

My mother's calm demeanor proved she already had this information.

"He sounds like he's doing okay. I'm going to send money for a bus ticket so he can come home by Christmas."

"Come home to stay?"

"Of course to stay, or at least until he leaves for State," my mother answered. "Your father explained the deferment to him and he was relieved, wasn't he, Eugene?"

"Well, I believe he understood what a stupid stunt this has been."

The response they were describing did not sound like the Donald I'd envisioned between the few lines of his letters. But I didn't counter their comments. I wanted to see Donald too and was happy to imagine his homecoming.

Chapter Twenty-Six

❧

"This is it," I said. Mr. Douglas stopped the car in front of Venetia's house. The colorful lights on a Christmas tree blinked in the front window. I felt on the cusp of things, smug in my experience of having been here before.

"Pick you up at 10:30?" he asked.

"Yep! Thanks, Dad!" Claudia leaned over the front seat and planted a kiss on his cheek.

"Have fun!" he said, as I thanked him for the ride.

Going places was never a big deal for Claudia. Her father remained unfazed with our social life, and didn't mind being our transportation. It was never that easy in my house. I'd learned to be comfortable "owing" more rides than I gave. Claudia made me feel better, saying I paid double when my parents drove or when I had to jump through so many hoops to use my mother's car.

"You came!" Venetia hugged us when she opened the door.

"Told you we were coming," Claudia said.

"So did Ben and Allison, but they haven't shown up yet." I peered into the living room. Claudia and I were the only white kids there.

"You'll be fine," Venetia said, watching my face. "Fergy and

261

Deloris are wandering around somewhere."

Claudia knew more people than I did and wasn't self-conscious about her whiteness. But the smugness I'd felt in the car disappeared as soon as I stepped into the living room and couldn't spot Fergy or Deloris in the dark crowd. My pale face became a beacon.

"Hey, white girl!" Hands reached from behind me and covered my eyes. I jumped.

"It's me, stupid!" Deloris whirled me around. She was stunning in her platform shoes and purple bell-bottoms. Her ebony skin shone against her gold blouse and I was so relieved to see her broad toothy smile.

"You look like a model, Deloris!"

"Maybe I'll be one someday," she tossed her chin upward. "This is still a mess." She moved my hair around with both of her hands. "One day I'm gonna put some of my Afro Sheen on you and you're gonna be surprised."

We laughed. I had missed Deloris. Since she went to Madison I'd only seen her once since school started, when she came to the coffeehouse with Venetia.

"You and Fergy ever get together?" she asked.

"No."

"What is wrong with y'all?" She put her hands on her hips and stared me down.

"We're just good friends."

"Uh-huh." She shook her head. "That works 'til one of y'all starts goin' with someone else, and then the other one will get all hurt feelings, realizing the missed opportunity could've changed your life. Poof!" Her hands made a circle like a magician casting a spell. I changed the subject.

"So how's Madison?"

"Girl, that school sucks." Deloris's face lost its brightness. "But I might not be going there much longer."

"Why?"

"The damn city's taking our house for that new highway.

They're trying to move us to some place east of town. If that happens, I'll be wishing I was back at that nasty Madison."

"But how can they take your house?"

She glared at me and tilted her head.

"You don't know nothing 'bout how the world works for black people."

It was like someone snapped their fingers and Deloris turned into a different person. Her shoulders dropped. Her eyes became slits. Her nose flared. I bit my lip and tried to think of what to say.

"Want something to drink?"

She shook her head and walked away. Someone put a Jackson 5 album on the record player and the room started dancing. I backed against the wall and tried to make myself inconspicuous.

"Well looky here."

A guy I'd never met towered over me.

"We got us an integrated party!"

I could smell his beer breath.

"Why you look so sad, white girl?"

"I didn't know I looked sad," I said.

"That or scared. You scared, white girl? You scared of black boys?" I wished Venetia or Deloris would find me. Or Claudia. She knew how to deflect comments like that.

"Of c-c-c-ourse not."

He laughed. "Maybe you should be." He stepped even closer to me and put his arm against the wall above my head, humming along to "A, B, C, easy as 1, 2, 3."

"Want to dance, white girl?"

"I'm n-n-n-ot a good dancer."

"Oh, everybody can dance." I looked under his arm and caught Venetia's eye from across the room. She didn't smile. She didn't mouth any advice. She didn't make a move.

He gyrated and thrust his pelvis in a circle. "See, all you gots to do is listen to the beat. Your body does the rest." He was so close our hips were almost touching. I flattened against the wall. It would've been better if I'd laughed and gone along with his dance moves. Edith or Claudia would have. But I couldn't make my body do that. When his hand went to my waist I stiffened.

"Lamont, you quit makin' my friend uncomfortable!" Venetia appeared and admonished him like a mother.

"I jus' was inviting her to dance is all," he said, pulling his arm off of the wall and taking a step back.

"She'll dance if she wants to, and she won't dance if she doesn't want to." Venetia stood with her hands on her hips and stared Lamont down. His face that had been so intimidating a moment before was now the face of a contrite child.

"Yes, ma'am," he said, restoring some cockiness to his voice. "Let me know if you want to dance later, white girl." I tried to smile.

"He didn't mean any harm, Nell. He's just full of himself, and I don't think he knows any white girls, so he's testing you out."

I nodded, still shaken but pretending it wasn't a big deal.

"But, that's the way you do it," she said to me. "That's how you take care of your friends."

December had begun with a dusting of snow, the anticipation of Donald's homecoming, and the renewal of my mother's holiday mania. It would have never descended on her if my father hadn't sent the bus money to Donald. On the last day of school I went with my father to the same tree lot, and he asked Fergy to pick out another cedar for us since we had enjoyed the last one so much. While Fergy was making cuts in the bottom of the tree my father went to buy hot chocolates.

"Here you go," he said and handed one to me and one to

Fergy.

"Wow, thank you, Mr. Randolph," Fergy put down his saw and took the Styrofoam cup from my father's hand.

"I figured you get mighty cold when you're out here for hours."

"Yes, sir."

"Is your father around, son?"

"Yes sir, somewhere." Fergy pointed. "He's probably over by the truck, unloading more trees." My father nodded to Fergy and walked in that direction.

"Why does he want to see my father?"

"I have no idea," I said, sipping on my hot chocolate. "But I don't think it'd be anything bad. He wouldn't have bought you hot chocolate if he was upset with you." I held Fergy's cup while he lopped off a rogue branch.

"Good to go?" My father rubbed his gloved hands together. "It's a cold one tonight. Hope you have on some warm socks, Fergy."

"You sound like my mother!" he chuckled. "She made sure I was wearing two pair." He picked up the tree by the freshly cut trunk. "Which way is your car, Mr. Randolph?"

Fergy hoisted the cedar on his shoulder and my father led us to the car. I held both hot chocolates until they had tied the tree on top of our station wagon, passing the rope back and forth and feeding it through the back seat.

"Better drink this while it can still warm you up," I said. His hand covered mine for a brief moment as I gave him the cup. He winked at me and I was glad my father was busy checking the security of the tree on top of the car.

"Thank you for your business, Mr. Randolph," Fergy said, "and the hot chocolate!" He raised the cup as if he were making a toast to my father.

"You're welcome, Fergy. Merry Christmas."

When we got in the car I switched the heater on full blast, but it blew cold air. My father turned it down. "You have to wait for the car to warm up first." We were quiet until the first stoplight.

"Why did you want to see Fergy's father?" I asked.

"I wanted to meet the father of such a hardworking young man," he said.

"Why?"

"I wanted him to know he has my respect."

"Why would he need to know that?"

"Even though my name has been in the paper a few times with this annexation and housing mess, I wanted Mr. Sutton to know I'm not part of an angry white mob. I respect his family and I want Fergy to have the same opportunities as my own children." He turned up the heater and it blew warm air on my feet.

"Even while my own son wants to throw away an enormous privilege."

"But Donald's coming home, and that will all be fixed, right?"

"Yes. But Donald's first choice was to throw away an education. I'm sure Fergy would never do that."

"No. Fergy's working all the time to save money for college."

"Perhaps they've got it right. You only value what you work for. Perhaps I didn't require enough from Donald for him to value it."

"I don't think that's it," I said.

"We'll see when he comes home, won't we?"

But we didn't see. Donald was not on the bus we went to meet or on the next one from up north. My father called the number from the little scrap of paper over and over. After hours of trying someone finally picked up on the other end, but it wasn't Donald.

"Tell him to call collect," my father said, his voice more desperate than angry. "Tell him it's fine for him to call collect."

He hung up the phone. My mother and I waited to hear what had been said on the other end of the line.

"Well?" my mother said.

"That was one of his roommates. He thinks Donald's at work. All of his stuff is still there so he hasn't left."

"Why hasn't he left?"

"Marjorie, the kid doesn't know why he hasn't left!" The anger came then, hot and loud and percussive. "I guess Donald accepted the money with no intention of using it to come home!"

He took both fists and banged them against the wall. He left them there and pushed his head against them. My mother trudged up the stairs and into their bedroom and closed the door. I wanted to put my arms around my father but I wasn't bold enough to take the few steps towards him. I wonder if we had weathered that awful moment together, if it would have made a difference. But we didn't.

The next day was Christmas Eve and my mother never left the bedroom. I heated up soup from a can and took it to her room and left it on the bedside table. I don't know if she was asleep or faking sleep but she didn't budge when I came in. My father and I ate our soup at the table.

"I guess we're not going to midnight Mass tonight?"

"I'm not," he answered. "You can go if you want."

"What should we do about dinner?" I had rummaged through the refrigerator; it was full of ingredients for the dishes my mother was going to make for Donald. I could manage to fix potatoes and beans, but I didn't know how to cook the meat. My father put down his spoon and pushed his chair back from the table.

"I'm sorry, Nell. All of this shouldn't be put on you. It's your Christmas too."

I was grateful for those words. "I don't mind cooking," I said, "But I don't know how to cook what she bought."

"Why don't I pick up pizza?" My father didn't even like pizza, but he knew I did.

"That's fine, but what about tomorrow? Nothing will be open on Christmas Day."

"Let's hope your mother snaps out of it by then."

I spent the afternoon trying to make some of the casseroles for Christmas dinner, because I needed something to do and I wasn't at all sure my mother would reappear, even on Christmas Day. I found recipes in the metal box that held the 3 x 5 cards where my mother wrote out all the instructions in her perfect handwriting. I made the green bean casserole without too much trouble. She'd already started the layered Jell-o salad, but when I poured the next layer it made the green Jell-o dissolve into the red. I wasn't skilled with a knife so the potatoes were uneven, making some too soft and others too crunchy when I dumped them out of the boiling water for the scalloped potato recipe. The kitchen was a mess after all my attempts. My father helped wash the dishes and I thought about Claudia and her dad, and wondered if this was how it was for them all the time. We put the uncooked casseroles on the back porch to stay cool until they were cooked the next day, which was my mother's way in the winter when the refrigerator was full.

My father and I ate pizza for supper. He took some up to my mother, but didn't stay in the room with her. He tried to call Donald. I kept thinking Donald would show up, like those Christmas stories where travelers pushed through all the odds of wind and weather to get home by Christmas Day. I tried to find a show to watch but it seemed wrong to watch TV on Christmas Eve. The evening dragged and as it limped its way towards eleven, my father and I heard movement upstairs. My mother came down dressed for church. Her appearance was impeccable; no one would suspect she had sequestered herself for two days in her room, barely eating. Her ashen face, in contrast to her stark red lipstick, would be the only sign of her distress. Her flattened hair that was usually teased in a bouffant around her face was hidden when she put on her black lace chapel veil.

"I'm going to Mass," she said.

I jumped up, "I'll go with you. I can change in a sec." I ran up the stairs and scrambled into a dress and hose.

"Nell, why don't you drive?" my father said when I was ready. My mother didn't object. I drove us to the church in silence. I remembered the last Christmas Eve when Donald and I sat in the same pew, with our parents and grandparents, smug in our familiarity with the new folk music they hadn't heard before. Had it only been a year?

The Mass held little mystic satisfaction for me that night. The loss of respect for our priest that my father experienced planted seeds of doubt for me. As I watched Father Richard handle the sacred elements I kept picturing the man behind the curtain in *The Wizard of Oz*, making all the people believe in his power. I understood why my father could not come with us. My mother followed the Mass with automaticity, kneeling and reciting the liturgy, but she said all of her responses in the Latin of her childhood indoctrination, not in the English of Vatican II, her mantilla drawn over her face like a woman in mourning.

Chapter
Twenty-Seven

My father tapped on my half-closed door, and poked his head in. "Nell, do you think you could stay with the Carpenters a few days?"

"Why?"

"Your mother and I have decided to fly to Canada. There's one week before the term begins at State. I've got to find Donald and talk some sense into him."

"Can't I go with you?" I thought I'd be an asset, a bridge. "I can make up anything I miss in school, which won't be much."

"I think it best you stay here."

His shoulders slumped and he hadn't ventured past the doorway. Yet his presence still commanded my respect.

"Yes, sir." I knew Mr. and Mrs. Carpenter would welcome me, but I wasn't sure Sally would. "I wouldn't be scared to stay here by myself."

He sighed, "I guess you could. I trust you, but I'd be more comfortable if someone were here with you."

"So I can ask a friend to stay instead of going to the Carpenters?"

"I guess so." He walked away.

270

I peered out my window into the dark. The glass was cold and I shivered thinking about Donald shoveling snow in a frigid Canada. I wondered how they would convince him to go to college. I'd never told anyone how I'd helped him in school. Then a flash of Donald in uniform jumping out of a helicopter with a gun on his shoulder played through my mind like a movie, like what I'd seen on the news. I found my father at the antique desk in the corner of the living room.

"I know why Donald didn't go to State," I said.

My father riveted his head. "What?"

"I know why Donald doesn't want to go to college." I took a breath and said it all at once. "He told me he was afraid of flunking out and once he flunked out he would have to go to Vietnam. And the reason he would flunk out is because he had such a hard time learning. I helped him write all his papers in high school and I would read things to him instead of him reading them himself." My face was hot by the time I spewed out the years-old secret.

My mother appeared and stood at the other end of the living room. My father studied his hands like something was written there.

"How often did you do this?" he asked.

"He brought me his homework almost every night." My eyes were filling with tears from the guilt of being accessory to a crime on top of worry for Donald. I felt my neck turn splotchy and my stomach turn somersaults.

"When did this start?" he asked, his orderly questions befitting his attorney style.

"I don't know. I guess when he went to junior high and he wouldn't let mom help him anymore."

"How did he pass his tests?" my mother asked.

"He memorized a lot. I think he may have cheated off other kids' papers sometimes. And he sweet-talked teachers and they let him make corrections and stuff. He faked broken fingers sometimes and the teachers let him answer the questions orally instead of writing them."

"Why haven't you told us?" He stood with his hands on his hips, exasperation in his voice.

"I don't know. I promised Donald I'd never tell. He didn't want you to think he was stupid." My heart pounded. "He's not stupid, you know. He's actually pretty smart. I kept telling him he should tell y'all, that maybe there was something wrong with his eyes that could be fixed." I sucked in a breath. "And now he's going to hate me for telling you." I turned to leave the room.

"Wait, Nell," my father said, "we're not finished here. Sit down." I obeyed.

"Do you think there's a teacher of Donald's who could verify what you're saying?"

"I don't know." I tried to remember the names of some of Donald's teachers. "I know he tried the broken finger with his history teacher, Mrs. Clarke. She liked Donald."

"What are you thinking, Eugene?" my mother asked.

"I'm thinking I need to get as much information as I can before we get on that plane. I need to get to the bottom of this, and I need the truth, the truth from everyone." His eyes drilled into mine. "Is there anything else, Nell? Anything at all you haven't told me?"

"No, sir."

"You're sure?"

"Yes, sir."

He nodded as a way of dismissal. I didn't feel the relief I had when I gave him Donald's letter. That was revealing a location. Now I had exposed who Donald was, and betrayed years of his trust in me.

The lights were still on downstairs when I went to bed.

My parents were supposed to be gone for three nights. They came back after two and they came back without Donald. Whatever they experienced in Canada became a secret they would not share with me. My questions were halted and I was told not ask them again, that Donald had made his choice. The door to Donald's room was left closed. Skipper sometimes slept in front of it, but after awhile he found other places to nap. The heaviness in our house became a thick mud we all trudged through; unable to pick up our feet. My father worked most nights. My mother stopped doing any real cooking and bought instead the frozen meals that were partitioned into aluminum compartments. They owned the cute name of TV dinners, but I never ate mine in front of the TV, because my mother was eating hers there.

My father stopped going to church after he went to Father Richard's study and coerced Donald's address from him. Since he was not born a Catholic his absence from Mass did not wound his conscience like it did my mother's. She began going to early Mass on Sundays to avoid encounters with those who had sat in neighboring pews for all our growing up years. She kept to her gloves and her head coverings as younger women were shedding theirs. I took my questions about Donald to Father Richard, the only other person who might have known what was going on.

"Father Richard, may I talk to you for a minute?" I asked when the flow of teens coming into the church basement slowed.

"Of course, Nell. What's on your mind?" He flashed his movie star smile, which should have put me at ease.

"I want to ask about Donald."

"Do you have a letter for me to mail?" He reached out his hand but I had nothing to give him.

"No. I can mail them myself now."

"Of course," he remembered. "I hear he's doing fine," he added in a reassuring tone.

273

"Did you know my parents went to visit him and he refused to come home with them?"

His face darkened for an instant, then he readjusted it. "They did? And how was he?"

"I don't know because they won't tell me. What could be so bad they can't tell me?"

Father Richard studied the floor. He cleared his throat.

"Nell, as Donald's priest, I will always safeguard anything he has confessed to me. But I can assure you I believe Donald is within God's grace."

"But it's like my parents won't even admit they have a son! They won't talk about him. They've closed the door to his room. It's awful!"

His blue eyes held compassion in their gaze. "I will pray for your parents. Donald's choice to avoid the war is not the choice your father would make. Your parents will need to come to terms with that."

"But they have! There's something else wrong. I know it!"

He placed his hands on my shoulders as if he were pronouncing a blessing, then left me to assist the kids on stage who were calling for him. I could not figure out what sin was within God's grace that my parents found unforgivable.

Chapter Twenty-Eight

~***~

The college letters arrived. I was accepted at the three schools where I applied, but on the day I received the thick envelope from State the memory of Donald's acceptance the spring before was too raw for mine to be celebrated. Even though it was a year premature, my entrance was a foregone conclusion for my parents, and my attendance there was assumed by them and by me. My mother only attended two years of college before she married and thought more about the social aspects of a campus. My father believed a degree from State looked the best on a resume if I didn't get married and had to support myself.

"This is so weird," Sally said on the bus one afternoon.

"What?" I asked.

"I always thought you and I would be going off to college together, but now you're going to State with my brother instead."

"You'll be there next year."

"Yeah, but I'll be the lowly freshman and you'll be the know-it-all sophomore," she moaned. "I wish I'd known about graduating early and gone to summer school. Next year is going to be *so* long, waiting to get away from this."

275

"I feel bad about leaving you. You'll still have Allison and Laurie."

"I know. But I have two classes left to take. It's going to be so boring!"

"Maybe you can get a cool job in the afternoons and only go to school in the mornings."

"And what kind of cool job can a seventeen-year-old girl get? Babysitting?"

I could not find a way to make Sally feel better. She hated Stonewall. She would have done well at St. Mary's. She would have made friends there and the nuns would have liked her. If she'd only been Catholic.

"Maybe you can convert and I can pass on my lovely St. Mary's uniform to you," I tried to joke with her.

"I still don't get why you gave that up for this." I'd managed to keep my dismissal from St. Mary's a secret from Sally and let her believe it was my choice to transfer back to Stonewall. The truth about it didn't seem to matter anymore.

Venetia had planned to go to Howard. Both of her parents went there, but she would have been accepted on her own merit even if they hadn't. She and a cousin had already made plans to be roommates.

Fergy had been accepted to the local college where most black students went as soon as he applied, but the day he received his acceptance letter with the promise of scholarship funds from State his family had an impromptu party. He called me later that night, basking in the glow of his family's celebration of him.

"All my cousins were here and the neighbors heard us and came over." I could hear the excitement in his voice. "You would think I was famous!"

"That's so cool!" I tried to match his excitement, but I couldn't help but compare it to the lackluster response to my own acceptance. I listened as he told me what people said, and how his mother baked a special cake. His grandmother made a toast with her sweet tea that Fergy repeated to me word for word. By the time we hung up I was gripping one of the sage pompoms I'd twisted off my parents' bedspread.

One day Mrs. Hayes asked me to eat lunch with her. She'd taken turns spending time with the seniors that way. No one ever turned her down. With any other teacher it would have felt like a punishment; with her, it was a privilege.

"So are you going to State for sure?" she asked, pulling two student desks to face each other.

"Yeah, I guess so."

"Why?"

"Why? I guess because it's the best school, and I got accepted there?"

"You said that like a question," she smiled. She sat down and a trace of her perfume reached me.

I squirmed. It was like she was asking one of her deep literary questions about an underlying theme that I had missed. A sense of relief had come with a decision my parents supported; a feeling of being included when I followed everyone's expectations of me. Mrs. Hayes was the first one to question my decision.

"I want to make sure you're choosing what's best for you, and not just doing what everyone expects you to do."

I'd told Mrs. Hayes early in the year about my experience at St. Mary's, including my dismissal. She was the only one I'd confided in and I was certain she'd kept that information confidential. Her concern for me felt authentic.

"You think I could make a better choice?"

"Oh, I have no doubt you can handle the workload at State. But you're a forward thinker, Nell. I wouldn't want you to get swallowed up in an old Virginia institution that wouldn't encourage that independent thinking."

"Swallowed up how?"

"Remember how you felt at St. Mary's? How everyone there thought the same way and wouldn't even allow you to be seen in public with a black boy? You were forced to dress the same way and they tried to teach you to think a certain way. I'm afraid that could happen to you at State and you would be a frustrated soul longing for some freedom."

"But State is NOTHING like St. Mary's!"

"Not on the outside."

I put down my sandwich and recrossed my legs, swiveling my body to the open side of the desk. Mrs. Hayes reached over and put her hand on top of mine.

"It was not my intention to upset you." She waited for my response. She was like that when we talked. She didn't try to fill the empty spaces with more words. Sometimes the silences were uncomfortable, but students grew to expect them. She wasn't waiting on a response; she was waiting for me to digest her words. My eyes leaked tears.

"I don't know why I'm crying," I said, wiping my eyes with the back of my hand. Mrs. Hayes stepped over to her desk and brought back a tissue box.

"I'm tired of being the different one. I didn't fit in at St. Mary's. Most of my white friends, like Sally and Allison, don't understand why I like to hang out with Venetia and Fergy. But I'm not black, and I know I won't ever really fit in with them either. When I go to State I think I'll finally fit in somewhere."

"I understand," she nodded." I think you've handled all the change in your circumstances remarkably well, with more openness than most white students." Her kind eyes rested on me and waited for me to absorb her encouragement.

"What I want you to understand is most of the people who go to State are the white people who have been raised to think like Sally and Allison."

I stared at my half-eaten sandwich.

"You need to read the news and also read between the printed lines," Mrs. Hayes continued. "Students all over the country are standing up against injustice on their college campuses. But there has not been one newsworthy protest at State this year. What you can surmise from that is those students aren't thinking about the war or civil rights or even women's rights. Most of them are there to follow in their parents' footsteps. Do you think you will fit in with them?"

My eyes filled again and I yanked another tissue out of the box.

"Mrs. Hayes, I'm not sure I'm the protest type either."

"You don't have to be, Nell. But I don't think you want to be with people who would not want Fergy or Venetia as their friends."

"So what do you think I should do?"

"You'll know when it comes to you. I'm only encouraging you to examine your options and think about the people who'll be going to the schools where you've been accepted. You'll be happier if you go where there are like-minded students and where the professors encourage independent thinkers, rather than feel threatened by them."

She glanced at the clock on the wall.

"You might find a group of friends at State who are like you. But promise me you'll look at all the angles when you decide this next step, and not automatically go with what you think is the obvious choice. Because this decision can determine the track of the rest of your life."

The bell rang and I gathered my trash.

"Thanks, Mrs. Hayes."

She gave me a quick squeeze as I left for fifth period.

"Did I miss any gossip at lunch?" I asked Sally on the bus ride home.

"Nope. How was your lunch with Mrs. Hayes?"

"It was fine." I didn't feel comfortable telling Sally about our conversation.

"I hope I get her for English next year. When she talks, she doesn't even sound black."

Sally's words felt disrespectful to me, but I didn't counter her. There was so much more to Mrs. Hayes than her speech. I don't know if I stayed silent because she surpassed any defense I could offer or because I knew Sally wouldn't get it.

As soon as I got home I ran up to my room and pulled out the three college acceptance letters and packets I'd received. Winchester College, tucked away in the mountains of Virginia, was my mother's favorite. It boasted the best training for teachers, but I didn't think I wanted to be a teacher. It had a beautiful campus, and the pictures of students hiking made me think of the camp summers I'd always wanted. There wasn't one brown face in any of the brochures and I doubted there had been any protests on that campus. My litmus test that day was asking myself if Deloris or Fergy or Venetia would be welcomed there.

The State brochures had pictures of black students. Fergy had been accepted there. I was a little irritated at Mrs. Hayes for casting doubt on my choice and making me unsure of what I thought was the best decision. State would be a better option than Winchester.

My third college acceptance had been to Keller College in Massachusetts. Mrs. Burrows, the guidance counselor, had handed me the application one day and asked me to apply. "They want more students from the south," she said, "and you and Denise Brown are the only ones I can think of who could handle their academic rigor." Denise was a studious senior, black and shy and brilliant. We had both been accepted.

I hadn't visited the campus. My parents had told me to go ahead and apply to see if I got in, but they didn't consider the school a viable option. They didn't know anyone who went to college in Massachusetts. It would be complicated to get back and forth. It wasn't necessary to go that far away.

But now I studied the materials for the first time. Keller was a small school. The students had the fresh-faced look of kids who were outside a lot, not those who always had their noses in a book. Some of the professors dressed like hippies, in jeans with no ties, wearing beards and longer hair. The girls in the pictures were wearing jeans, not the plaid skirts of the girls at the Virginia schools. I wondered if my parents would take me there to visit, to make sure. I put the Winchester stack back in its manila envelope and left it closed, but took the State and Keller brochures and left them side by side on my desk.

I'd learned from Donald how to present a case to our father: be sure all the questions were answered before he could ask them, and offer all my reasons in a way that appealed to his logical mind. I practiced my case, even wrote down my talking points, before I went to him with my request to go to Keller College for the weekend they reserved for accepted students. As it turned out, Donald had been a wise teacher.

"I think that's an excellent idea, Nell." He lowered the open newspaper down to his lap.

"Really?" I hadn't made my way through half of what I'd planned to say.

"Yes. I think it's a good practice to evaluate all the options before you commit to State."

I gave him a grateful smile.

"But I don't think we need to pay for two airline tickets," he continued. "Would you be alright flying up there by yourself?"

"Yes." I'd never flown before, but that didn't matter.

"Write down the dates for me and I'll get the firm's travel agent to make the reservations."

I was so excited I wanted to tell someone. I tried to call Claudia, but no one was at home. Venetia answered and sounded genuinely excited for me, even though she admitted to being jealous of getting an airplane ride out of it. I wrote to Donald too. If I ended up at a college in Massachusetts, maybe I'd be able to visit him.

I had to run to catch up to Venetia between classes.

"I got my plane ticket to Boston!"

"Great" she muttered, picking up her pace.

"You okay?"

I'd thought she'd be excited for me. We reached her locker. She fiddled with the lock and jerked it open.

"Don't you know what happened to Deloris?"

It was an accusation. Fear of the unknown that would soon become known made my heart race. She studied my face.

"The city took her house." Venetia threw a book in and reached for another. "My father has been defending those families for months. City Council told him they thought it was important to save the neighborhood too. Then they up and took their property anyway." Her breath came out like a raging bull.

"How is that legal?"

"It's not. But if you get enough white men together that want something to happen, they find a way to make it legal." Venetia slammed her locker shut. "Ask your father. He'll know how they did it."

I felt my whiteness like the day I wore the yellow dress. I pulled my books close to my chest and watched Venetia storm down the hall.

I called Claudia that night, thinking she might have talked to Deloris.

"Yeah, I talked to her before it happened, but I haven't since," Claudia said. "I don't have her new telephone number."

"Where did Deloris's family go?"

"The city built some cheap apartments on the east side. Said having a new place more than compensated for their old house, but you know that's not true."

"Did she have to change schools?"

"Yeah. Madison's too far for her mom to take her and get to work on time."

"It's so not fair," I said.

"How do you not know this stuff?" Claudia asked. "It's been all over the paper."

Mrs. Hayes words about reading the news flashed through my mind.

"My dad and I went down there to stand in front of the bulldozers," Claudia said. "But they wiped out all these people's houses anyway. There's a big pile of rubble sitting in the middle of the city on a block that used to be Deloris's address."

Deloris was all I could think about. Deloris, with her big heart and her big smile. Deloris, with her home mangled into a pile of debris. The knot in the pit of my stomach tightened. Why did Venetia tell me to ask my father? He would never be involved with doing that to a family, I felt guilty. Guilty for being white. Guilty for living in a nice house no one was going to take away from me. Guilty that in some way I had been responsible for Deloris losing her home.

I searched for information about the razing in the stack of papers tied up for the next newspaper drive. I found an article with two pictures: one of a rundown abandoned house, and another of a new cinderblock building with a smiling white man handing keys to a black couple with three children and a baby. The article praised the city for providing better housing and sanitary conditions for sixty of the city's poorest families. I took the newspaper to my father. He was reading in his chair in the living room when I thrust the pictures in front of him.

"Were you involved with this?"

I glared at him, waiting for his response.

"My firm defended City Council's plan for the placement of the highway." A tense face looked up at me.

"I have a friend who lived in one of those houses that was torn down. How can the city do that? Just take people's homes without their permission?" My voice came out too high and reedy. I don't know why talking to my father made me nervous.

"It's a complicated situation, Nell." He lowered his newspaper and uncrossed his legs. "First, a new highway is being built, and it has to go through the city some way. This block inconvenienced the fewest number of people."

"It's more than an inconvenience for Deloris's family," my voice came out stronger this time.

"Second," he continued, "most of those homes were terribly inadequate and unsanitary. The city invested in another property and built brand new apartments for those families."

"Did you see the houses yourself?"

He shook his head.

"Because maybe Deloris is poor, but she's not unsanitary. She always looks beautiful and put together, like a model. Her clothes don't smell. How could you be like that if your house was unsanitary?"

"Nell, I'm sorry for your friend. But wherever this highway goes is going to displace someone and that person will be someone else's friend who has to move."

"It's not fair! I thought you were on their side!"

For the first and last time in my life, I walked out on my father.

Chapter Twenty-Nine

I didn't get reprimanded for being disrespectful. Instead, my father made arrangements or me to be met and driven the forty-five minutes north of the airport to Keller's campus. He circumvented my mother in making the plans. Ever since the day my mother and I walked out of St. Mary's, she'd pulled away from me. At first, it felt like punishment or even banishment. But I learned to regard her distance as a new freedom. When Donald left she stopped quizzing me about phone calls, and quit asking me where I was going. I knew her attitude towards me was not newfound trust, but disinterest. Maybe it was a display of grief in losing Donald. But I didn't understand why if you lost one child you would give the other one up too.

The day of my flight to Boston was also my seventeenth birthday. My father, who was unused to planning for such things, decided we would all go out for breakfast before my flight. But a migraine took control of my mother sometime in the night and she stayed in her darkened bedroom and left the celebrating to my father. Before I left, I slipped into her room, delivering an ice-cold washcloth for her head as my goodbye. I doubted she wanted to go to my birthday breakfast, but I couldn't imagine she would choose to be alone with her pain over being with us.

Neither one of us said it, but we were relieved to not have to make conversation with my mother during our breakfast. My father didn't tamp down my excitement, didn't raise an eyebrow at my order of eggs and pancakes, and didn't fuss when the nervousness about my first flight left most of my breakfast untouched. He walked me through what would happen when I got on the plane and what I should do to find my ride to campus. He handed me more money for all of the "just in case" situations. At the airport he carried my suitcase to the desk where I checked in, then we watched the planes taking off and landing through the wall of glass in the waiting area. When they called for my flight he walked me to the exit door and planted a kiss on my forehead.

"Have a wonderful weekend, Nell. Take it all in, but stay safe."

"I will." I stood on my tiptoes to kiss his cheek. "Thanks for letting me go." He smiled and motioned for me to go through the door.

"I'll see you here on Sunday."

As I walked across the tarmac to the steps for the plane I sensed my father's gaze following me. I turned to see him standing tall and dignified, holding his hat in his hands. He nodded to me and waved.

When I think back, I can't remember one outstanding event that weekend that made the decision for me. I met some students, went to some classes, spent the nights in a dormitory, ate my meals in the dining hall. I wasn't the center of attention as I thought they might have treated their guest. Rather, I was included in each impromptu gathering as part of the group. The pair of jeans I'd packed in case I needed them became my uniform, while my skirts remained folded in my suitcase. No one wore makeup, so I didn't bother with it either. Boys and girls sat together at meals, but it didn't seem like any of them were couples. In the freshman discussion groups they talked about careers and politics and travel. When I applied my litmus test of whether Fergy or Deloris or Venetia would feel accepted here, Keller passed. Everyone seemed to be from somewhere else and that was their commonality.

"So how was it?" my father asked as I walked back into the terminal I'd left three days before. My mother wasn't with him so I was grateful defending my choice of jeans over a skirt on an airplane was not the first thing I had to do.

"I liked it," I said. "I really liked it."

"And why did you like it?"

"The kids seemed real and happy to include me. They had interesting conversations. The professors didn't lecture as much as they led discussions." He nodded and waited for more. "I think Fergy or Deloris or Venetia would be welcomed there."

"That's important to you, isn't it?" he asked.

"Yeah, I guess so."

"I'm glad it is."

We waited at the carousel, watching bags go round and round before my green Samsonite slid down the chute and my father grabbed it. Once we were in the car he picked up the thread of our conversation.

"Nell, I wish you could have had a more normal high school experience. I think and think about what I should have done to give that to you."

"What could you have done?"

"We could've moved, gotten you into one of the county schools. At the time I didn't think we should join the hordes of white people leaving the city. I thought I was being an example of a good citizen."

Both his hands gripped the steering wheel. His focus was straight ahead, staring at a point in the distance.

"There was another option for the highway. It could have gone through one of the country clubs. It would've taken a few holes off the golf course and made a noisy backdrop for a golf game."

I studied his face and saw the dark bags under his eyes and the deep creases in his pale forehead.

"Why didn't they choose that option?"

"I did, in the beginning. My arguments were politely dismissed at first. Then they were countered by all the economic benefits. I was told putting the highway there would solve two problems: transportation and safety; that clearing out the "slums" as they called it, would be a huge benefit for the city." His face crumpled and his shoulders drooped. "I didn't take the time to go look for myself."

I wasn't used to seeing my father look so vulnerable. It made me uncomfortable. I turned my head to the line of telephone poles out my window. I had the sensation that we were sitting still and the long line of poles were speeding past us.

"While you were in Boston, I went and looked at the new apartments the city built where your friend Deloris lives now."

"What's it like?"

"It's cheap. Cinderblock. No trees or grass. It felt desolate. I haven't really slept since I saw it, knowing I was part of that."

A motorcycle roared past us.

"Could you have changed their minds?"

"We'll never know, will we? I should have tried harder. I should have done my own research. I should have gone to look at the houses."

I was torn between sympathy for my father's angst and heartbreak for Deloris. His head turned towards mine.

"You're trying and I'm proud of you for it."

"Mom's not proud of me. I don't think she'll ever forgive me for getting dismissed from St. Mary's."

"Your mother was doing what she thought was best by sending you there, Nell. Remember that." I still thought my mother was doing what was best for her, not me, but I respected my father too much to voice that opinion.

"She's going to want me to go to State, not Keller." The car slowed to a stop at the red light and my father adjusted himself in his seat and looked at me.

"I'll take care of your mother. I want you to go wherever you want for college. I owe that to you."

The light changed and his eyes went back to the road. He flicked his signal for a turn that wasn't on the route home.

"I think we could use a side trip to Krispy Kreme."

The glaze-dipped doughnuts didn't feel celebratory, like I think my father intended. He was trying to honor my developing convictions. But the reality of his own decisions collided with his sense of justice and couldn't be assuaged. His confiding in me was akin to confession. Maybe he thought if I made better choices it would be his absolution.

I made the decision to go to Keller College. Few people understood. I could tell by the expression on their faces they thought I'd made an irrational decision to go to a small, expensive school up north when I had the opportunity to go to State. My mother never said a word about it.

After the weekend at Keller I went back to folk Mass. I sat in the pew and watched the late afternoon sun filter through the stained glass windows. There was an instant when I captured an overwhelming sense of peace, an acute awareness of being in God's protection. The guitar music began from the back of the church and as the musicians and Father Richard walked down the center aisle I had a flashback of this same experience from over a year ago, when it was new. There were so many more kids sitting in the pews now. In the beginning we had worn church clothes: dresses, pantyhose, slacks, and ties. Now we were in jeans with uncut hair. In the beginning we were timid with our voices. Now we sang the familiar tunes by heart.

But when Father Richard stood at the altar and spoke with his charismatic voice a sense of unease crept in. His beautiful veneer had begun to chip. I was on edge in his presence, with his knowledge of Donald's secrets he could not share. In the beginning he had brought Donald and me closer together. Now it felt like he stood between us.

The undercroft was full when Claudia and I walked in.

"Man, our little coffeehouse sure has taken off," she said as she scanned the room.

I saw clusters of teenagers I'd never seen. "Do you know these kids?"

"Some of them. I think we've gotten cool, Nell!" We laughed as we went to get snacks. Younger teens were pouring the cokes and popping the popcorn.

"Father Richard's new protégés," Claudia said.

"Just in time for us to go." I filled up a cup with popcorn. "Are you ready to leave?"

"I've been ready!" She took in the crowd. "Aren't you getting tired of this?"

"I hadn't thought I was, but tonight I feel kind of antsy."

"You've had the speed version of high school," Claudia said. "It's understandable if you're not quite over this yet."

"I don't think it's that," I hesitated, but then plowed on. "I don't feel close to Father Richard anymore."

"He's got so many kids here now, he can't pay much attention to us."

"Maybe that's it." I knew it wasn't.

Father Richard hopped onto the makeshift stage. He welcomed everyone with the same exuberance he'd exhibited a year ago. His blonde hair now went past the top of his white collar. His jeans were no longer an anomaly. There were sandals on his feet. He introduced some college students, who invited us to join in a war protest on Saturday.

"Are you going?" I asked Claudia.

"I can't. I'm going to go see my mother next weekend. Are you?"

"I don't know. What good does it do?" I thought about all the protests across the country and I couldn't see how it had changed anything except make people more antagonistic. The war in Vietnam kept going and Donald kept hiding from it in Canada.

"Hello, Nell and Claudia!" Father Richard greeted us with his magnetic smile. "I've missed seeing you the past few weeks. How are things?"

"Fine, Father," Claudia said, "I've been visiting colleges and stuff."

"That's excellent. You too, Nell?" His gaze caught me and held my eyes in his unique way.

"I went up to Keller College last weekend."

"Keller? I don't think I know that one."

"Most people don't. It's a small school in Massachusetts."

"Did you like it?"

"Yes. I think I'm going there."

"Congratulations! Making that decision is a huge step." He turned to Claudia. "And have you made a decision too?"

"I'm going to North Carolina University. My mom lives in North Carolina and I can get in-state tuition there. I promised I'd go to college close to her."

He put his hand on Claudia's shoulder. "I'll miss seeing your faces around here." He surveyed the groups of teenagers in the undercroft. "And I will always remember you were the ones who got this coffeehouse off the ground." He patted our backs before he moved on.

❊

"Look who just walked in," Claudia said and nodded towards

the door. It was Fergy. We could tell something had happened by the expression on his face.

"What's wrong?" Claudia beat me to the question.

"Remember all that celebrating when I got into State?"

We nodded.

"It was for nothing."

"What do you mean?" I asked.

"I can't go there."

"They already accepted you! They can't take it back!" Claudia said.

"Yeah, well, the admissions office told me not to worry about the cost because they were certain the scholarship would cover most of my fees." He made quotation marks in the air when he said *scholarship*. "Turns out that was crap. They're offering a stipend that would pay for my books, nothing else."

"That's not right!" Claudia said. She tried to pat his arm but Fergy shrugged her hand off. "What are you going to do?" she asked.

"The only thing I can afford to do—stay at home and go to the college where all the other black kids go." His hands were curled up into fists and his body was so tight he trembled. His watery eyes darted around and I couldn't catch them with mine. I'd never seen him like this. I reached over to touch his arm and he jerked away from me too.

"I'm going to get you a coke," Claudia said and left us alone.

"I'm so so sorry, Fergy,"

He leaned against the wall. His body slid down against the cinderblock like slow dripping paint. He slumped onto the floor and splayed his legs out. I sat beside him.

"Why would they promise me something they couldn't give me? Why would they let me get my hopes up?"

"I don't know. Maybe they didn't have as much money as they thought they did."

He glared at me, the whites of his eyes eclipsed with anger.

"I think they got money for white boys, but not black boys."

I said nothing.

"I think they accepted me 'cause they had to, 'cause my grades and my test scores were just as good as anybody's. That way they can say they accept black kids just like they accept white kids. They can brag they are color-blind."

"You're smarter than any of the white boys I know." He ignored me.

"What I want to know is who got that scholarship money? Were they color-blind about that? I don't think so."

Claudia walked up and handed Fergy a waxy paper cup filled with coke. He took it without acknowledging her.

"So Miss Nell, you think about me when you're walking around that pretty campus next year." The bitterness in his voice was palatable.

"I won't be there next year."

"You won't? What are you doing?"

"I'm going to Keller, in Massachusetts."

"You get a scholarship for that?"

"No." I watched the expression on his face as he calculated what my father must be paying for me to go to a private college so far away. The burden of guilt I felt for not having to worry about money doubled its weight.

"I see." He swallowed his coke in one go, crushed the cup in his hand and stood up. "I'm out of here. Don't know why I came. This place is just too white for me."

Claudia and I watched him push himself through the crowd and leave through the basement door.

I didn't know it at the time, but that would be my last conversation with Fergy. We'd been eager to find our commonalities. We'd connected in our love of plays, in what made us laugh. We both craved the respect of our parents, maybe he more than I. We'd danced around our sometimes attraction to each other and settled into safe flirtation. We'd wanted to ignore our races. We both looked past our differences: me feeling uncomfortable in his drug store, him rolling up the windows in my neighborhood; my brother avoiding the draft in Canada while his uncle served in Vietnam. But the loss of Fergy's scholarship shone a spotlight on all of it. I'd thought the coffeehouse was neutral territory for us. It had been so freeing to have Fergy and Venetia and Deloris come there. I was right in that no one cared they were black. I was naive to think they didn't feel the color of their skin when they were there. They felt their race everywhere, whether they were in a church or on a bus, or a name on a piece of paper passed around a college admissions committee.

Chapter Thirty

There was a coffeehouse night at the end of May to recognize the seniors. Deloris walked in with Venetia.

"Deloris! I'm so happy to see you!" My overzealous greeting met her cool demeanor.

"What's up with you, girl? You're acting like I've come back from the dead." Her proud face stopped any questions from me.

Venetia led the game of pretending nothing unusual had happened to Deloris, and I played along. We talked about Fergy instead. I'd given him a long letter between classes one day but he hadn't responded. I didn't even know if he read it.

"You can't make that boy feel better, so you may as well stop trying," Venetia said.

"But it's like he's taking it out on me, and I want him to understand I really wish he was going to State. I'm on *his* side."

Deloris put a handful of popcorn in her mouth. "Girl, you're white, and that is always gonna land you on the white side of things." She took a big gulp of coke. "What Fergy is wrassling with now is he is black, and even as smart as he is, he has still landed on the black side of things."

Venetia nodded her head in agreement.

"That's not fair!" My voice cracked with emotion. What I thought should be met with solidarity was held at arm's length.

"It ain't never been fair, but that's the way it's always been." Deloris wrinkled her nose like she smelled something rotten.

"I wish Fergy could go to Keller with me." I kept pushing. "He could have gotten a scholarship."

"It's too late for that," Venetia dismissed my idea.

"Do you think Fergy will end up happier at a college with all black kids?" I asked.

"Like you were happier at that school that had all white girls?" Deloris snapped back.

She had a way of slapping the truth down in front of me. Venetia turned away and stared at the swirls she'd painted on the wall, tugging on her hoop earring.

"Are y'all going to pull away from me too because I'm white?"

Venetia kept her eyes on the paisley swirls. "I already told you what I had to say on that subject," she said, "at my Christmas party."

I nodded, reminded of how she saved me from Lamont, and how I hadn't done the same for her with Mike.

Deloris stood up from the spool table and put her hands on her hips. "Nell, we're friends. And as long as you treat me right, I'm gonna treat you right."

A dart pierced my conscience. If she knew the part my father had played in the loss of her home she would know she hadn't been treated right by me, by way of him. I prayed that truth would stay buried.

Deloris touched my hair and gave me a half smile. "I still want to see if I can make an afro out of this stuff, or maybe some bush balls."

I laughed and pushed her hand away from my hair. "I'm still not ready!"

She pulled a pick out of her back pocket and lifted her afro with it. She stood tall and queenly and her aura made kids around us take notice.

"People think trying to be color-blind make things better." She was a teacher delivering a lesson. "I think you and Fergy been trying too hard *not* to see that one of you is black and one of you is white."

"So what can I do to get Fergy to talk to me?"

"You can't make somebody talk to you if they don't wanna. You gotta sit tight and wait for him to come 'round."

Deloris put the pick back in her pocket. "He might or he might not."

If I had been a good friend to Deloris I would have asked about the experience of losing her home or at least told her how sorry I was. But I couldn't face the discomfort of it. I couldn't expose my father's involvement with the situation. I used Fergy's misfortune to try to demonstrate my compassion for their race. But I was ignorant of the many roadblocks they faced, and not brave enough to bear the truth of them, even if I could have mustered the courage and the heart to ask.

My graduation from Stonewall High School was neither ignored nor celebrated. One warm day in June I put on a thin white gown that was too long and had a stubborn zipper. The matching mortarboard had a tassel that didn't quite reach across the top and hung at an awkward angle. I was placed in line alphabetically, next to classmates with whom I had never shared a class. "Randolph" was not too far from "Sutton", so if I turned around I could see Fergy two rows behind me. All I wanted from that day was to be with Claudia, Fergy, and Venetia; to laugh with them, to remember with them, and to capture into an untarnished memory this one part of my high school experience that had meant something to me.

My grandparents reasoned that since they couldn't attend Donald's graduation they shouldn't attend mine, so my parents sat alone in the bleachers. Sally's entire family was there to celebrate David, like they'd all been together for Nancy's graduation from Lee the year before. Claudia's mom came. She had red hair like Claudia and sat with Mr. Douglas, not seeming awkward, like I thought divorced parents would be. I scanned the bleachers until I found Fergy's family. His blind grandmother sat between his stoic parents. Sadness, anxiety, and regret washed over me as I watched them.

After the ceremony started Deloris walked in. She wore a mini skirt and platform shoes that made people turn their heads. I was so glad to see her magnificent afro that was as big as I'd ever seen it. My strange concoction of high school friends were all in the same room together.

After the ceremony Mrs. Hayes grabbed Fergy and brought him over to where Deloris, Venetia, Claudia and I were talking. She arranged us and focused her camera.

"Smile, thespians!" she called out above the racket.

There was a flurry of hugging after the picture. I wasn't sure when I would see them again. Claudia was moving to North Carolina. It would be harder to see Venetia without school as our meeting place. I didn't even know how to get in touch with Deloris.

"What are you going to do now?" I asked her.

"I'm figuring it out." Deloris said. She wrapped her arms around me and I smelled her coconut scent. "Take care of yourself, white girl."

Fergy slipped away, without a word or a hug. I tried to find him but he disappeared into the crowd. I didn't see him again.

Mrs. Hayes mailed me a copy of the photograph with a poem about keeping your dreams by Langston Hughes. I memorized it, and mainly thought of Fergy and Deloris when I said it to myself, like a prayer. Venetia and Claudia were on the way to following their dreams. Fergy and Deloris had been barricaded by the "too-rough fingers of the world". There were no roadblocks for me, but I couldn't define my dreams either. It made me feel like I was squandering the advantages I'd been given.

I have often studied that photograph. Claudia looks poised and confident, like she was used to having her picture made. Venetia is smiling in a formal, dignified way, and Deloris is laughing, her head cocked to the side, the joy of being finished with school revealed not only in her face but in her body. I am between Claudia and Deloris in the picture. I look young and not quite happy. Fergy is on the end next to Deloris. His copper face next to his navy-blue graduation gown makes it more difficult to discern his features. He isn't smiling and his glasses camouflage his eyes. It is the only picture I have of Fergy.

I wish I had one that revealed the fun, caring person who had been my friend and confidante. I wish I had one that showed the cute boy of an off and on secret crush. I wish I had one that proved a black boy and a white girl can be friends. Even if we hadn't come past one of us being black and one of us being white, unscathed.

Judith Bice

The Dream Keeper
by Langston Hughes

Bring me all of your dreams,
You dreamers,
Bring me all of your
Heart melodies
That I may wrap them
In a blue cloud-cloth
Away from the too-rough fingers
Of the world.

Epilogue

Even though my mother has turned Donald's old bedroom into a proper guest room with a poster bed and a reading chair in the corner, I prefer to stay in my old room when I visit. My mother may try to change our family story by erasing the remnants of Donald's room, but sleeping in my twin bed by the window makes my better memories of Donald and my dad come flooding back, and I welcome them.

I think if my father had lived longer he and Donald would have made their peace. They didn't hate each other. If anything, they loved each other so much the gulf that was created by their deep misjudgment of the other could not be crossed.

Donald's life has not been easy. We have seen each other a handful of times in the last fifteen years. At first, our conversations were weighty and teary. Over time the truths that once shocked us have become our normal, but our times together have never regained the closeness we had growing up. I think Donald believes me when I tell him I don't care about his lifestyle choices or his political beliefs, but I am still a reminder of a painful past he will not revisit. Our conversations are the polite interchanges of adults.

He obliged me by walking me down the aisle when I married, even though he wouldn't stay for the reception. Once, he accepted my invitation to spend Christmas with us, but we couldn't get it right. He appreciated my efforts to make recipes from our childhood, but a deep sadness came with the smells and tastes and it was easier to leave it alone than to navigate through it.

I have tired of my fractured family and have stopped trying to put us back together. But lately, my mother has started tagging on "and what do you hear from Donald?" at the end of our long-distance phone calls, and I wonder if it is my duty to be their bridge.

That is not why I'm visiting. It has become less disruptive to my own family's life to fly down from Boston every few months to check on my mother, rather than arrange for her to visit us. She has managed stoically since my father's early death from a heart attack, caring for the house and gardens. I've tried to get her to sell the house and move somewhere smaller, safer. The nice parts of the neighborhood have shrunk. Our street looks mostly the same, only more tired and worn. Not many of the old neighbors are there anymore; even Sally's family moved to the suburbs. Three streets over the shabbiness has crept in. Houses in need of paint, yards in disarray. But change is difficult for my mother. She stopped changing anything after my father died: no new curtains, no fresh paint color, no updated hairstyle. I take her shopping when I come, but she chooses to buy the same version of what she already has, from the same stores, even though they have lost their more sophisticated clientele. Her behavior doesn't feel like that of a grief-stricken widow; it feels like that of a woman who has no confidence or will to make a decision on her own.

I go to Mass with my mother when I visit, even if I haven't kept the Mass obligation on my own. I can't quite see the point of it in my current life, but I don't mind when I'm in Richmond. There are fewer people in the pews, and most of them are old, their aging faces vaguely familiar. Being there brings back sweet memories for me, and sometimes I catch a fleeting sense of the divine, like a trace of perfume that transports me for a nanosecond, then is gone; the same feeling we used to chase with folk music and coffeehouse nights.

My last trip to Richmond was in May. I like to go then, to experience the warmth of spring while Boston still requires sweaters and long pants. I go hoping to hear the awakenings of the katydids and witness the maiden flight of a lightning bug. I'd completed most of the list of going with my mother to doctors' appointments, stocking her pantry and freezer, and balancing her checkbook. I had a few more errands to run and she stayed home while I took Dad's old sedan to do them.

"Can I help you find something?" a deep silken voice said behind me. I'd stopped in the local hardware store to pick up some gardening gloves and flashlight batteries.

"I always forget. Do flashlights take B's or C's?" I said without turning around.

"Usually C's." A long brown arm reached beside me and took a package of C batteries off the pegboard hook.

"Thank you." I looked up to that kind copper face, with a grin that showed a familiar gap in the front teeth. Fergy Sutton.

"Nell Randolph!"

We embraced without a pause. A strong, tight squeeze of a hug.

"Oh my gosh, you haven't aged a bit!" I said.

"Look again, girl," he smiled. His eyes crinkled around the edges, making little crow's feet behind his glasses. His hair was cropped short and the small scar on his chin had darkened with time. He was a filled-out version of his teenage self, but that was all. He was still Fergy and I was so happy to see him.

"You haven't done so bad, yourself," he said.

I pushed my hair behind my ears, and wished I'd put on lipstick before I'd dashed out of the house. Fergy's way of holding you in a gaze had not changed, and I sucked in my lips.

"Still biting your lip, I see." He chuckled.

"I guess some things don't change." I laughed and pushed the attention away. "How are you? What are you doing now?"

"You want me to sum up the last fifteen years just like that?" He caught my eyes again and wouldn't release them. His immediate intensity threw me off kilter, like the first time he sat down beside me in the auditorium and introduced himself as my dead father.

"I'm only in town until tomorrow morning, so it'll have to be the short version."

A teenage boy wearing a polo shirt that matched Fergy's appeared at the end of the aisle. "Mr. Sutton, there's a man up front asking about getting his chainsaw sharpened."

"Tell him I'll be right there," Fergy answered. He turned back to me. "Meet me for a drink after I close up?"

"Sure." My mind speed solved the logistics of the evening with my mother. It was Thursday. She watched game shows and *The Cosby Show* until nine and then *Dallas*. She would be as happy to watch without me and I would be relieved to not be subjected to the blaring TV.

I was a high schooler again, telling my mother I was meeting up with an old friend, without revealing who it was. Even now, I think the mention of Fergy's name would make her uncomfortable. I prepared a meal of steamed vegetables and leftover roast beef for her preferred dinner time of five thirty. She'd poured her wine an hour before and her edges were softened by the time she sat down to eat. By definition, my mother was probably an alcoholic, but I couldn't think of what I would ever do about it. I never saw her drink into oblivion; she just drank every day. My father had frowned on daily drinking, and that wasn't their habit when I lived at home. I'd gotten her to switch from martinis to wine. That was somewhat better, I reasoned.

Fergy had chosen a little restaurant in my neighborhood, not far from the hardware store. I showered and put on makeup. My wardrobe consisted of work suits and jeans and not much in between, so I wore my jeans. He was wearing a button-down with khakis when I found him chatting with the bartender.

Fergy stood when I walked up and motioned to the stool beside him.

"What will you have?" I checked what he was drinking.

"A beer would be great." I never ordered beer when I was out with my girlfriends; I still didn't care for it. But I asked for it without thinking, as if I were at a high school party and didn't want to risk being different. My beer arrived and we clinked glasses like a toast.

"So...ladies first," he said.

"This lady chooses to go last." I sipped my beer.

He nodded and launched into his summary of the years since we graduated.

"I got a degree in business, worked at a few places around town and saved up what I earned. My dad and I bought a little hardware store. Then we bought another one. And now we own three, and I work to make them profitable."

"Wow. That's a lot of progress in a short amount of time." His presence exuded intelligence and confidence. I was proud of him. I nodded to the gold band on his finger. "You're married."

"Yes. Cassandra and I've been married for ten years. Two boys—seven and nine."

"Is that it? You could have given me that in the store today."

"That's it for now." He finished his beer and nodded to the bartender for another. "So where have you been for the last decade plus?"

I reached for the pocketbook still hanging on my shoulder

and hung it on the back of the bar stool. He smiled. "Oh good, you're settling in."

I took a swallow of beer.

"I graduated from Keller College."

"Yeah, that hoity-toity school up north. I remember," he nodded.

"I remember you being angry about it."

"I wasn't angry you got to go there. I was angry I couldn't go to State. Still am." His expression went flat, like a veil had been pulled across it. "But it's your turn. Keep going."

I rushed back in to escape his sadness. "I joined the Peace Corps and spent two years in Ghana, then came back and went to law school."

"A lawyer? My, my, that's something."

I couldn't tell if he was teasing or showing admiration. I hadn't meant to brag.

"I met Ted when I was in law school. We got married and have three little kids: twin girls, who are six, and a four-year-old boy."

"Is Ted a lawyer too?"

I shook my head. "He's a business guy, like you." I gulped my warming beer.

"Bad thing is—after all that work to get through law school, I didn't enjoy being a lawyer. I think I did it to try to be like my dad. I worked for a large firm for a short time, but that's all I did. Having twins was a good excuse to get out."

Fergy nodded. "It doesn't surprise me you wanted to be like your father. He was a fine man. You know, when my dad and I were getting into the hardware business he went to bat for us."

"What do you mean?"

"We wanted to buy property where no Black person had bought before. He made sure the higher powers approved it." He made quotation marks in the air for "higher powers."

My eyes filled with tears and the sudden emotion surprised

me. It had been such a long time since I'd talked with someone who had known my dad. Even Ted never got to meet him.

"Your dad always treated me with respect," Fergy said. "His death was such a shock."

Tears leaked out of my eyes and I brushed them away. Fergy took my hand and squeezed it.

"I came to the funeral Mass."

"You did?"

He nodded.

"Why didn't you come speak to me?"

"I thought it'd upset your mother if she saw me and I figured she didn't need that." His thoughtfulness endeared him to me even more. We sat with our memories and it didn't feel awkward to not talk, until it did and Fergy rescued the moment.

"So what do you do now? Stay home with the kids?"

"My life is mostly about the kids, but I work part-time providing counsel for a couple of small nonprofits in Boston."

"I'm sure your father would be pleased about that." He spoke like he was proud of me. I was at home with him.

We ordered burgers and my second beer tasted better than the first. We stayed at the corner of the bar instead of getting a table. He knew the latest on anyone I asked about. Venetia was practicing law in D.C., Claudia was living in Europe, the last he'd heard. Renay was a principal of an elementary school.

"Whoa—I'd hate to be one of the kids sent to her office!" I said.

He laughed his big stage laugh.

"Venetia's the one to be proud of." He leaned back and smiled. "She's giving those Washington politicians a run for their money, challenging every education practice in the book. A few more like her and I wouldn't have to pay all that tuition for my kids to go to school."

"Your kids are in private school?"

"Yep. They need a good education, and they're not going

to get it in the city schools. We're lucky to be able to give them one."

I was curious, but hesitant to ask him more.

"Don't you keep in touch with anyone?" he asked.

"Venetia and I wrote letters when we first went to college. Claudia's just not the keep in touch type. Then after Dad died, I stopped trying to feel connected to anything in Richmond. Looking back on high school...I just never really belonged anywhere."

Fergy's eyes squinted and he started to say something but stopped himself.

I finished my beer. "What about Deloris?"

"You don't know?"

I shook my head.

"She died."

"What?" I felt light-headed. I gripped the edge of the bar. Fergy put his hand on my back to steady me until my breathing slowed again.

"What happened?" I asked.

"She got some decent modeling gigs for awhile and I thought she was going to do really well for herself. Then she got caught up with the wrong people. 'Tia and I both warned her that what they were offering sounded a little too good, but she was bound and determined to make some big money. They took her to New York. We heard she died of an overdose, but no one really knows what happened."

She had such big dreams, such style. Of any of us, she had the most resilience. I could still see her flashy smile and hear the way she called me "white girl."

Fergy's hand resting on the bar made a fist. His knee jiggled like an unbalanced washing machine. "Moving her family to the projects was the worst thing that could've happened. That shouldn't have been legal. She saw some stuff. She spent the rest of her short life trying to erase that part and she lost her way."

I never went to see where Deloris lived, but the look of disgust on my father's face when he described her new home was seared in my memory. A panic shot through me, wondering if Fergy knew of my father's compliance with the city's decision.

"My father said the city council was misled into believing that newer housing would be better." My response to Fergy's guarded anger came out as a veiled defense. I bit my lip.

"They knew what they were doing." Fergy looked past me at the mostly white patrons in the restaurant. "Even if it'd been nicer, their neighborhood was ripped in two. They not only obliterated her house, they took her away from her people. It's like they constructed a roadblock with the rubble."

The Fergy I'd run into at the hardware store had brought back the little bit of excitement I'd had in my high school life. This Fergy was the one who'd stomped away from me at the coffeehouse, the one who made me uncomfortable, who made me feel so White. I wanted to coax the first one back. And I wanted to push thinking about Deloris to another time. It made me too sad. I ordered another beer and searched for subjects to connect us and make us laugh.

The restaurant was almost empty when Fergy asked for the check.

"Fergy, let me pay."

"No way, girl. My momma taught me to always pay for the lady." His eyes caught mine in one of his intense gazes and my pulse quickened.

"How often do you get to Richmond? Ted ever come with you? I'd like to meet him someday."

We had talked about everything except the undercurrent that had kept our conversation flowing all evening. I'd had enough to drink to not let anything go unsaid.

"You know what Deloris used to tell me all the time?"

He shook his head.

"She thought you and I were made for each other. I always

309

told her we were just friends. She thought we were star crossed lovers that were too scared to admit it to each other."

"She was something else, wasn't she?"

It wasn't the response I was hoping for.

"Fergy, are there any mixed marriages in your wide circle of friends here?"

"Not among the kids we grew up with. But there's a couple who moved here about a year ago. He's Black and the conductor of the symphony. His wife is White and their kids are a beautiful warm shade of bronze. "

I took a deep breath. "Could we have done that?"

He handed his credit card to the bartender. "Living in Yankee land has sure made you bolder, hasn't it?"

I thought he was teasing, but he didn't follow his question with a smile. Maybe I'd gone too far, and now had spoiled what I'd salvaged from earlier.

"You know, there are only three other Black kids in our school. We pay full tuition, volunteer, and do the fundraisers."

I waited for him to continue.

"Cassandra and I are doing this to give our boys a quality education. But I'm not sure if living in a white world all day is the best thing for them."

I tried to follow his line of thought, but couldn't. I couldn't see the downside of a better education.

"Everyone is friendly, welcoming, supportive—to a point. But the boys don't get many invitations outside of school. Cassandra and I aren't included in dinner parties. People are afraid to ask us about our jobs—and Cassandra's a pediatrician!" He shook his head and his shoulders slumped. "It's like a subtle version of my scholarship to State being revoked."

My stomach lurched at that memory. I searched his face and found more sadness than anger in his eyes.

"When you and I were talking on the phone all the time and writing notes and flirting, my daddy sat me down and told me I needed to think long and hard before I let myself fall for a White girl."

He smiled. "I used to think he was being too old-fashioned. But I've come to believe he was right. There's a lot we can't understand about the other."

He signed the bill and put his credit card in his wallet. "It's not that we're prejudiced, or unwilling to learn, it's just our cultures have taught us differently, and it's like the differences are stamped on our DNA. Maybe not forever, but it's going to take time and work and depths of understanding we don't have yet, for that stamp to fade. And just me sending my kids to a White school is not going to do it. The White people are gonna have to try too."

"It's doesn't feel like that in Boston. Our neighborhood's diverse. The twins have playdates with kids of other races and nationalities." I wanted him to know there were places it could work.

"Well this town has a hard time changing." Our eyes locked. "You say you never belonged in high school. But your belonging was a choice. It's never a choice when you're Black. Sometimes I want to move my kids out of here. Move them where it's easier to be Black, if there is such a place. But then I think if I move, who's going to change it for the ones who are left?"

A wave of admiration and fondness for Fergy and his beautiful soul came over me. Then a pang of guilt. I'd left home because it was too difficult to stay. Fergy, who would have had an easier time of it somewhere else, had stayed.

"My dad thought it would take a few generations," I remembered from our conversation in the fancy restaurant so long ago.

"Let's hope that's all. And in the meantime maybe you could take what you've learned in Boston and Ghana and bring it back here. You're an attorney. Get in touch with Venetia. Do what she's doing from the white side." What I had sensed as Fergy's admiration for my accomplishments now revealed a tinge of resentment, even a feeling of exasperation."

He stood to go. I stayed seated.

"What do you mean?"

"Come back home. Live here like you lived in Ghana and Boston. Let your kids play with my kids. Maybe we both send them to public school. Change things from the inside out. Let other White families learn from yours."

I'd never considered moving back to Richmond; it would be like going backwards. A heaviness was hijacking what I'd envisioned as a nostalgic evening. I didn't want to deal with the responsibility that Fergy was placing on me. I'd wanted the fun side of him, the Fergy that made me laugh and flirted with me. I didn't want to be reminded of the issues that had kept me away.

"Nell, I think you'd like Cassandra. I bet I'd like Ted. There's a lot that needs to change for Black folks. But we need White folks to help with the changing." Fergy had added wings to the heaviness.

We were the last to leave the restaurant. Moon shadows outlined the giant oaks on the sidewalk and a spring breeze carried the scent of daffodils. The flowering pear trees glowed in the moonlight. My heart ached at the beauty I had missed by not being here. Fergy walked me to my dad's old sedan. I wasn't ready to leave him. He was the thread to my younger self, maybe my purer self. He made me remember that feeling of hope that comes with the spring. He made me want to be a better version of myself, to raise my children to appreciate all the shades of who we are. To quit pretending to be color-blind, like Deloris had preached to me years ago.

Fergy opened the heavy car door and I slid in and rolled down the window. With a sparkle in his eyes he said, "Maybe it will be us in another lifetime, white girl," and kissed me on the cheek.

Acknowledgements

The journey of writing this book has not been a solo one. From classes at the VMFA Studio School with Susan Hankla to summers at Nimrod with Sheri Reynolds and Charlotte Morgan, I owe much gratitude for the wisdom, guidance, and encouragement that has been generously shared. Even though writing is a private endeavor, the love of books has been a shared joy with my book club of thirty years. I have learned so much from you, about literature and about life.

Wolfgang, my first reader, first cheerleader, and occasional nudger, I thank you. Jen, Jay, and Mary Katherine, you all shaped my early drafts with your unique insights and candor, giving me the boost to keep working. Anne Westrick, your early editing helped me define my path. Nick Courtright and the team at Atmosphere Press, not only have you given me the opportunity of a lifetime, you matched me with the brilliant Asata Radcliffe, an editor of remarkable intelligence and mettle. To you all—my heartfelt gratitude.

To my friend Ann, who never stops believing in me or being excited about making art in any form, your constancy is a rock. Janis, your courage to be honest with the white girl that had not become your friend yet has been a priceless gift. You continue to enrich my life.

And to Tim, Kate, and Becca—my deepest love and gratitude of all. You have given me the space, the support, and the assurance to become more of myself through the power of the pen.

To my hometown of Richmond, and to all our hometowns, may we learn from our pasts and forge our futures with grace, honesty, and compassion.

About
Atmosphere Press

Atmosphere Press is an independent, full-service publisher for excellent books in all genres and for all audiences. Learn more about what we do at atmospherepress.com.

We encourage you to check out some of Atmosphere's latest releases, which are available at Amazon.com and via order from your local bookstore:

Twisted Silver Spoons, a novel by Karen M. Wicks

Queen of Crows, a novel by S.L. Wilton

The Summer Festival is Murder, a novel by Jill M. Lyon

The Past We Step Into, stories by Richard Scharine

The Museum of an Extinct Race, a novel by Jonathan Hale Rosen

Swimming with the Angels, a novel by Colin Kersey

Island of Dead Gods, a novel by Verena Mahlow

Cloakers, a novel by Alexandra Lapointe

Twins Daze, a novel by Jerry Petersen

Embargo on Hope, a novel by Justin Doyle

Abaddon Illusion, a novel by Lindsey Bakken

Blackland: A Utopian Novel, by Richard A. Jones

About the Author

Judith Bice was born and raised in Richmond, Virginia, where she has enjoyed a dual career as an educator and a musician. Her first novel, *Hey, White Girl,* is inspired by her own busing experience, her return to the classroom as a teacher, and her growing awareness of what it means to be white.

6/2022

CPSIA information can be obtained
at www.ICGtesting.com
Printed in the USA
LVHW091801030522
717857LV00016B/2661

9 781639 882076